CW01635761

Brainrack

Kit Pedler and C[illegible] aking series *Doomwat*[illegible] gedies that modern science could engender[illegible] wide. For *Dr Who*, possibly the longest running science fiction serial in the world, they created the Cybermen – today's space age monsters.

Kit Pedler is a doctor of medicine and a research scientist of great distinction. He has thirty-eight original research papers on the eye and vision to his credit, has written a number of short stories, and has broadcast on current affairs on radio and television.

Gerry Davis has engaged in practically every branch of show business from English provincial repertory theatre to making documentary films for the National Film Board in Canada and the UK. For the past few years he has been responsible for editing and writing television scripts for a number of popular British serials and series. These include *United*, perhaps the only successful serial about a sport – in this case soccer; *The First Lady*, a series about small town politics in Yorkshire, and *Softly, Softly*, the highly popular and very long-running police series.

By the same authors in Pan Books

Mutant 59: The Plastic Eater

Brainrack

Kit Pedler and Gerry Davis

Pan Books London and Sydney

First published in Great Britain 1974
by Souvenir Press Ltd
This edition published 1975 by Pan Books Ltd,
Cavaye Place, London SW10 9PG
© Kit Pedler and Gerry Davis 1974
ISBN 0 330 24590 2

Made and printed in Great Britain by
Hazell Watson & Viney Ltd,
Aylesbury, Bucks

Conditions of sale: This book shall not, by way of trade
or otherwise, be lent, re-sold, hired out or otherwise circulated
without the publisher's prior consent in any form of binding or cover
other than that in which it is published and without a similar condition
including this condition being imposed on the subsequent purchaser.
The book is published at a net price and is supplied subject to the
Publishers Association Standard Conditions of Sale registered
under the Restrictive Trade Practices Act, 1956

One

The huge bulk of Flight 697 loomed out of the industrial murk to the north-east of Paris and, as the port wing of the great jumbo jet dipped, slanting beams of bright sunlight swept like spotlights down the tightly-packed passenger compartment and across the laps of Mrs Oates and her three children. The sudden brightness jerked her out of a doze and she looked up sleepily at the rows of heads in front of her and then down at the jumble of white plastic cups and knives on the seat tables folded down in front of her children. Only another hour, she thought, then I'll be able to get a good wash and a decent cup of tea. For a moment she tried to rub away the stiffness in her neck, until the subdued rumble of the engines and the relaxed chatter of the other passengers gradually lulled her back into sleep. As her eyes closed, she was totally unaware that the lives of her family and the three hundred and seventy mothers and children packed into the charter plane *en route* from Majorca to Heathrow, London, were moving inexorably into the balance. For the next one hundred and twenty seconds her survival lay in the hands of a twenty-eight-year-old man.

The man was one of eight operators seated at a complex of multi-coloured instrument consoles in a long, underground room near Deal on the south coast of England. The room, in contrast to the bright aircraft interior, was in almost total darkness except for small pools of light picking out each man and his set of console panels. Stretching along the entire wall in front of them was a curved, illuminated screen showing a bright green Mercator projection of Great Britain and the North of Europe. The outlines of the map shimmered. Criss-crossing the outlines of the land masses was a maze of curved blue lines and along each line a deep ruby spot moved slowly. There was a background hum of ventilating fans and in the air there was a faint smell of hot electrical machinery and the tarry, hessian smell of new carpet.

The room housed the newly-opened control room of ACE or Air Control Europe where each and every civil aircraft movement over Britain and Northern Europe was monitored and controlled. Flight 697 was under the guidance of a computer complex controlled by twenty-eight-year-old operator number two.

Dr Alexander Mawn fingered the orange press badge on his jacket lapel uneasily and edged clear of a small knot of journalists to get a clearer view of the operation. He was entirely preoccupied with the complex patterns of red and green signals appearing and disappearing in rapid succession on the consoles in front of the operators, and paid no attention to a small moving red light which had appeared on the extreme left of the screen. Neither did he particularly notice, at that moment, that operator number two's behaviour was any different from the other seven. As he watched the kaleidoscope of colour patterns scurrying over the banks of indicators, he began to visualize the logical designs behind them. He concluded that of all the similar systems he had examined that year, the ACE network carried the highest potential hazard from overload.

The atmosphere in the control room was quiet and controlled and if there was any sign of strain on the face of Cartland, Deputy Air Traffic Control Officer, standing silently behind the operators, it was not due to the complexity of the multi-million dollar installation under his direction, but to the two television cameras on each side of him, and the presence of Sheldon Peters, probably the most exposed television face in England. Cartland tried to listen to Peters's commentary with one ear and at the same time made an effort to keep an eye on the movements on the wall map. He was only able to pick up isolated phrases.

'. . . through that wall is one of the most advanced computers in the world, and it's logging all the flight paths of every aircraft as they are transmitted from airports all over Europe. When it's sorted them out, it puts them up as those blue lines and red spots you can see on the screen. The whole system was built by the Gelder Consortium and must be the most modern and up-to-date system in the world. In fact Mr Brian Gelder is here watching it all . . .'

One camera swung out to a slight, dark haired man, standing beside Cartland. Despite the air-conditioned chill of the room, Gelder wore a lightweight shirt and a jacket slung casually around his shoulders. He smiled easily as the camera focused in on him.

'. . . so the ACE system,' Peters continued, 'has entirely dispensed with any routine voice communication between pilot and ground control and so cutting down the risk of faulty communication . . .'

Alexander Mawn picked up the red spot now moving in over the map boundary. He quickly did some mental arithmetic. Too fast for a civil jet, much too fast, he thought, must be a military plane . . .

Flight Lieutenant James Hodgson hunched down in the cramped cockpit of the Dassault Mirage six, trying to ease the tension in his limbs. Familiarization runs were always nerve-racking and he was already looking forward to a large scotch in the mess, back at Abingdon. He looked down at the flight plan on his knee pad, checked the next procedure and pushed the twin throttle quadrants forward. Immediately the giant vacuum cleaner noise from the engines behind him swooped up in pitch and the seat pushed with massive force into the small of his back. Looking downwards he could see the Dover cliffs slide away behind him and, as he eased the controls to the right, he winced at the sickening G force as it tried to drag his body downwards to the left. He checked the Course Deviation, Turn and Bank indication and Mach reading which had already climbed to 1.8, a speed which would have enabled him to overtake a rifle bullet at more than four hundred miles an hour.

Mawn glanced anxiously at control officer Cartland, but he had already seen the intruding ruby light. He pressed a button on a small panel beside him and a light flashed on the control panel in front of operator two. The backs of the other operators were straightening.

The light on number two's panel flashed again and Mawn caught Cartland's impatient glance at the operator. There was sweat on the back of the man's neck and, as his hand came into view, Mawn saw that it had a coarse tremor more like the jerky movements of an old man. Mawn moved closer, the light had illuminated the instruction: 'Manual over-ride'. Operator two pressed a square yellow button, the instruction winked out and the remaining light signals abruptly changed into a new pattern.

On the screen the red light was visibly converging on another and Peters was directing a camera towards the screen while attempting to explain the situation, caught by the sudden tension that had gripped the room.

'... It's almost certainly an Air Force plane. In this situation the computer is controlled directly by the operator in charge of this sector ...'

In front of operator two, a row of five coloured signals had appeared – green, red, red, green, red on the computer read-out screen. As Mawn watched, the operator again lifted his hand, his arm seemed to move stiffly as he punched out the instruction that was to be relayed directly to the Flight 697 giving it an immediate change of course.

Green, red, green, red, red, green. Mawn caught his breath, surely that was wrong. Incredibly, the simple code had been misread by the operator.

Captain Andrews on Flight 697 glanced at the incoming signal from operator two on a small screen set between the banks of dials in front of him. It stated in bright green letters: 'Starboard two four zero'. He moved the controls until the signal went out.

On the control room screen the red blips moved closer on a collision course that was now clear to everyone in the suddenly hushed room. Even Peters was silent, waiting for the red spot that was Flight 697 to break away on its new course.

Abruptly a shrill repeating tone sounded in front of both

operator two and Cartland's desk and a panel flashed: 'Error function positive'. 'Error function positive'.

Operator number two was now visibly shaking, his hands tightly clenched on the console.

Again the row of colours flashed up: 'Green, red, red, green, red'. Again the operator's hand moved up to the controls, the fingers searching clumsily. 'Green, red, red', the man hesitated, his left hand brushing away the sweat coursing down his brow. As Mawn watched incredulously, he punched up 'red, green'.

The shrill tone sounded again. With a horrified glance at the screen where the two spots were now almost together, Cartland slammed down a fluorescent orange switch and seized a microphone.

'Voice over-ride, voice over-ride.' His voice was thin, high, like a whiplash in a confined room. '697, 697, do you read, aircraft converging, starboard level – north seven five one. You should see it. Over.'

On the flight deck of Flight 697, Captain Andrews, jerked into sudden attention by the voice, peered ahead through the blue-tinted screen. The co-pilot shaded his eyes against the sun. They both picked up the thin vapour trail of the Mirage streaking towards them.

'There it is, fighter, port high!' Both men simultaneously grasped their control columns and pulled them hard over.

Flight Lieutenant Hodgson looked up from the instruments. The giant, wheeling shape of the jumbo almost filled the sky. Over or under, left or right?

In the last few seconds, he registered the swing of the giant plane downwards and wrenched the control column back into his stomach. As the Mirage shot upwards, he felt the anti G air roaring into his pressure suit. His vision ebbed as blood drained away from his brain like mercury, suddenly weighing six times the normal.

Flight 697 lurched into a nearly vertical bank and the scene inside the flight deck abruptly changed from relaxed anticipation to horror. A torrent of white plastic cups and trays cascaded into the aisles, followed by a jumbled struggling mass of screaming women and children, desperately grabbing for support as their world turned round. There was a metallic resonant grating from the grossly over-stressed air frame and for a moment the giant plane seemed suspended from one wing with its massive weight holding it in that position. There was a sudden, deafening explosion from the shock wave of the Mirage as it blasted past overhead, then the cabin began slowly to right itself.

Mrs Oates, weeping and half crushed under a mass of struggling passengers, began desperately to pull herself clear and to search for her children in the screaming, hysterical shambles around her. Over a bulkhead, the 'fasten your seat belts' sign lit up.

Flight Lieutenant Hodgson's vision gradually returned through red and then grey as he pushed the control column forwards to lessen the almost vertical climb of the Mirage and to relieve his body from the near intolerable stress.

Inside the control room, tension suddenly broke as the ruby lights converged into one and then parted again. A hubbub of voices broke out. Then, from speakers overhead, came the sudden roar of Captain Andrews's voice: 'ACE control, do you hear! What in Christ's name was that? We nearly . . .'

Abruptly Cartland cut the pilot's voice off. The journalists clustered round and Peters thrust his hand microphone towards the distraught controller. 'Exactly what happened, Mr Cartland?' Notebooks were out and ball points raised. The controller fought himself into calmness: 'It looked more dramatic than it really was – the red blips on the screen are enormously magnified – there was no danger . . .' Gelder had joined the two men. '. . . there was a considerable safety margin between the two planes . . .'

Peters broke in: 'The pilot didn't think so, Mr Cartland!'

Mawn was pushing his way towards Peters. Cartland glanced up at the screen, the two spots were diverging again. His voice showed visible relief: 'As you can see, Flight 697 is now cleared as far as the Kent coast and . . .'

'Just how close was it?' Peters held the microphone expectantly. 'Was it an official near-miss?'

'Can't say yet,' Cartland replied. 'We'll have to examine the tape logs first.'

'I am sure there was no danger, Mr Cartland had the situation well under control.' Heads turned to Brian Gelder. 'In fact now you've all seen the flexibility of the system – there was a need to over-ride the computer and everything functioned entirely as it should have done.'

'You can honestly claim there was no danger?' Peters persisted.

Gelder paused, but before he could speak, the tall figure of Mawn appeared in front of the camera. 'No danger! You could hear the noise of the other plane in the pilot's intercom. That wasn't a near-miss – it was damn nearly a disaster!'

Cartland moved forward to usher Mawn away, but he angrily shrugged him away. Peters moved forward with the microphone: 'No, let him speak, who are you please?'

'My name's Mawn – Alexander Mawn.'

Peters glanced at Mawn's lapel press label. 'Which paper do you represent?'

Mawn ignored the question. 'I'm in computing science at Plymouth University and I'm interested in the failure rate of machines like that one.' He pointed. 'I've a lot of evidence now that the basic design is faulty and has got to fail sooner or later and it just did!'

'Why must it be the computer?' Peters demanded. 'There are eight men working it.'

'It involves both. The faults in the man-machine interface – the relationship between the computer and the operator. It's a growing threat – the Caird Oil Company and the American NALA computers, they're all having the same problem.'

The clamour of voices from the listening journalists rose to a tumult of questions. Cartland moved forward, beckoning to security guards who had entered the long room. 'I must ask you all to go now, you're making work impossible.'

Outside in the corridor Mawn felt a touch on his arm. Peters was smiling. 'You'd better take cover for a few days.'

'How's that?'

'When that programme goes out tonight in front of X million people, they will see you accuse a multi-national company of almost killing a plane full of people. If you're right, the public will make you a super hero. If you're wrong, the Gelder people will have you in court.' He gestured not to reply as Gelder caught up with them, his face pale with anger: 'You're not going to use any of that?'

Peters smiled: 'I have to.'

'It was completely slanderous.'

'Mr Gelder,' Peters continued. 'Whether you like it or not, that whole episode is going to be in the late editions of the evening papers and all over the national dailies tomorrow, so it will go out on my programme tonight. If you'd like to come to the studios, you're welcome to oppose it.'

Gelder turned on his heels and was gone. Peters turned to Mawn: 'You know my programme "Nightstyle"?' Mawn nodded. 'I want you to come on it and say what you said today.'

Mawn paused: 'Yes, I will, it happens to be the truth.'

'Good, that's fixed.' Peters's face grew serious. 'But I'd be a bit careful if I were you.' Mawn looked puzzled. 'You've stamped on some fairly big toes today.'

Mawn looked through the side window of his car at the dark silhouettes of the trees and hedges sliding past. In his mind he compared their quiet composure with the unending stridor of the past forty-eight hours. First there had been crowds of reporters in the hotel lobby, then an urgent demand for a radio interview, followed by a two minute interview on Sheldon Peters's 'Nightstyle' programme, where he had simply repeated what he had said at the ACE centre. The newspaper headlines had varied between the relative sobriety of *The Times* which had given one inch of column space under a headline: 'Scientist Accuses Major Consortium of Shoddy Control Systems' to the two-inch banners of the *Clarion*, alongside a picture of the passengers: 'Did these families miss death by inches?'

He looked at the dashboard clock. Tina Hale should be at home by now. He decided to ring her from a callbox in the next village to see how the experiment was going. He reflected that a few days' solid laboratory bench-work would cure his over-stimulated nerves.

Tina Hale sat feet up in front of the television set and realized she was only half watching the screen. In the back of her mind there was a nagging, hollow anxious tug of something forgotten. She got up, flicked off the set, swallowed the remains of a gin and stared at the dwindling spot of light, trying to search for the cause of the anxiety. Laundry – no; phone Richard about the new ordering system at the lab – no; the lab! the experiment! – something in the experiment – something not complete.

She tried hard to recall Dr Mawn's instructions and began almost immediately to wish she worked for a more reasonable boss. He had poked his head round the laboratory door and rapped out a few terse sentences and then disappeared without even waiting for her reply. She reflected that laboratory technicians were in short supply and that there were plenty of other jobs . . . perhaps one of these days . . .

The laboratories had been built inside the shell of an old Victorian vicarage set on the edge of the campus. A three-storey grey-stone folly with a carved stone porch and garishly coloured stained glass windows, it was in almost satirical contrast to the tidy anonymity of the new University blocks. It was not Mawn's first choice for a new computing science department, but it had the one great advantage that it was a long way from the administration building and the watchful eye of the Dean of Science. In any case, he had been given no choice.

The car drew up quietly in the lane outside and a thick-set man of medium height got out. He eased the door closed and, for perhaps two minutes, stood absolutely still beside the car. Finally he walked through the open gate, treading only on the grass.

. . . Reaction temperature – the condensation columns! Tina Hale quickly opened a loose-leaf folder and started to thumb through a list of physical constants. Reaction temperature –

fluor – hydro – carbons – tetrafluorethylene bromide 118 to 123° centigrade. With a dull hammer of real fear she remembered the connections Richard had made between the columns. They were polythene. Polythene softens at 80! She snapped the book shut and began to dress quickly.

The man was standing beside a large rhododendron bush holding a small case and looking up at a first floor window on the side of the house. He stood listening, sensing the air like an animal, and then began to climb up on to the flat roof of an outbuilding beneath the window. Supporting himself on the sill with one hand, with the other he pulled out a small pen-torch and ran the beam round the edge of the window. It was a sash window divided transversely into two halves and bolted by a single central lever.

He attached a short, thin blade of metal to the end of a threaded rod about eighteen inches long, put one end of the rod against the edge of the window frame and slid the metal blade up into the gap between the two window halves. With a short ratchet lever he began to turn a nut, forcing the metal blade along the threaded rod until it moved the central lever bolt of the window. Finally it clicked over parallel with the window frame. He slid the lower half of the window silently upwards and eased himself into a small office room, then reached out for the case on the sill and pulled it in. The office door was open. He picked out the name: 'Doctor A. Mawn' printed in Dymo-tape on the outside. Sweeping the thin probe of the pen-torch ahead of him and carefully keeping it below window level, he began to search through the building methodically.

After a while, he opened one file labelled: 'Barfield figures' and laid out its typed contents on separate sheets. Then, one by one, he fed the sheets through a slit in a small oblong metal box a little larger than a pencil case. After about six seconds, the sheets emerged from a slit in the opposite side of the box. Attached to each sheet was a transparent plastic film. On the film was a perfect copy of the words on the typed sheet.

As the headlights of the car picked out the signboard: 'Kramer

Computing Science Laboratories', Tina saw the dark shape of the car in the lane as she turned into the forecourt. The tyres crunched loudly on the gravel.

The man jerked up at the sound, clicked off the torch and felt his way quickly to the door. He put the copies back into his case, closed it gently and retraced his way up to the first floor . . .

Tina walked up the wide stone steps, turned the heavy deadlock and pushed the great oak door open. The noise echoed in the front hall . . .

The man darted quickly into a laboratory and crouched down behind a bench. He glanced up apprehensively at the equipment surrounding him. There was a maze of interconnected glassware connected to blocks of electronic apparatus. Each unit glowed softly in the darkness with a single neon eye. One tube led past a long dark green metal box. On the box was a hastily-scrawled warning: 'Danger. Laser light'. From a small aperture at one end of the tube a coruscating pencil beam of light reflected an intense ruby glow from the ceiling. He could feel the warmth from the heating mantles round the flasks as he crouched down out of sight. There were faint clicking sounds as the equipment heated and cooled. A motor whined abruptly and a pen-trace recorder spewed out a length of squared paper covered in a series of irregular traces. He flicked round anxiously as a solenoid-operated tap clacked and buzzed. A large flask began to drain its contents automatically into a tall vertical condenser column.

Tina opened the door and switched on the lights. For a moment, the overhead fluorescent tubes flickered and then struck, flooding the room with light. The man screwed up his eyes in the glare and hunched down against the wall. Tina began to examine each connection between the complex leashes of glassware, turned off a glass tap isolating one segment of the condensation column and cut away a plastic tube connecting two convoluted tubes with a razor blade. From a drawer she withdrew a coil of milky white tubing, severed a short length and reconnected the open ends of the glass tubes. She checked through the connections of the experiment and compared them with a rough flow chart scrawled on a nearby blackboard. Finally she began to realign the gas laser, altering its setting by turning heavy, knurled controls on its base mounting. Then she hesitated for a moment, opened a drawer and took out a pair of heavy goggles with dark glass filters, put them on and then unscrewed a panel on the side of the laser tube. Immediately the room was flooded with a grainy red fire, which sparkled off all the metal fitments. She replaced the panel loosely.

A telephone sounded harshly, echoing through the deserted building. A red light flashed intermittently over the door. She picked up an extension attached to an amplifier.

'Kramer lab.'

'Tina! That you?' Mawn's voice boomed out on the speaker, clear and immediate. 'I tried to get you at home. All well?'

'Yes, thank you Doctor.'

'I'm at Bacton, on my way home. I'll drop in for a few minutes.'

'All right, Doctor, I'll wait for you here, goodbye.' The man raised his head slightly. She hung up and took a mirror out of her handbag surveying her face.

The man stretched a cramped leg and moved a cable lying on the floor behind him. The cable flicked a jack plug from the side of the pen-recorder. Immediately a buzzer sounded angrily and the paper tape began to pour out of the recorder in an uncontrolled stream.

Tina whipped round, gasping at the noise, and saw the man's head bobbing above the bench. Stiff with fear, she inched backwards towards the door, fumbling behind her for the extension phone, her eyes fixed on the man.

'What are you doing? Who are you?' Her voice was a constricted whisper. He stood up, and they faced each other, poised.

Suddenly the man lurched past the apparatus, making for the door. His hand struck the long green laser tube and its nozzle broke away from the optical bench and swung round towards him. The deadly red pencil of light slashed round the room like a solid red-hot bar and raked his face.

The beam lanced into one eye and, like a wounded animal, he screamed and staggered along the bench blundering through the complex of tubes, shattering flasks and sweeping electronic apparatus to the floor. Tina screamed and sprang forward, trying to save the tottering remains of the experiment, as the man staggered by her through the door and was gone.

Trembling and weeping, she knelt beside the shattered experiment, ineffectually trying to rearrange the broken tubes. Suddenly her breath caught in her throat and she clutched her mouth and tried to scramble to her feet. Blindly she grabbed for the edge of the bench and tried to drag herself up but her head started to arch backwards, then her neck, and finally the whole of her body curved into a grotesque spring bow and crashed down on to the broken apparatus. Above her body the angry red pencil of the laser beam swung round in the swirling fumes and came to rest on the side of a black plastic screen.

Mawn swung the car along, sensing rather than seeing the dark, winding contours of the lanes ahead. The night was clear and starlit and he drove with both windows down, enjoying the bland rush of the country air over his face.

About two miles away from the laboratory, he slowed before the last turn. Abruptly, the empty lane was filled with the glare of headlights and a car bucketed round the corner, tyres squealing. Mawn jammed on the brakes and swung into the hedge. The other driver also braked and slewed sideways, off-side wheels churning along the grass verge. In the beam of his headlights Mawn caught a momentary glimpse of a pale startled face with a gloved hand holding a handkerchief over one eye.

The driver double-declutched, straightened up and blasted off down the road behind him. Mawn gingerly backed his car out of the hedge and drove on. With almost clinical detachment, he felt the adrenalin surge through his body, his face turning cold.

He recognized Tina Hale's car but, as he got to the front door and put his key into the lock, it swung open. He called out, switched the stair lights on and then saw the thin white fumes curling down through the banisters into the hall. With a handkerchief against his nose, he tore up the stairs and into the laboratory.

The pen recorder was still ejecting rolled paper which had collected in a folded pile on the floor. Under the pile he saw an arm. Tearing the paper, aside, he picked up Tina's body and staggered out of the room and down the stairs coughing and retching. Finally he laid her gently down on the steps outside the front door and put his ear down to her mouth. For about half a minute he knelt still, listening for any sign of respiration, then quickly pulled her jaw down and applied his mouth to hers, breathing into her lungs, taking a deep breath and repeating the action rhythmically. He kept the cycle going and felt with one hand for the pulse in her neck. Even in the light coming through the open doorway he could see her face putty white. He got up, raced into the hallway and dialled emergency then leapt up the stairs back into the laboratory. He looked quickly round through the fumes, only half registering the red pencil of light from the laser, made certain there was no one else in the room and then ran back down the stairs and back to Tina.

In the laboratory, the black plastic screen was beginning to soften and run under the fiery onslaught of the laser.

Mawn was still applying mouth to mouth resuscitation when the ambulance arrived. A uniformed attendant put his hand gently on Mawn's shoulder: 'We'll take her now sir, if you don't mind.'

The two men lifted Tina's body on to a cloth stretcher and strapped it on to a frame inside the ambulance. One of them pulled her head back and took down a mask attached to a portable respirator, put it over her mouth and switched on the gas flow from a cylinder. The other watched in silence. Their eyes met.

In the fume-laden laboratory, the black plastic was bubbling and running down on to the bench. Smoke began to curl up, followed by a small yellow flame. The flame caught the edge of a bunch of notes clipped on to the edge of a shelf above. The paper flared, flames licked round the bottles on the shelf. A bottle cracked and broke.

Outside, the two men swung round at the muffled thump of the explosion. A window glowed bright orange, then with a succession of blasts the glass flew out and great tongues of flames billowed and licked hungrily at the eaves of the old house.

Mawn was on his feet as the glass showered down over him. He rushed back into the hall and groped his way up the stairs. Dense black clouds of smoke were pouring along the upstairs corridor and down over the hall. Pulling a foam extinguisher off the wall, he ducked down into the fumes, feeling his way along the corridor wall towards the laboratory. Gradually, as he stumbled through the murk, his movements began to weaken and he staggered, dropped the extinguisher and dropped to his knees. Somewhere behind him he could hear the discordant cry of a fire-engine. He turned and crawled painfully back along the corridor towards the head of the stairs and dragged himself over the edge and began to flop down like a fish out of water. Dimly he felt rough hands grab his legs and shoulders.

Somebody was gently slapping his cheek: 'Hello there – back with us are you?'

He felt cold air in his throat. There were flashing blue lights and men shouting, unloading ladders and paying out rolls of hose. He tried to get to his feet.

The attendant put a restraining hand on his shoulder: 'It's all under control now. Nothing you can do sir.'

Mawn spoke hoarsely: 'We've got to get the files out – years of work – we've got to get them out.'

'The fire boys will save all they can sir, don't you worry.'

'Tina Hale, where is she?'

'They've taken her off to the Plymouth General, sir.'

'How is she – is she all right?'

The man exchanged a glance with his companion: 'We'll get you off there now, sir, if you don't mind.'

The two men supported Mawn over to a waiting police car,

eased him down into the back seat and closed the door. The uniformed deputy fire chief turned to the two men: 'Have to make a special on this one.'

'How's that?'

'Christ! You should have seen what they've got upstairs. All the flammables stacked over the electric stuff. They must have broken every regulation in the book. Could be manslaughter.'

The glow of the fire reflected on Mawn slumped back in the car, his eyes closed.

'Mild bronchitis from the fumes and a first degree burn on his forearm, nothing more . . .' The words filtered dimly into Mawn's mind. He struggled against an overwhelming torpor and then listened again, keeping his eyes closed. Another voice with a characteristic inflexion – quiet, meticulous: 'Poor old chap – must be taking it very hard.' The Dean of Science! His nightmare was true. Tina Hale was dead. He seemed to have known for hours, as though the news had filtered through to his subconscious while he was asleep. He opened his eyes cautiously.

He saw a white hospital counterpane, sunlight streaming through a high window and a doctor with an array of pens and a chromium torch sticking out of his white coat pocket. Keith, the Dean of Science, stood at the end of the bed, his red, regency face rounded off like an avocado.

His tongue was dry and gummed to the roof of his mouth and he found it difficult to raise his head. The doctor spoke breezily: 'Good morning – you've got a visitor.' He watched Mawn struggling with his senses. 'It's almost 15.30, you've been having a splendid nap. In case you're wondering where you are, my name's Wilkinson and you're in the Plymouth General Hospital.'

Keith put both hands on the bedrail. The note of solicitude in his voice was almost perfect: 'Alex, what a ghastly business. I'm really so sorry. Miss Hale was dead on arrival here.'

Mawn took a long drink from a bedside water glass. His voice rasped: 'Is there anything left?'

'Oh, yes indeed. It was mainly confined to the central lab and your office, they managed to get it under control quite quickly.

But I am afraid the roof structure is weakened, at least so they tell me.'

'What about all the files and the records?'

The Dean's face took on a well-modulated gravity. 'There's considerable loss Alex – considerable loss I'm sorry to say . . .'

'Are they all burnt?'

'I am really not sure, but your secretary's office was badly affect . . .'

'All that work!' Mawn cried out.

'Alex, we do have a more serious problem – I – er – want to have a word before the – the police do . . .'

Mawn felt his heart leap: 'Police?'

'Yes, Alex. I really don't want to worry you with it now but – well the police have made a very clear suggestion.'

'What do you mean?'

'They think that you hadn't really adhered to the fire regulations properly. Of course I told them they were wrong, that the most stringent care is always taken . . .'

Mawn met the protuberant eyes, they were saying: see where your carelessness has got us now! He gathered speed. 'To be frank, Alex, I'm worried. As you well know, we've given you a completely free hand with your department – indeed you've had a great deal of encouragement throughout. You see this is all bound to reflect very badly. I can't help . . .'

'Just what is left?' Mawn sat up abruptly cutting the Dean off in mid-flight.

'I'm not sure.'

'Haven't you been there yet?'

'Well no, I haven't really had time, but . . .'

'Jesus!' Mawn threw back the bedclothes and got out of bed unsteadily. He put his hand out to the bedside table for support but it rolled back on castors against the wall. He almost fell.

'For goodness' sake man!' The doctor reached forward.

Mawn brushed past him and began to take his own clothes from a chair.

'Alex, this is most unwise.' The Dean put his hand out in restraint.

'I'm all right.' He winced as he hit the back of his bandaged hand against the chair. 'I'm going to the lab.'

'What am I going to tell the police?' The Dean's voice was strained and petulant. 'I told them you were *here*.'

'Well they can find me at the lab. That's where they should be anyway, not sniffing round the fire regulations.'

'What do you mean?'

Mawn's voice was muffled as he pulled a polo-necked sweater down over his head: 'There's something bloody odd about that fire – if you want it straight I think it was started deliberately.'

'The police didn't mention anything. What are you talking about? Have you any proof?'

'Not yet.' Mawn paused by the door. 'But I tell you, when I get it I shall expect cooperation from the University. Whoever it was is a murderer. He killed Miss Hale.'

'If you want to discharge yourself you'll have to sign the waiver form.' Dr Wilkinson broke in after a glance at Keith.

'You sign it.' The door slammed and Mawn was gone.

Wilkinson spread his hands: 'I can't hold him against his will you know.'

Keith shook his head angrily: 'Really the most intemperate man. I have to put up with a great deal. The television business was bad enough...'

'Television?' Wilkinson looked puzzled, but Keith didn't reply and started to lead the way out of the ward.

Firemen were still working inside the gutted house, bringing out burnt and twisted laboratory equipment. Mawn quickly established his credentials with a bored police constable standing by the front door and walked in.

It was like walking into the rib-cage of a giant. One side of the building was a bare, charred framework, with the edges of the upper floor tilting down at an angle from the outside wall. One of the laboratory benches was perched precariously on the end, ready to slide off down into the hallway below.

Mawn clambered over the charred joists and beams and found the door leading down to the basement computer room.

At the bottom of the stairs he saw that emergency lighting

had already been rigged and some men were working on the units of the computer. For a moment he thought that they were there on behalf of the University, to move the machine to new premises. Then he caught sight of Duckett, the computer firm's trouble shooter.

'Bad business, Doctor,' he said as Mawn approached. 'Still, could be worse. Fire didn't reach this computer luckily.'

'You mean it's all right?'

'This part is. I've checked as much as I can. OK as far as I can see.'

'Thank God for something!' Mawn's relief must have been evident and the release from tension made him sway a little.

'Here, take it easy.' Duckett caught his arm.

'I'm OK.'

Duckett nodded and turned away a little uneasily.

'Anyway, what're you doing here?'

'Ah, well you see, Doctor,' he saw Mawn's pallor and hesitated, 'we've been asked to remove it – much as we can anyway.'

'Remove it! On whose authority?'

'Came directly from the Dean I understand.'

Mawn understood. The return of the computer would finally draw his teeth. It would all be neatly minuted at an emergency meeting of the Academic Board. He imagined the Dean at the meeting: 'Of course the building is quite unsound – we couldn't conceivably leave all that equipment there, the whole place might collapse – I'm sure Doctor Mawn would approve if he were here.'

He looked around sadly at the twisted and blackened racks of tapes and files. Years of hard, hard work and now what?

'Mr Mawn?' A policeman was standing at the bottom of the stairs shielding his eyes against the light from the naked bulbs.

'Mr Mawn? There's a man upstairs asking for you.'

Mawn turned and slowly made his way up the stairs.

After the sour acridity of burnt wood, the fresh air outside was a benediction. He screwed his eyes against the dazzle of the sun and saw Sheldon Peters standing by his car.

Two

Peters waved Mawn in through the open door. Mawn followed down a thickly carpeted corridor opening on to a living-room which blazed at him like a sun.

It had all the signs of a carefully-arranged stage set. The walls were hung with brown linen panels leading down to dimpled, black leather cushions set informally around the floor. In the centre stood a low, plate-glass table, with chromium frame, and hung on the cloth walls were large, abstract paintings chosen more for the current vogue of the artist than their quality. A European Television Award statue shone under its own light in a small alcove. The floor was of soft oatmeal-coloured carpet. One side of the room was hung with heavy curtain drapes part surrounding a baby grand piano. Mawn looked about with an increasing sense of incredulity. A place to dazzle, he thought, living in it would be like trying to be comfortable in a hotel lounge.

As his eyes adjusted to the glare, he became aware of a tall, slim girl standing by a table. 'Alex, meet a friend of mine,' Peters said. 'Marcia Scott, Alex Mawn.' Her grasp was firm and he saw cool, green eyes appraising him, framed by full, black hair swept evenly back. He had an immediate impression of probing intelligence. He put her age at a little over thirty.

Peters waited until they were settled into soft white leather armchairs, then turned to Marcia: 'You know the mess Alex has got into?' She nodded. 'Well, I've got an idea, I'll put it up – just to see what you do with it. Briefly, I think Alex is the first English victim of the environmental backlash. First there was Nader in the States when that motor corporation tried to nail him, now we've got the Japanese environmentalist Nickimodo – he has to ride about in a bullet-proof car – not because of ordinary people, but because of threats from large corporations. Now Alex goes and accuses three large consortia of incompetent production, his lab gets burnt down and an assistant dies.'

'OK, so big business is very nasty and protective, but that

doesn't make a case.' Her voice was low-pitched and she spoke with a mild Boston inflexion.

'Maybe not,' Peters continued, 'but – and here I declare myself – it'll make a tremendously powerful piece for my next "Nightstyle" programme.'

Marcia put her drink down and laughed: 'Shel – you're a real media pro, if you don't have a case – make one, is that it?'

Peters saw Mawn give a tired, wary glance at the American woman and anticipated his curiosity. 'Marcia and I have known each other for years – reason why I got you both together is that I think you've a common interest . . .'

'Which will lead to an even better TV show!' Marcia drawled.

Peters smiled: 'Give it a rest, love.' Then to Mawn. 'Marcia is a research psychologist and she's been doing some performance tests on certain groups of workers here in England. Now I felt when you went off on TV at the air control place there might be a common thread. Alex, are you too tired to go over it again – for Marcia?'

'Don't you think maybe some other time?' Marcia looked anxiously at the large Englishman, his head sunk on his chest in near exhaustion, his coat still blackened from his search in the ruins of the laboratory.

Mawn raised his head: 'No, I asked Peters to get moving. I'd much rather talk than think right now.'

He drained his glass and watched Peters refill it before continuing: 'I'll try and explain – if it just seems too bloody obvious to you, then shut me up. I've been interested in the man-machine interface, that's just a long-winded way of describing what happens when a human being operates a machine. If you like, the interface of a typist is what goes on between her fingers and the keys she hits. Why she makes mistakes there and so-on.

'Well, my work has been around human operators and complex machines like computer . . .'

'And aircraft control systems!' Peters interposed. 'By the way, how *did* you get your press badge?'

Mawn waved his drink: 'Dead simple. A reporter I go drinking with at Plymouth. He's on the local rag. I wanted to see the system at first hand. I borrowed his, that's all. Anyhow, I've been gathering a lot of data about mistakes which are made between operators and control machines – it's absolutely horrifying. There's an information jam across it. Start with the abacus. The operator slaps his beads around and does very quick arithmetic. If he makes a mistake he can see the whole guts of his machine in front of him – just beads on wires – so he can see the mistake and put it right.

'Now, we make ourselves computers and do massive sums very, very quickly. Sums which we couldn't even begin to do with our heads however long or hard we tried – interrelation of complex variables for example – if the machine goes wrong – we probably *can* put it right – but it takes a very long time. The point is we can't *see* the source of the error like the beads . . .'

'But you can find it,' Marcia intervened.

'Yes, we can, but that was in the first and second generation machines. Now your hard technologist is a greedy bastard. He says to himself – my last machine did its sums in X seconds, now I can make it do them in half of X seconds – so he does it – not because anyone really needs it – but because it will be a very good selling point. So he has to develop more efficient and much smaller computing elements. First we had the monolith blocks, now micro-monolith and so-on . . .

'. . . but that's not enough by itself. The designer's got to think up new ways of increasing his machine's performance – just to keep ahead of the field – so he takes a look at the human brain to see whether it has any little tricks he can copy and he finds it can learn. So he starts to make circuits in his machine so the machine can learn – that is, improve its future performance as a result of past experience.'

'All of which is a good thing, surely?' Peters interjected.

'Yes, but there's a snag – this search for ultimate performance has a cost in reliability. Everyone's madly squeezing the last ounce of work from their circuits and so they start to take risks.'

'What kind of risks?' Peters asked.

'I've done quite a bit of work on this,' Mawn went on. 'Putting it at its simplest, there are conditions where one error makes two, two makes four and so-on. Sometimes it's even more severe and it can go two, six, eleven, etc.'

'A sort of mechanical brainstorm,' Marcia said.

'Yes, that's it. We're getting so incredibly lazy as a species we give more and more of our functions over to the tinware – we no longer worry about the fact that we're taking more and more materials out of the earth – things we can *never* put back – just to make computers which are so bloody smart we don't even know how they go wrong. Nobody needs the damn things except maybe hospitals – they're just an electronic phallus – a technological status symbol.'

'Oh, really, that's just polemic,' Marcia said.

Mawn continued without appearing to have heard her: '. . . So here you've got your machine wallowing in its own complexity, desperately trying to retain its efficiency in the face of its own man-built unreliability. It's a dinosaur . . .' He gestured with the glass. 'The great lizards grew very large and they had little pea-brains. Now a small brain with slow conducting nerves can't hope to control a vast body like a dinosaur – so the poor beasts had to develop a second brain down by their backside – that still wasn't enough. They slopped about in mud and finally got extinguished, because they were uncontrollable. I've called it "the dinosaur effect".'

'That wasn't the only reason, surely?' said Peters.

'All right, that was simplistic, but we're making more and more complex machines and they are definitely getting more unreliable – they make faulty products and tell their human operators that the product is not faulty . . .'

'You've no evidence of that surely?' Marcia said.

'Everything points to it, and we'll get more things like that – bound to happen – just a matter of time. Greed and opportunity that's all!'

After he had stopped speaking, there was a long silence. Peters seemed to be mentally appraising how Mawn's performance would look on his TV show, Marcia Scott was on the edge of her seat, her face flushed and excited, waiting to break in:

'Hey, that's fantastic! But excuse me, you're way off on the wrong track about the fault lying in the space *between* the operator and the machine. The fault isn't there. You see I've been working on . . .'

Mawn, who had moodily slumped forward in his seat and did not appear to have heard a word, suddenly broke in:

'Of course!' He turned to Peters, oblivious of Marcia's annoyed stare. 'I've got it. The laser burn! We can track that bastard.' Mawn was practically hugging himself with pleasure, oblivious of the other two.

Marcia rose and Peters saw two high spots of colour on her cheeks. 'I don't think Dr Mawn is in any condition to hold a two-sided conversation right now, Shel. If you'll excuse me I'll get along.'

She walked to the door, followed by Peters. Mawn could hear him trying to soothe her down in the hall before the front door of the flat banged behind her.

'What's the matter with her?' Mawn looked up in bewilderment as Peters returned.

'She got the impression you weren't very interested in her views on the subject.'

'Oh!' But Mawn's mind was obviously on other things. 'Can I use your phone?'

'Of course. Use the flat as your own while you're staying here. I'm seldom around anyway.'

'I'm going to phone a friend of mine, he's an eye doctor. I've an idea he can be very useful right now.'

To Mawn the pub exemplified all the more repellent aspects of the twentieth century. Black plastic beams complete with artificial grain ribbed the ceiling and were hung with crude, brass-plated, replica horse-brasses. Around the melamine-surfaced bar, groups of men in anonymous executive uniform huddled in earnest confederation around glass tankards. The walls were lined with artificially-aged replicas of theatre bills and the barman himself looked theatrically Dickensian as he wheezed stertorously between customers. The smoke-hazed air smelt of hot pies, after-shave and beer.

Mawn looked down at his watch. Peter Brookman was late.

Brookman had been a last long-shot following the agony of

the inquest. Mawn had spent several days trying to reconstruct the details of the laboratory layout, so he would be able to answer the coroner's questions. He had noted down the position of the experimental apparatus on the bench relative to the inflammables stored in Winchester flasks on the shelf nearby. He had also made a complete breakdown of all the wiring and electronics apparatus and talked it out with Peters at his flat. Peters had given him his spare room and was negotiating a contract with the BBC on his behalf for a forthcoming television programme.

He had made his allegation about an intruder just once. The coroner – an elderly doctor – had received his statement with a stony politeness which was more insulting than a direct denial and had hinted that it was an excuse he frequently heard from people who wanted to avoid possible charges of negligence.

The police had behaved in a determined and suspicious way and had gone to considerable lengths to suggest that there might be a civil case for the University to answer.

The Dean of Science had appeared and, without overtly saying so, pointed out to the coroner that Mawn's department was separate from the main University buildings and that Mawn had been given more of the responsibility for its safety than the heads of other departments. It had been a beautifully phrased buck-passing performance, elegantly terminated by a short speech of sympathy for Mawn.

The coroner had then asked who deputized for Mawn when he was absent. He had answered that there was nobody since they all worked together as a team. The coroner then read from a copy of the University Regulations and pointed out that it clearly stated that, in the absence of a head, departments were to be officially deputized in writing.

Towards the end, it had become clear that the coroner had not been able to gather enough evidence to implicate the living so he turned to the dead.

Methodically he went through the evidence supplied by members of Mawn's department and began to construct a picture of Tina Hale as both over-worked and careless. He recalled the comments of one student who had said that she was 'a sort of string and sealing wax worker' and another who called her 'the artful bodger'. Mawn himself knew that her slapdash methods were his own responsibility and due entirely to the overwhelming pressure he himself had created. He listened with a dull anger to the liturgy of inefficiency intoned by the coroner.

The verdict had been preceded by a long moralizing homily by the coroner about the need for increased vigilance in laboratories. The word to Mawn sounded cold and empty: 'death by misadventure'.

In the University, Mawn had suffered the full consequences of the loner. He had never troubled to keep within any particular corridors of power and had openly expressed his contempt for those who did. It was the view of many of the staff that he had been negligent, with the result that the good name of the University had been tarnished. He remembered one comment he overheard at the faculty club bar: '. . . nice bloke, but he's so damned erratic – too much time with his Arctic penguins I suppose – he'll catch it now – the Deanery's been looking for a chance like this for ages.'

He recalled his last conversation with Dean Keith about his personal chair which the academic board had already approved in principle. 'This sort of thing is so difficult, Alex. I really don't think we must rush things at this stage, do you?' The blue watery eyes held about as much concern as a professional assassin.

He began to think about looking for a new job. Back to the Arctic? No, never again. Television science pundit? Teaching? Medical research?

Well, first he had a job to do. He had reasoned that the man who had driven past him in the lane had held a handkerchief to one eye. Lasers burn the back of the eye and so the driver, if he was the intruder, might have retinal burns from the laser in the lab. He had contacted Peter Brookman who ran an ophthalmological department in a London teaching hospital and specialized in industrial eye injuries. He had asked whether there was any category in Brookman's records including laser burns and if so had anyone sent in any cases of laser burns to the eye within the past four weeks.

'Sorry I'm late, Alex but one of my old ladies decided to have a bleed – lots of drama. How are you? It must be ages!'

Mawn looked up: 'Peter, good of you to come, thank you.'

'I was curious – just to see how you're doing. Saw you on the box by the way – jolly interesting – do you really believe all that rhubarb about – what was it? – your "dinosaur effect" – people not working their gadgetry properly?'

Mawn smiled: 'Yes, as a matter of fact I do.'

'Well, all I can say is that I hope it doesn't get into my operating theatres – it's all so computerized nowadays. Can't do an ordinary common or garden cataract extraction without punching up some damn programme or other – that looks nice beer you're drinking . . .'

'Sorry. What'll you have?'

'Half of best bitter, please.'

Mawn went over to the bar and came back with a small tankard. 'Don't want to rush you Peter, but did you get anything out of your records?'

Brookman patted his briefcase which was lying on the bar counter between them. 'Yes, I did – three altogether. One got his burn in Edinburgh, the second is female so they're both out . . .' He opened the briefcase and took out three stiff brown envelopes labelled 'Clinical Record,' '. . . . and the third is – well – a possible.'

He put the envelope down on top of the briefcase. 'But we've got a little problem, Alex.'

'What's that?'

'Well you see, these are all confidential – the seventy-three Privacy Bill and all that.'

'Oh!'

Brookman put the tankard down: 'Trouble with this stuff, always puts me in mind of a piddle – where is it?'

Mawn pointed to a plush velvet curtain: 'Through there.' Brookman eased himself off the bar stool and pointed to the envelopes.

'Look after those while I'm gone, will you?' He walked towards the curtain.

Mawn scanned the notes quickly, eliminating the two Brookman had already mentioned, he opened the third envelope and read:

'TELLER, George. Age thirty-four. Heat burn to right eye. Gives only a general account of how he did it. Says he was involved in work with infra-red beam. Now says he can't see properly and the eye is continuously watery. On examination the right eye shows some circum-limbal injection and a mild vascular reaction. *Ophthalmoscopy*: There is a small punctate lesion on the temporal side of the fovea, it extends forward into the vitreous and is typical of a coherent light (laser) burn. His story of how he got it must therefore be regarded as false . . .'

Mawn scanned quickly through the rest of the notes and turned the page. On the back, he read: Home address: 14 Dreighton Gardens, London SW9. Work address: Director, Teller Intelligence Services, Pomeroy House, Edgware Road, London A41ZO.

Mawn scanned quickly down the slotted nameboard near the glass swing doors. The individually lettered titles included an accountant, a psychiatrist, a firm of insurance brokers and a dentist. He picked out 'Teller Intelligence Services'.

He looked through the glass doors at the main foyer of the building, thickly carpeted, with a long, low black couch and a magazine-strewn glass table facing a long curved desk, with a small switchboard and an impersonally pretty receptionist. A medium height, thick-set man in a light brown car coat was talking to her, leaning across the desk. Mawn hesitated before going in. What was he to say to this man Teller, even supposing that he was the man in question.

After leaving Brookman he had walked through the busy London streets towards the Edgware Road without a clear idea of how he would tackle him. He glanced at his watch and, almost with relief, saw that it was 17.45. Teller would surely have left his office by now.

As he glanced up the man by the desk turned for a moment and, with a shock, Mawn saw that he had a pink eye shade over one eye. His mind racing, Mawn eased back against the wall, waiting.

Finally, after what seemed to Mawn an intolerable wait, though it could hardly have been more than two minutes, the man came towards the glass doors and shouldered them open, waving back at the receptionist as he did so.

Almost involuntarily Mawn stepped forward and touched him on the arm. The man turned and, with a shock of recognition, Mawn thought he saw the face he caught sight of in his car headlights that night. Surely it was the same large, startled blue eye, the same lank strand of black hair framing a round moon face. And, to Mawn, the sense of instant recognition was mutual. The man's remaining eye seemed to register first shock then apprehension before he regained control.

'George Teller?' Mawn's voice sounded high pitched and uncertain to his ear.

'Yes?'

'My name's Doctor Mawn. I'd like to speak with you, if I may.'

'I'm sorry, you've caught me on my way out – to a function. I'm late already. If you'd like to phone me.' Teller was impersonal, quick and smooth, he edged past Mawn and made for the outside doors.

'No wait!' Mawn sprang ahead of him, blocking his way. 'I must speak to you now.' He felt shaken but determined. 'It's very urgent.'

Teller looked at him coolly, almost with amusement, noting his confusion. 'Make it quick then.'

'Your eye. It looks bad. How did you damage it?'

Teller smiled: 'What is this? Professional interest, Doctor Mawn?'

'I'm not that kind of doctor. I'm a research scientist with a lab down near Plymouth,' Mawn scanned him closely, 'which was burnt down by an intruder a couple of weeks ago.'

'Really?' Teller's eye showed only a slightly puzzled impatience. 'What has this to do with me?'

'My research assistant, Tina Hale, was killed in the fire. There could be a charge of manslaughter against this intruder.'

Mawn seemed to see a slight flicker pass over the other man's face but Teller's voice was entirely steady when he replied: 'How does this concern me?'

'The intruder caught a laser beam in the eye, this leaves a very definite scar recognizable by any doctor. Attempts to pass it off as an infra-red burn won't work.'

Again the shadow passed over Teller's face, but he merely glanced at his watch. 'Look, I'm late. Can't we cut this short. I take it you're working up to some form of accusation?'

'Not yet. I'm just warning you to have a better story ready.' Mawn was gaining confidence, the other man seemed nervous, his hands fiddling with a bunch of car keys. 'Lasers are only found in labs.' Teller frowned: 'What exactly do you want?'

'The name of the man, or firm, who sent you.'

There was a silence for a moment, then Teller spoke abruptly: 'You don't need me, chum. You need a psychiatrist!' He gestured towards the nameboard. 'I recommend Dr Brown – you might just catch him in.' And before Mawn could stop him, he was out the doors, down the steps and walking along the street. With a sudden premonition Mawn opened the door and looked after him. Teller walked into a side road opposite, unlocked and climbed into a parked car by the long row of meters. But which car it was Mawn couldn't make out.

Then a car edged out of the line of parked vehicles and drove up to the end of the street, its side blinkers winking. Mawn shaded his eyes from the late sun and stared. There was no doubt about it now, it was a BMW 2002, the same car that had so nearly driven into him in the lane.

With a new sense of purpose, Mawn turned back through both sets of doors into the foyer. The pretty receptionist was standing up holding a small mirror and delicately outlining her right eye with a brown pencil.

'Sorry to trouble you but Mr Teller has asked me to make an appointment with him, this week or next.'

'Oh!' She looked slightly put out, but bent down, unlocked her desk drawer and brought out an appointments book. 'Let's see.' She flicked over the pages. 'Thursday afternoon any good to you?'

'No. I'm afraid not.'

'Well, there's early Friday morning?'

'No, can't make that either.'

This time she was definitely annoyed. A buzzer sounded on the switchboard and she went over to answer it. Mawn leant over and took Teller's appointment book from the desk. He flipped back through the pages and ran his finger down the appointments between his television appearance and the fire in his lab. The first page yielded only a couple of names unfamiliar to Mawn. He turned over – there it was! Almost with a sense of incredulity he read 'Gelder – King's Head'. Brian Gelder could it be?

He flicked quickly through the pages leading up to the present date – there it was again. 'B. Gelder' this time, 'King's Head' and once more it appeared in the 13.00 column.

'Do you mind?' The girl, angry now, was back. She snatched the book out of his hands. Mawn smiled at her: 'I'm afraid Mr Teller is far too busy for me during the next couple of weeks. Perhaps you'd tell him I'll be phoning him . . . Dr Mawn's the name.'

He turned and started towards the door, oblivious of the girl's irritation. As he went out he mentally dismissed Teller. Another name was recurring much too frequently – Brian Gelder.

Peters put the highly polished tray down on the glass table. Marcia noted with a wry amusement that it looked exactly like a full colour advertisement from a glossy magazine. On the tray there was a mound of hot steaming croissants, gleaming white bone-china and carefully folded blue linen napkins. It was laid for three. Peters saw the query in her expression. 'Alex Mawn's staying for a few days.' He started to pour the coffee. Marcia frowned. 'Then can I just leave the stuff I've dug out for you, I'd like to be away by the time he appears.'

Peters smiled: 'Hey I've asked you to research a programme and work with him, that's all. Not to go to bed with the man!'

Marcia flushed slightly. 'He doesn't seem much interested in either right now. We get a ten minute monologue then wham, that's it. The great man has spoken! Sorry, I've had your provincial English academic before. It's worse than being back in grade school.'

'You don't think much of his dinosaur effect then?'

'I didn't say that. It's just his polemic I can't stomach. There certainly is something peculiar going on in the balance between man and machines – but – oh, it's just the result of years of soft student audiences – he can't see there's another side to it.'

Peters handed her a coffee cup. 'He's a pretty angry character right now. He's lost most of his records, one of his technicians is dead and his own university wants to disown him as quickly as possible.'

Marcia put the cup down: 'Look, Shel, this is a tremendously real problem. You know my work. I think it very probably fits in with his, but right now he's on some private revenge kick!'

Peters got up and walked over to the door, closing it gently. 'Perhaps it will help if I tell you a little about Alex. I had one of our researchers do some digging. He's quite a man, this red-brick don of yours. To begin with he's quite a bit younger than he appears behind the beard and tweeds.' He gave a slight grimace of distaste. 'He's only just over forty.'

'You've got to be kidding!'

'Nope – forty-three he is. He runs the computing science unit at Plymouth but he's got himself obsessed with the environmental crisis. He's written dozens of articles condemning hard technology – pollution and so-on. That's why he's in bad odour with his university. Apparently he spends half his time doing measurements on local pollution issues, when he should be teaching students computer logic.'

'Well, it's a good racket these days. Quickest way to grab some free publicity.'

Peters wagged his finger at her: 'That's unfair, Marcia, no, the key factor was probably his father – he was a foreman at a lead-smelting works. He got chronic lead poisoning – they were very close apparently, and poor Alex had to watch his father die in a particularly horrible way. Just to cap it all – the firm challenged that his father's condition was due to lead and paid him off – there was no worker's compensation then.'

'I see.' Marcia leant back thoughtfully. 'That does alter

things. I guess it explains the chip, the need to hit big industry – OK, Shel but I still can't work with him. He's probably been waiting for a chance like this all of his life. I'm not going to supply data for a hatchet operation.'

'You surprise me,' Peters smiled. 'I thought I'd got through to that elusive heart of yours!'

'Really, I'd expect you to know me better by now.' Marcia looked back coolly at him.

'You still misjudge him. Apparently he also spent two years in the Antarctic . . .' Peters broke off as Mawn appeared at the door and walked in. To Marcia his appearance had completely changed. The previous day he had appeared lumpen and awkward. Now she noticed for the first time a powerful chest under the thick pullover and heavy set shoulders as he walked easily across and sat down by the table. He poured coffee and, with a brief nod, acknowledged Marcia's presence.

'Did you find your one-eyed burglar?' Peters asked.

Mawn helped himself to a croissant before replying: 'Yes, and he's not a burglar. He's an industrial intelligence consultant, whatever that means.'

'It can mean a great deal.' Peters went over to a line of box files on a low shelf hidden by a thick Heal's curtain and pulled one out. 'We did a programme . . .'

'Say, a licence to break in, destroy a man's lifework and even commit murder!' Mawn's voice was not particularly loud, his face was down and he was pouring a second cup of coffee for himself with a rock steady hand but Peters and Marcia turned involuntarily towards him. For the first time Mawn took on a certain presence, the inner power of the man came through to them from the shambling provincial academic. There was a sense of strong will and an inner drive that was almost elemental.

Then the moment passed and Peters smoothly continued; 'This is research we did for a programme about a year back. There are well over twenty firms in England specializing in this particular line of business. It's a nice twentieth-century euphemism for industrial spy.'

'What, bugging, that sort of thing?' Marcia asked.

'Goes far beyond that. Nowadays they're professionals. They can plant or extract almost anything from a firm – bugs, an informer, agent-provocateurs – you name it, they'll do it – for a price.'

'Legally?'

'Oh, yes. They're completely legit – on the surface anyway. They advertise protection – "we'll help you to be secure". What they don't advertise is that they'll also do the reverse – nothing in writing and for cash. They're the technological jackals – scavenging for profit, sales figures, new processes, weaknesses in marketing structure, mistresses, kinks, the lot. People who employ them get an OBE for services to industry. They occasionally get nicked.'

'Why would they want to know what I do?' Mawn asked.

Peters smiled with an effort: 'I don't know whether you're joking or not . . .' Then, as Mawn frowned, 'Alex, you nailed three groups of industrialists in front of an audience of eight million people. You've pointed your finger at probably seven per cent of Britain's industry. You didn't give a theoretical spiel to a bunch of academics, you told some hard-headed opportunists that the way they got their bread is irresponsible and dangerous. What did you expect? Of course they're going to find out what you're doing, and how? – By putting a man on to you, what else?'

'You mean the Gelder Consortium simply held a board meeting and minuted a note to send this man Teller!' said Mawn.

There was a sudden silence. Peters's voice was quiet, almost icy: 'Who mentioned anything about Gelder?'

Mawn looked up at him. 'I was just about to. I've identified the man all right, George Teller . . .' He described his meeting with Teller and his finding the name 'B. Gelder' in the appointments book.

'Could you substantiate any of this – in a Court of Law?' Marcia broke in.

Mawn shook his head: 'I doubt it. My word against his, the coincidence of the laser burn, the car. No. I think I've scared him pretty badly though.'

Peters, who had been pacing to and fro, turned and broke in

with a new urgency in his voice: 'I think I see it now. It would be a private cash arrangement between Brian Gelder and Teller, meeting informally at that pub – what was it – the King's Head? Also I very much doubt that they meant to destroy your lab. Much more likely that they were looking to see what you had on file and how much was bluff.'

'Yes, but how could that affect Gelder?' Marcia asked.

'Depends on what Alex *has* got.' Peters looked at Alex querying. '*Had* you much?'

Mawn replied: 'It's all in ashes now.' He looked down.

'Enough, anyway, to show that he'd had a series of failures in some of his installations which would make a small business fold up altogether.'

'Gelder heads an enormous European consortium,' Peters put in. 'Their main line at the moment is building nuclear power stations. Things like the ACE control centre are relative flea-bites. He's got all the family money behind him – it's a merchant bank – so he can more or less print his own money. He's done extremely well so far, built his light-water reactors all over the world – Japan, Germany, the States, even Albania – right Alex?'

Mawn looked up and nodded: 'They're just taking advantage of the energy crunch and making a profit. You see – the writing is pretty much on the wall for fossil fuels – the States have run out of natural gas, the price of oil is rocketing – so every country is saying, where the hell do we get power from? So they build nuclear reactors, it's obvious. What isn't obvious is that the type they're putting up is the cheapest.'

'So?' Marcia queried.

'Cheapness has got to mean reduction in safety standards,' Mawn continued. 'Nobody can successfully test the safety systems anyway, but if you cut costs – you're bound to make an untested safety system less safe. I've got information that they've had to spend so much money putting faults right in stations they have built that their profits are likely to be almost nil this year. And now they've started up this giant new station at Grim-Ness in the Orkney Islands.'

Peters was standing by the window looking out at what promised to be a fine, clear June day. He turned: 'The European Government, in their wisdom, have decided that there is going to be a chain of nuclear power stations all across Europe and that they can be contracted out to consortia like Gelder's. They are supposed to supplement our own gas-cooled reactors which, incidentally, have got a very good safety record.'

Marcia leant forward excitedly: 'So this place in – where did you say?'

'Grim-Ness – good name for it!'

'So it's a kind of test station?'

'Much more,' Mawn intervened. 'Information is that if it doesn't come in on time and they have to do the same sort of fault clearing, they may run out of cash.'

'If Mr Gelder was a poker player,' said Marcia, 'I guess it would be "go for broke", right?'

Mawn nodded. Peters, slowly, almost unconsciously, began rubbing his hands together in excitement. 'So the last thing he wants is any unfavourable publicity right now, when the British Government is deciding whether or not to buy his new type of power station. It begins to make sense.' He looked over at Mawn, obviously enjoying the whole situation. 'I wonder how far a thirty-five-year-old boy-wonder tycoon will go to protect his interest? Alex, we're going to have to be very, very careful with you from now on.'

'And we're going to carry on with the programme?' Marcia's eyes were lit up with excitement.

'Why not?'

'They're big boys, we'll have to be pretty damn sure of our facts.'

'Agreed,' said Peters. 'But a scoop like this is what makes my job bearable.'

Mawn looked from one to the other, the mercurial, very slightly effeminate commentator and the trim, almost severe New England psychologist with her hair drawn back from her handsome bony face. They both seemed to have forgotten him in the excitement of the moment and he suddenly wondered what he was getting into. The phone rang. Peters sprang to answer it.

'Hello, hello.' He was almost jocular, then his face changed as he listened, his eyebrows rose as he looked back at the other two and he sat down carefully.

'Yes, fine.' He put his hand over the receiver. 'Richard Lodge, Under-Secretary at the Ministry of Science. I've done a couple of programmes with him but he's never called here before.' He took his hand off the phone.

'Yes. Hello, Richard. Yes, I can talk, go ahead.' As Peters listened the boyish smile dwindled, his body became rigid and the others could almost feel the tension. Apart from an occasional affirmation, he did not reply. Finally he put the receiver down and walked thoughtfully over to the window.

'Please,' said Marcia, unable to bear the suspense. 'What did he want? Was it about Alex?'

Peters nodded: 'Yes, in the nicest possible way he suggested that we didn't go on with your dinosaur effect. Apparently not only would it not be in the national interest, that's the standard Ministerial line, but,' he turned to Mawn, 'it would not be in the interest of mankind as a whole.'

Three

Gelder put the lap chart down on the pit-counter. He was sitting alongside the main straight of the Brands Hatch motor-racing circuit. Behind him stood Ian Caird, Managing Director of the Caird Oil Company.

The main straight separated the two men from the packed grandstand opposite to them. Along the edge of the stand was a notice proclaiming: 'Caird Formula 5000'. The public address loudspeakers blared: 'Now we come to the main event of the day – a fifty-lap race for Formula 5000 cars, the Caird Oil Trophy. Any moment now the cars should be coming out for the warming-up lap . . .'

The echoing voice was swamped in the harsh calico-ripping snarl of the cars as their engines fired up one by one in the paddock. Marshals swung back the gates and urgently beckoned. One by one, like wild beasts released from a cage, the long-snouted projectiles probed their way on to the circuit and, one after another, howled off down the track in a haze of bright blue rubber smoke, the drivers hunched down like astronauts in fully enveloping helmets. As the last car disappeared round Paddock Bend, for a few moments there was silence, then a high pitched whine announced the arrival of the first car as it slowed down from the warming up lap and began to nose into position on the white painted squares of the starting grid. Marshals peremptorily beckoned the remainder into position until finally an official held up both arms and signalled to the race marshal's box.

Engines snapped off as mechanics rushed on to the track, surrounding their charges like bees round a queen. A man in white overalls walked out in front of the cars and held up a board with the legend: '5 minutes', a klaxon blared and the mechanics quickened their activities anxiously.

Caird turned to Gelder. He spoke with the soft, rather meticulous care of the Highlander: 'How was your car this morning?'

Brian Gelder pointed to a driver leaning back in a low blue and white car in pole position on the front row of the grid: 'Mark got down to one minute two in practice.'

'Will you be winning?' Caird smiled thinly.

'Doubt it. Anderson's on good form, he did a minute dead this morning – can't do much about that.'

'You said you had a problem.' Gelder smiled and nodded. The pit Tannoy over their heads crackled: 'Clear the grid – three minutes – clear the grid.' Mechanics gave a last polish to windshields, banged their drivers on the shoulder in encouragement and began reluctantly to move away towards the pit-counters.

Engines crackled and banged unevenly into action, drowning all conversation, as the one minute signal went up and the starter walked to his rostrum with a furled Union Jack. The driver of the blue and white car turned briefly towards the pit where

Gelder sat, nodded his helmet briefly and settled back in the safety harness twitching the steering wheel.

The starter unfurled the flag and slowly raised it. The movement was accompanied by the rising scream of the engines. Suddenly he whipped the flag down and the air exploded with a physically painful blast of sound hammering into chests, drowning all thought. The cars leaped forward as if tied together. One snaked through the pack from the rear, tyres touched. Drivers wrenched their mounts back into line.

Suddenly the whole pack was gone, thundering away down towards the bottle-neck of the first corner. Over the grid the air swirled and eddied in the wake of the cars and clouds of acrid dust and smoke blew over the crowd.

Gelder's face was alive: 'Christ, I wouldn't miss that.' He turned to Caird: 'The problem's called Dr Alexander Mawn.'

'Never heard of him.'

'I'll tell you. There's champagne laid on – let's go and get some, besides there's someone else I want you to meet.'

'What about your car?'

'It's fifty laps yet, come on.'

The marquee could have been at a motor race, a country farm show or Royal Ascot. The surroundings were similar and many of the densely-packed crowd seemed to be identi-kit copies of the bored and affluent afficionados who throng the upper reaches of spectator sports.

There were long wooden folding tables covered in white cloths. Rows of glasses, plates of tired canapés and a red-faced throng buzzing with animated conversation. Nobody reacted to the intermittent scream of the cars as they rocketed past outside the tarpaulin walls.

Gelder walked over to a short, almost completely bald man in a light Alpaca suit. He wore rimless glasses. Caird followed. 'Carl, glad you could make it.' The bald man turned and raised a glass of champagne, smiling: 'Hey, this is pretty good material for an oil company!' His face was flushed.

Gelder turned to Caird: 'Ian, this is Carl Bellamy. Carl, Ian Caird, who provides champagne and oil.' The two men shook hands, eyes moving expertly, assessing. Gelder continued: 'Carl heads NALA computers.' Caird smiled: 'Yes, of course, glad to meet you at last.'

The bald American smiled: 'We surely ought to have met – we've done enough dealing over the years.'

Caird picked up a glass of champagne and turned to Gelder: 'Your problem, Brian?'

'Yes.' Gelder looked down at his glass. 'Dr Mawn.' Gelder turned the glass. 'Ian, you fired the mate of the *Yarmouth Pier* tanker pretty damn quick, didn't you? After the Southend grounding.' Caird stiffened and put his glass down slowly: 'Pardon?'

'And Captain Osborne of the *Scarborough Pier*?'

'How?'

'All those people on the beach never realized how close they came to being fried did they?'

There was a long silence broken by the coughing snarl of a car in the paddock nearby. Caird's sallow face seemed to have elongated, his skin looked grey in the filtered light of the marquee. 'We've known each other a long time, Brian. Hadn't you better explain?'

'That is right, isn't it?'

'Yes.'

Gelder turned to the American: 'Carl, some of the computing elements you supplied to the Bijon coal mine were proved faulty by an independent team of investigators. And then there was the test of the control gear for the French Epourentail anti-missile missile. Ten people died in that village when it went off course didn't they?'

The American stood quite still, his eyes searching Gelder's face. His voice was silky but without inflexion: 'I'd sure like to know where you got all that, Brian. Have you changed your line of business?'

'It came from just one source, Doctor Mawn.'

'Jesus Christ!'

'What I've just told you came from his files.' Gelder continued, 'One of my employees is almost certainly involved.'

Caird nodded grimly: 'Impressive!'

Gelder picked up a champagne bottle and filled their glasses: 'You've very little need to worry, those files – are now quite safe. My point is – where do we go from here?'

'I'm not entirely with you?' Caird replied.

'This Mawn – how did he get to all that?' Bellamy asked.

'I'm not sure yet, I'm looking into it,' Gelder replied. 'But people like him automatically attract all the people with a chip, say disgruntled employees, one you may have fired. They get their own back by taking him some of your confidential material and delude themselves they're doing good to the environment at the same time. Then Mawn gets adopted by the media and we've got trouble.'

Bellamy spoke sharply: 'What use is he going to make of it?'

'Propaganda. To force more restrictive legislation on us. He's one of your zero growth people – stop using depleted resources – stop industry chasing the profit motive alone – all that.'

The American relaxed: 'We've got lots of these characters back in the States. They're always holding teach-ins, sit-ins; it's OK, it gives the students something new to put on their placards. Soft Liberal bullshit. Why give it a thought?'

'This one's not just an econut. I've met him. He's hard-thinking, he's a scientist – he knows exactly what he's talking about and he's prepared to fight. It's not just you he's after. He's done a complete – in depth – study; economics, safety, the lot, on the nuclear reactors and control gear my consortium makes. We're three-quarters complete at my new station at Orkney. I've got to bring it in on time. If I don't – we've got so many penalty clauses against us it could jeopardize the whole deal.'

The American nodded: 'I wondered why you invited me down. We're pretty deep into that project ourselves.'

Caird spoke: 'He's taking a big risk using all that stuff. He must know it's actionable under the Privacy Bill. What does he want?'

Gelder put his glass down: 'For us all to go back to the cave. Look, consider this, ever since that man went on the media, he gave half the small investors of this country a nervous breakdown. They've been selling like the devil and buying unit trusts. You see, every investor in this country is already tremendously nervous about high technology groups like ours. You've seen the Stock Exchange Index, just one man in two days, by scare tactics, has wiped approximately four and a half-million off our stock value. Oh, we'll recover all right, but he'll do it again. Every word Mawn utters costs all of us here thousands!'

Caird smiled thinly. 'You obviously have a suggestion to make, let's hear it.'

'You agree he should be stopped?' Gelder looked at the two men. Bellamy nodded.

Caird raised his eyebrows: 'Stopped?'

'I'd like to talk to you both about it. Perhaps we could meet next week at my place in town?'

'By all means,' Caird nodded.

'Sure. I'll still be around I guess.'

Gelder looked over at Caird: 'Incidentally – did you fire those two men?'

'Nobody fires senior union men these days. But, yes – they're not with us any longer.'

'That cost you!' said Bellamy.

'I can't tolerate that sort of inefficiency,' Caird went on. 'We're plagued with it. Reliability – production standards, it's very, very bad.'

'You can say that again,' Bellamy went on. 'In one production line of ours we've had to make up an entirely new work force. Just inspectors. None of the products are fully operational any more . . .' He broke off, remembering he was talking to customers.

Gelder nodded: 'The most dangerous thing about the Mawns is that they're having increasing influence. They teach, they give lectures. There is the basis of a really dangerous movement here. It's almost an "invisible college" without a campus. You never know where they're going to crop up. They're getting organized, and it's time we did.'

'I'll drink to that,' Bellamy said.

Gelder looked the two men over carefully. 'But we can't

publish any prospectus.' He raised his glass. 'Call it the invisible board.'

Mawn threw the papers down on the table and leaned back, realizing that he had been only half concentrating on the lists of figures he was preparing for the 'Nightstyle' programme. First of all he had been glad of the work, glad of the chance to do something, to be away from the blackened ruins of his work over the last twelve years and the hostile atmosphere of his college where he was suddenly an outcast, a loser, a man who had got the university into disrepute both by his appearances on the media and by his carelessness which caused the death of a fellow member of the staff and destroyed their only computer.

Campus opinion, which had started out by being sympathetic to Mawn, had now finally hardened, and the echoes were apparent at his club and the London college he frequented. A guarded politeness and hastily-remembered appointments were all he found when he tried to engage them in conversation.

Sitting in another man's living-room drinking his whisky and living, as he bitterly put it, on BBC 'charity', Alex Mawn realized that he was for the first time in his life totally disorientated, out of touch, a spectator waiting for something to happen. He went over the previous crises in his life, the struggle to pass his finals at Cambridge, the first Antarctic expedition, the long months of privation. Then, his marriage to Gwen, the gradual drift apart, the mess of the divorce, with one harmless infidelity brought up in Court and hammered home until the girl, a former research student, was forced to leave the University . . .

There were voices outside the main door to the flat and he quickly pulled his mind back to the present. Peters entered, followed by Marcia, shaking the rain from a small folding umbrella.

Peters opened a rather damp evening paper and put it down on the table. 'Might interest you – a piece about Brian Gelder. Our friend is off on holiday with the Club Méditerranée. There's a picture of him here complete with doll on arm, taking off for Dubrovnik – looking jet-set and smooth.'

'You're kidding!' Marcia broke in. 'What's a millionaire doing with the straw hat and twenty pounds a week brigade?'

'You're wrong about that,' Peters continued. 'I went to the Cefalu place in Italy once. A lot of very well-heeled people go there. One Swiss millionaire flew his whole family down in his own plane. The food's terrific and the whole place reeks of wine and sex.'

Marcia shook her head: 'I still can't buy it. He's your sub-Onassis type. If he wanted that he'd probably buy his own island and import fifty guests by jet. There's got to be another reason . . .'

'Just a moment!' Peters broke in excitedly. 'Do you remember that news story a few months back. There was some report of increased radiation in the air over – where was it? – yes, by God it was, over the Adriatic! Some French research vessel picked it up. I remember now, there was speculation whether the Yugoslavs or someone had got the bomb and done a sneak test.'

'What was the result?' Marcia asked.

'Oh, nothing.' Peters went on. 'There was no confirmation – someone else denied the figures and the story died the death.'

'And there's a Gelder-built station in Albania,' Mawn said. 'Supposing they blew it up. I remember when they were building it, they gave several news stories out. Come to think of it they went very quiet about it after a bit. They're normally pretty tight, but – yes they did – they cancelled a visit by some of our science people. I should think they probably wrecked it then got a rocketing from their Chinese advisers. That's their main entente now, at least for technical and scientific help. It also probably embarrasses them ideologically that they did a financial deal with a Western European group.'

'But if Gelder wants to visit Albania, surely there's an easier way, isn't there? I mean, he'd just go,' said Marcia.

'If he's going to Albania,' Peters replied, 'presumably he doesn't want to be seen going. Maybe he's just *persona non grata* there. If they have blown the whole thing up they'd never make anything public, it was too much of a showpiece. I remember, because they told a lot of half-truths about the origin of some of the equipment.'

'Suppose they have had an accident,' Mawn said.

'We're not sure of that.'

'Right. But what would they want from Gelder if they had?'

Peters smiled: 'Their money back – with interest. And they'd search for ways of putting the screws on him, too.' He leant back thoughtfully. 'It occurs to me that I've got a way into it.'

'How's that?' Marcia asked.

'Look, I'm in Turin next week. We're doing an incredibly boring thing on the motor show there. If I go a couple of days earlier I can drop over to the Club Méditerranée and nose about a bit.'

Marcia smiled: 'Drop over! Are you taking your Walther PP2 in its underarm holster? It'll take you a month just to get a visa. Watch it double-o-seven.'

Peters laughed in return. 'No . . . there's a man I once helped out when I worked in the Washington office. He was a health physicist in Los Alamos. He nearly got crucified by the late, unlamented Joe McCarthy. Interesting man – Arnold Chen-wa. Would you believe?'

'No, I don't,' Marcia laughed.

'No, really,' Peters continued. 'That's his name. He was in charge of radiation checks in an isotope lab. He's a really sweet character as a matter of fact, Chinese, American-educated, a theoretical Marxist rather than a dyed-in-the-wool party man.'

'I'm not with you,' Mawn intervened.

'Well, it fits in rather nicely, I heard from him a few months back – he's in Albania. Didn't give me any details about what he was doing, but it's a reasonable shot. He's a radiation health physicist, he's in Albania and Albania puts up its first atomic reactor.'

'I don't like it,' Marcia said. 'I'll be quite frank, I think we're all building up stories. All we really know is that Teller has contacted Gelder and Teller may have broken into your lab. We can't even prove that!'

'Two days after Alex accused the Gelder concern on the air?' Peters interjected. 'Anyway, we've got the next show to put on. Alex, you're going to be on the spot – we might just as well get all the facts we can – you're going to need everything you've got to defend your "dinosaur effect".'

Mawn rose abruptly from the table. 'Marcia's right. I've stuck my neck out. Don't think I'm not grateful, you've helped me tremendously. But it's just that I've gone back over my own stuff and I'm beginning to think it may have been over the top . . .' His voice fell away. He looked tired, sick and dispirited.

There was a silence, then Peters spoke gently: 'Alex, I don't think it is all in your head. That's just what the opposition would like you to think. They'd like to make you feel isolated. If you face them believing that, they'll stamp all over you. Look, I didn't tell you this before, but I've had a lot of very interesting reactions from the first programme, from several sources. There's a very definite attitude filtering down from management. They're not actually saying "don't do the programme", but they're letting it be known very clearly that they are not in favour of it. Nothing overt – they're just making life generally difficult for my directors – no studio facilities – you know the sort of thing.'

'I'm sorry – I'd no idea,' Mawn began.

'Don't worry about it, it's part of the game. I haven't had so much attention paid to a programme of mine since a series on abortion I did in the sixties. You've really stirred them up with this theory of yours and I'd love to know why. And look at the phone call from Lodge. Even the Government says we should dry up.'

'It won't do you much good,' Marcia protested.

'I really don't mind. It's about time I cooked up a real blockbuster. Thing is, I shall have to leave you two to get on with the preparations for the "Alex Mawn Show". My editor at BBC can help you but I want you to reassemble all your lost data and harden up a concise effective presentation.' He looked at the two of them, the slender New England spinster, her stiff stance belying the promise of her attractive body and the large, bearded academic. 'You've really got to start spending some time together and ironing out any differences of approach.'

'I've been given no real opportunity to put my side of it yet.'

Mawn hesitated. 'I'm sorry if I've . . .'

'Oh, forget it,' Marcia snapped. 'What really riles me is that you've got yourself fixed on this man-machine interface – this dinosaur effect of yours. It's a good dramatic title, but you've completely missed the point!'

'Oh, yes?' Mawn began to show interest at the sound of attack.

'Let's define your position,' Marcia continued. 'You say that machines are just growing too complicated for people to operate, right?' Mawn nodded. 'More to it than that.'

'OK, but that's basically it. You see, you're just bound up in the hardware – you can't see beyond the nuts and bolts. What about the operators?'

'Well, they're trained obviously for a particular type of machine. They pass tests, they have to. No one's going to let an untrained idiot near a million pounds' worth of equipment.'

'Right! They're trained on paper, yes,' Marcia said. 'But how do you know what happens to them once they start actual work.'

'The mistakes would show up.'

'No, they wouldn't either! First of all you know as well as I do it's quite often impossible to trace the cause of a computer fault, and second, no operator's going to admit it if he does press the wrong button. He's got his job to think about.'

'This is all amusing speculation . . .' Mawn began.

'Speculation be damned,' Marcia flushed angrily. 'Like all hard science buffs – you don't think psychology has any part to play at all, do you?'

'Right.' Mawn began to grin at her anger. 'Applied fantasists!'

'It just so happens that I've been getting good, statistically copper-bottomed evidence about a repeatable and good observation which if you can put down – I'll tear up. I've been at work on it now for nearly three years and I can show you that groups of certain types of people show a uniform loss of intelligence!'

The smile drained off Mawn's face: 'What?'

'Something like a ten per cent loss. Now look, will you come to my lab at the Institute and look at it for yourself?'

'When?'

'Tomorrow. We've an open-day happening but that shouldn't get in the way. There's a Parliamentary Secretary coming to give us the once-over, but once he's had the red-carpet treatment we can get down to work.'

Mawn nodded sombrely: 'You've just got to be wrong!'

Four

Marcia led the way past the discreetly-lettered brass plate: 'Institute of Psychology' and on up a curved flight of stairs to the first floor. 'We're all polished and sparkling, you'll never see us so tidy again – it's open day.'

Lining the corridor there were multi-coloured sheets of peg-board on blackboard trellises supporting large black titled labels, carefully drawn graphs and tables of figures. The doors of the laboratories leading off the corridor were open and Mawn could see huddled groups of scientists in clean pressed white coats waiting anxiously inside for their first visitors. Marcia led Mawn through a door labelled: 'Ergonomic & Behavioural Studies'.

Howard Venn, Marcia's Head of Department, rushed forward, his manner excited and nervous. 'Marcia, where in heaven's name have you been? The Under-Secretary's been here for about an hour. He's on the second floor already . . .' He broke off, seeing Mawn. 'Oh, sorry . . .'

'This is Dr Mawn, he's interested in our work,' Marcia said.

'Yes, yes, good of you to come.' Venn looked around anxiously at the array of charts and apparatus: 'It's just that we've got a visit from the Research Council – they've brought along a Minister.'

'Have to do the same myself,' Mawn replied, gesturing at the display boards. 'They never remotely seem to grasp what you're doing, do they?'

Venn smiled, shrugged, and returned to a technician who was plugging leads into a flat aluminium box covered with red and green buttons. The leads connected with a small computer terminal and a large graphic read-out screen. Blocks of figures and numerals were flickering across the screen.

Mawn looked around and, with some amusement, saw that all the lettering over the display boards was a shade more perfectly executed than in the other labs he had passed. Venn had obviously farmed them out to a display artist. It looked more like an advertising campaign than a scientific display. Over the box with the array of buttons the legend on the label read: 'The Venn portable intelligence meter'. Again he smiled to himself as he saw that the letters were bigger than any others in the room.

There was a sudden sharp crack and a thin column of smoke drifted away from the back of a complicated block of apparatus. Venn's voice was sibilant with rage: 'You idiot. How many times have I told you not to turn the power pack on before lining up!' The technician began fumbling nervously with the leads.

Mawn turned to Marcia: 'What's all the fuss about?'

'Bread! His grant application is up for the next quinquennium. The guy who's coming round is on the board.'

A girl in a white coat stuck her head quickly round the door and spoke in a loud stage whisper: 'They're here!'

There was a brief commotion in the corridor and then a small rotund figure wearing gold-rimmed glasses bustled in, followed by a tall, grey-haired man. The handkerchief protruded at exactly the right height out of the coat pocket and the suit was from the right end of Savile Row. His hands were clasped behind his back and he wore a fixed expression of intelligent interest as the Director started to describe the exhibits in the laboratory. Finally the Director turned and, almost as an afterthought, said: 'And this is Dr Venn. Dr Venn may I present Mr Lodge, Under-Secretary of State to the Science Office.'

The tall man leant slightly forward from the hips with his hand outstretched. 'How d'you do, Dr Venn.'

Mawn reacted. Lodge! The name of the man who had phoned Peters and told him to lay off.

'. . . Now Dr Venn, I wonder if you could show the Under-Secretary your device . . .' He turned to Lodge, '. . . extraordinarily clever I think you'll find.' The Director tapped the top of the 'Venn portable intelligence meter' with an immaculate fingernail.

Venn spoke nervously, the words came out in staccato bursts. 'Well, it's really a very simple way of measuring some performances and skills – er – in the field.' He pointed to the box with the square array of buttons, took up a transparent slide and pushed it under a small screen set in the box to one side. He pressed a switch and the screen lit up showing a geometric pattern. 'It works by using a derivative of Karnaugh mapping with an automatic scoring logic attached to . . .'

The Director smiled thinly at the Under-Secretary who turned to Venn. He spoke gently: 'I'm afraid you'll have to treat me like a backward child of three.'

'Oh – yes – of course.' He paused, momentarily confused, then picked up the box: 'It's a sort of electronic noughts and crosses. We show various tasks on the screen by using these transparencies then ask the subject to press the appropriate buttons. For example . . .' He pointed to the screen. 'On this one, there are different shapes which have to be matched together, so the subject presses the buttons which he thinks will show the best matching pairs. Inside, there is a small arithmetic unit which automatically scores the subject and prints out his results.'

Lodge leaned forward and dabbed at the buttons: 'So it evaluates the performance of the subject automatically?'

'Exactly.' Venn, pleased at the apparent understanding, pointed to the underside of the box: 'There are miniaturized computing chips in here, which plot error frequency using a binomial function . . .'

'But that's invalid!' Mawn broke in suddenly.

All heads turned in Mawn's direction, noticing him for the

first time. Venn flushed as Mawn continued: 'Given the sort of paired values you're comparing – you'd have to use a "Poisson" distribution, binomials simply beg the very question you're asking the machine to measure.'

Venn spoke in tight control: 'It was considered good enough to be adopted as a standard method at the last European Psychology Conference.'

The Under-Secretary's eyes moved from one to the other. There was just the hint of a smile.

'Maybe,' Mawn continued. 'But that method for that task was thrown out years ago . . .'

'I think I've seen this down at Farnborough,' the Under-Secretary spoke deliberately as he walked over towards a screen showing an illuminated circle with a small light spot wobbling randomly inside the circle. Venn glared once at Mawn and then collected himself and followed Lodge over to the screen: 'Yes, it's a way of testing complex performance.' He pointed to a joystick control below the screen. 'The idea is that the spot is given a random movement by the machine and the subject sits here.' He pointed to a chair. 'And by moving this lever he tries to act against the machine and keep the spot in the circle.' He sat down, grasped the control in one hand and started to move it expertly back and forth, gazing at the screen. After a few seconds he managed to bring the spot, still wobbling, back into the centre of the circle and keep it there.

'May I try?' Lodge asked.

'Of course.' Venn slid out of the seat and the Under-Secretary took his place. Mawn noticed that, as he reached out for the lever control, his hand overshot and his fingers had a fine tremor. He was unable to keep the spot in the circle. Mawn suddenly recalled the inept operator in the ACE control room.

Finally Lodge stood up and looked down at his outstretched fingers. His laugh was slightly embarrassed as he turned to the Director: 'Don't think I'd make a very good airline pilot, do you?' The Director smiled and looked at his watch: 'I think we ought to be moving on.' He turned to Venn: 'Perhaps we could have a quick look over the ergonomics lab.'

Venn moved towards a door. 'Yes, of course.' He turned to

the Under-Secretary: 'Through here, sir, if you would.' The Director waved Lodge in front of him as they followed Venn out. Marcia wheeled on Mawn. She was furious. 'What did you have to do that for?'

'Do what?'

'God dammit! You made him look a complete dummy!'

'Not my intention. He's just using the wrong method. I told him.'

Marcia blazed: 'Don't be so damned British and uninvolved. You could have waited, couldn't you? You didn't have to nail him in front of the brass did you? Or was that what you wanted to do?'

Mawn paused for a moment: 'No, I'm sorry.'

'I told you before we began. Richard Lodge is on his committee and now you've sown the idea in his head that Howard is an incompetent. You could just have wrecked his whole grant application!'

'All I meant to say was that his maths are probably wrong.'

'So in the name of your holy truth you sent him up in public!'

'I have apologized.' Mawn turned abruptly on her and Marcia stepped back a pace. 'And I stick exactly to what I said. You can make any sort of sophisticated gadget you want and it's only as good as the theory you build into it. That thing's a typical high technology fix. You think you can just walk into a subject with a hundred and one different variables and with – what amounts to a souped-up adding machine – suddenly say you've put part of human behaviour into figures! Have you ever tested the reliability of the thing? How do you know it isn't distorting half the results you get out of it?'

Marcia frowned, suddenly anxious. 'That wouldn't invalidate the results would it? We spent months checking it out.'

'Who knows. It might only make a dent in them. Now if you don't mind.' He started towards the door.

'Alex,' Marcia's anger evaporated. 'Look, Howard's going away tonight – he's giving the Piaget memorial lecture in Paris. I've told you what I found, you said you'd take a look. God, I just can't tell you how vital it is. You can't cop out now.'

Mawn walked over to the long bow window, rain was streaming down the curved panes.

'Maybe you've too much to do?' Marcia asked.

'No, not a damn thing.' Mawn turned back to her. 'That's what riles me I suppose.' He nodded and smiled: 'OK, let's get to work.'

Peters lay back in the blue canvas deck chair with the white trident symbol, enjoying the bite of the hot sun and ruefully compared the city pallor of his own skin with the dark brown figures lying on the beach.

Near the water's edge he could see Gelder energetically playing volley ball against a crowd of young club instructors, with apparently, complete absorption. If he was using the club as a pretext, he was managing to enjoy the charade. He recalled their first meeting at the camp and Gelder's start of surprise, quickly suppressed.

It had been on the previous evening at the open-air bar, together with the half-dozen-or-so British contingent at the camp. Drink had flowed and Gelder had displayed an easy, almost insolent charm. Peters had found him difficult to categorize. Part of the time his manner had been open and laughing and then, every so often, he had caught a hint of watchfulness. There had been a crop of brainless bar games which had left Peters feeling every one of his fifty years. Gelder had been accompanied by a petite, exquisitely-shaped French brunette, nicknamed Minouche, who grew more restless and spoilt as the evening wore on. He remembered that when she had started to protest, Gelder had spoken to her savagely in French and afterwards she had stayed in the corner of the bar staring petulantly at her glass. From the others, Peters had learnt that Gelder scarcely ever left his hut until late in the afternoon, missing both breakfast and lunch at the open-air, vine-covered restaurant.

The next day, the first Peters had seen of him was in a long, red speedboat with a huge outboard screaming away into the distance across the bay.

He began to worry that their suspicions had been groundless, then he remembered Marcia's objection that if Gelder had wanted a holiday in the sun he could have bought the whole camp.

He had even searched along the well-worn path to the far end of the island where nude sunbathing and swimming were permitted. He had found the beautiful bare Minouche lying unselfconsciously on a towel among a small group of girls from the camp. She behaved differently from the other limp sun-drugged figures beside her on the beach and kept glancing at her watch. A persistent young German had eventually worked up enough courage to say something and had been immediately rebuked by a hard contemptuous stare.

It took Peters several hours, a long lunch and a free supply of wine to make her unbend. He had even mentioned a coming television programme in which she might be interested. Eventually she began to talk petulantly. Gelder did not in fact rest during the mornings but took off early in the speedboat without telling her his destination. He remembered her parting words: 'please don't tell anyone, I was told not to speak of this.'

Peters settled back in the chair. For the first time in years he felt the prickle of anticipation. His mind went back to his time as a European war correspondent. Now he began to feel something of the same mixture of apprehension and excitement. He looked down at his pale arms, the muscles showing the sag of years and remembered Marcia's jibe about double-o-seven. Perhaps contentment had to be paid for by taking a risk occasionally. Tomorrow he would find out.

Venn's normally immaculate laboratory was in total disorder. Mawn sat in shirtsleeves beside a bench strewn with files, computer read-out paper and card indexes. He completed a calculation, rushed over to the computer terminal, punched in instructions then waited impatiently until the machine began to clack out its reply. Marcia was kept running as she brought fresh material from the data files. Eventually he threw down his pencil and sat back: 'Well, that's that!'

Marcia flopped into a chair beside him: 'When I asked you just to have a look, I didn't expect a marathon.' She glanced at her watch. 'You've been going for over four hours – you know that?'

'Your Venn seems to have used fairly primitive circuitry but – I'm surprised, it only makes a marginal difference. Yes . . .' Mawn nodded, '. . . it's valid enough.'

'So your attack on his maths was completely unjustified?'

Mawn smiled: 'If you insist on making me crawl, yes.'

'Fine. What are you going to do about it?'

'What am *I* going to do about it?'

'You're not just going to leave it there, are you?'

Mawn was already studying a long table of figures. 'This your American data?'

'Yes. I asked you a question!'

Mawn looked myopically at her through his glasses then laughed. 'I'd better teach you both some decent maths.' He turned back to the table. 'This is interesting, at least so far as it goes. You say you chose a particular subject and defined him?'

'Yes, we selected middle grade executives. Same age group, salaries, educational levels, responsibilities, marital status and so on.'

'So providing the details they gave you were true, they should all have had a similar IQ?'

'Well, there are a lot of other factors involved, but that's about it I guess.'

'So, the first problem I've got is that your IQ thing is nothing whatsoever to do with intelligence! It simply measures the ability to do the IQ test.'

Marcia shrugged. 'That's an old one. Who's denying it? Nobody can define intelligence properly, but the tests we use are at least consistent in comparing individuals or groups.'

'Which is taking the easy way out,' said Mawn.

'No it isn't. We aren't measuring just the old IQ test like the Stanford-Binet, you know. We've got a little more sophisticated . . .'

'Or complicated?'

'Maybe. But we can build in the sort of Wechsler-Jackson idea – a measure of creativity. Also we can test motor skills.' She pointed to the joystick and the spot wobbling on the screen.

'Like that thing, or the pursuit rotor. The whole idea is to get a measure of a person's total capability not just his ability to solve paper puzzles – dominoes – matrices – that sort of thing.'

'But surely there are so many factors that can affect a person's performance – whether he's got a hangover – or he's frightened about something? Also if a person's got special gifts at expressing himself – he could use it to mask a relative dullness.'

'You've been reading the books. Yes, defects in reading ability, depression, consistency of the test itself – I admit all that. But you see Howard's test is basically non-verbal, so it should be free from that kind of error.'

Mawn persisted: 'The fact remains that your results are only as good as your observations and your figures. There's no compromise about that. You tell me that a group of subjects specially selected for the same characteristics should have shown very nearly the same intelligence, but they didn't. Well, that's no surprise to me. Statistics can either prove something fairly obvious or merely compound stupidity, you can take your choice.'

'Bullshit!' Marcia flared again. 'You have this colossal bias against us, just because we deal with people. You've got this amazing conceit that only you – the physicists – really do any measuring. What about your "dinosaur effect"? You say machines are becoming unreliable and you say you've proved it by showing faults in one machine system. I seem to remember a pretty shirty article in *Nature* accusing you of generalizing from the particular without enough evidence.'

'For every thesis, there's an antithesis.'

'Oh, don't be so trite! What you have to explain in our findings is that in some groups we tested, their IQ level was very much lower. Not just at the low end of the normal, scattered average but very much lower. And secondly, some of the people who were in this low group showed a second decrease in IQ when we tested them again.'

Mawn pointed towards the Venn intelligence meter: 'Well, that thing probably had a few off days.'

'Oh, swell! Now you use your dinosaur obsession to cover every conclusion that contradicts it. You can't blame everything on machines. I've described an effect – told you how we got it – you've read your Popper – one disproof is enough – so go ahead, disprove it.'

'Have you published any of it?'

'No, it's too much of a hot one – we have to be sure.' She went over to a file of computer print-outs. 'It's all over here.' She pulled one of the files off the shelf and brought it over to him.

'You've certainly done a lot of work,' Mawn sounded cautious.

'Which you say is a load of crap!'

'Now you're arguing emotively, like a woman.'

'And leave sex out of it!' She flung the file down on the bench and stalked away, slamming the door behind her.

Mawn opened the file and began to scan its contents. After a few minutes he reached for a pencil and started to jot down figures on a notepad beside him. He started talking to himself . . . 'Let's see – first approximation – P point six. Stupid bastards could have saved hours using sequential analysis – point five and then . . .'

After about a quarter of an hour Marcia re-entered and started to say something, but saw he was completely oblivious of her presence. Then, with all the delicacy of a mother leaving a sleeping child, she tip-toed to the door of the lab and left, closing the door behind her.

Peters completed his inspection of the boat, primed the carburettor and pulled the starter cord. The Mercury outboard engine immediately roared into life and, while it warmed up, he began incongruously to work out a way to include the cost of its hire in his BBC travel expenses. Half-way to the horizon he could just see Gelder's boat heading south, leaving a white fan of spray. He quickly cast off and headed in pursuit.

Replacing the hot clear skies of the previous two days, large black thunderheads had begun to build up over the high peaks of the mountains overlooking the bay and as he headed into open water he thought that it looked like a stage set of *Götterdämmerung.*

Following Gelder's boat around the spit of land limiting the bay, the straw huts of the camp standing out against the dark grey-green of the olive groves seemed almost a deliberate man-made arrogance set down to taunt the Albanians on the far side of the water. The horizon was made up by a stark, towering, half-circle of jagged peaks. It was as though the ancient gods were looking down on the presumptuous pygmies who clung to the thin green strip of land along the shoreline – looking down and waiting for a chance to shake them loose into the sea.

Peters snapped his thoughts back to reality as Gelder's boat disappeared round the point. He opened the throttle and immediately he could feel the thrust of the motor as the bows came up.

Rounding the bay into open water, he realized that he had closed too fast. He throttled back quickly, until the boat began to drift and waited until about a mile separated them; then opened up to about half throttle and settled down for the long haul.

Overhead the clouds were dense and, with a chill of anxiety, he saw whitecaps developing as the sea began to slap angrily against the sides of the hull. A distant rumble of thunder boomed menacingly off the mountains and a light warm rain began to sweep into the open cockpit.

Ahead he could just see Gelder's boat swing away from a tall craggy headland and head towards a small island about two miles off shore. In the rain he momentarily lost sight of the boat.

The island was one of many which dot the southern coast of Yugoslavia. At its centre was a ruined monastery built of great hand-cut stones lined by an orange-yellow terra-cotta rendering and topped by the remnants of a tiled roof. Protruding above the level of the surrounding olive trees was the spike of an old bell-tower.

As he closed on the shore he could just make out a dilapidated wooden landing stage partly overgrown with weeds and creepers. An old and battered fishing boat with a tall rectangular wheelhouse was moored there but he could see neither Gelder nor the crew.

He headed out to sea again and circled the island, but there was no sign of life among the stunted vegetation and crumbling walls. The fishing boat still rocked at anchor.

Spreading a map on the rear seat to pin-point the position of the island, he realized that the tall cliffs he had passed were Albanian. He remembered stories at the camp about pleasure boats whose unwary occupants had been machine-gunned for sailing too close to the Albanian coast. He opened the throttle hurriedly and headed back towards the Club.

He failed to see a man hidden in the trees near the landing stage pointing the long black snout of a telephoto lens towards his boat.

Five

It took Mawn two hours of machine time to analyse the data given to him by Marcia. He sat in front of the computer terminal in direct land line contact with a central machine complex situated over nine miles away at the National Physical Laboratory. As the machine clattered out its analysis of his data he scanned each line of closely-printed numerals comparing them with notes of his own.

Finally he punched in the 'log-out' instruction and shut down the terminal. The silence was intense after the peremptory racket of the machine. Mawn's features were pinched and drawn. He rubbed his eyes and stretched.

'I've shoved it through every routine I know and I can't put it down.'

Marcia waited without replying.

'There is one possible flaw but I can't think that it's crucial. You seem definitely to have shown that some of your groups of people confined to particular firms show a loss of intellectual performance.'

'So you believe it?'

'I wish I didn't. A general loss of intelligence seems impossible. I just can't begin to see why. But if the method – the Venn test – is right and I can't judge that – it's outside my sphere, you have a completely copper-bottomed case. Some people in some places are getting progressively more inept. Is there any precedent – anything like this known?'

'Lots of psychologists have suggested it. There used to be an idea in this country that the so-called "lower classes" had larger families, so when they grew up they bred larger families and the net intelligence of the human race would start to fall.'

Mawn frowned: 'Which assumes working-class people are less intelligent and that their lower intelligence is transmitted to their offspring.'

'Good old English class chauvinism.'

'And it was an American who first said black people were less intelligent than white?'

Marcia smiled: 'Ouch!'

Mawn picked up one of the files. 'These people in the firms showing the drop. You re-tested some didn't you?'

'Yes, and that's the real crunch. They showed a progressive fall.'

'What about the unaffected people? Did you re-test any of them?'

'Yes. There was hardly any change. Not so clear cut, there was a very, very slight downward trend – but it wasn't significant statistically.'

'Then you've got to test the worst affected for a third time? Three points on a graph and you've got the beginnings of a case.'

'That's under way. Two of Howard's PhD students are up North now, doing it.' Mawn nodded. 'Good. Let me know the results.'

'Not so fast,' Marcia smiled. 'If you accept the conclusion then you've got a big problem!' Mawn looked up. 'Your dinosaur effect. You've been producing evidence that computing and control machinery is becoming unreliable by itself with no other added factor.'

'Right. The study I did on the NALA system . . .'

'But Alex, you're forgetting the interface – the man-machine-interface – what do your people call it?'

'EMMIE – short for MMI.'

'Well, supposing some of these less able people of mine were operating a computer and supposing the computer started to throw up mistakes. How would you know who'd done it? Man or Machine?'

'Obvious. Test the operator.'

'There are two things wrong with that. First of all, our sample is pretty small and secondly people with mental defects can often mask it. A guy who's got a good retentive memory plus a good verbal facility can cover up for a real basic inability. Like some of the old "idiot savants". They could multiply two four-figure numbers together in their heads but the poor saps couldn't do their buttons up when they got dressed.'

'Why would they cover up?'

'Look Alex, if you're a computer operator and you noticed that you couldn't do your work so well any more you'd cover up wouldn't you? There aren't so many jobs in computers any more.'

Mawn waved his hand impatiently: 'You're trying to make a case for some sort of secret army of morons running our technology.' The image struck him. 'God, it's quite a thought. Somebody in charge of a missile silo growing inept and hiding the fact from his superiors.'

'Earlier on you mentioned a flaw in our data – what is it?' Marcia asked.

'Well, I was getting a bit desperate trying to find a way round your figures and it occurred to me that the buttons on the testing box are coded red and green.' Again, as he spoke, Mawn had a mental image of the ACE control desk, the sequence of lights – green, red, green, red and the operator's, nearly fatal, mistake.

'That was part of the . . .' Marcia's voice died away. 'Oh, boy, wait a moment, I think I see . . .'

'You didn't test your subjects for colour blindness!'

'Right, dead right. We didn't.' She stared at him fascinated.

Mawn continued: 'I don't have to tell you it's pretty common. It's a point for women's lib. About eight per cent of men and only one per cent of women have some colour deficiency of some sort, most red-green-grey confusion. They're called protanopes and deuteranopes as far as I can remember.'

Marcia got up and started pacing: 'Oh, my God! This could invalidate every solitary test we've done!'

'No. If the colour defective people are spread evenly over your affected and unaffected people then it could all even out, But if it's just the affected people . . .'

'I get the question . . . Is colour blindness more common in the groups with the falling IQ. Right?'

Mawn nodded: 'Where was it you said you got the subjects from?'

'Oh – from a junior management personnel firm. We tried first of all going to individual firms, but they weren't too co-operative. The personnel people were quite forthcoming – in fact we did a deal with them. They supplied us with guinea-pigs and they got free tests on applicants for jobs.'

'Well, we could start testing for defective colour vision – it's not very hard – we could start with the Ishihara test and if that doesn't show it up, put them on to split field tube of some sort . . .'

The laboratory door swung open and Howard Venn bustled in carrying an airline bag: 'Marcia, hello . . .' He glanced round the disordered room and at Mawn sitting with his feet up on the bench. His smile disappeared. 'May I ask what you're doing?'

'Marcia asked me to check through some of her figures.' Mawn slowly removed his feet from the bench.

Venn strode to the bench and snatched up a file. He shook it at Marcia. 'Who gave you permission to show these to him? They're completely confidential – you had no right, no right at all!'

Mawn gathered the computer print-outs together and stood up. Marcia stood silently between the two men. Venn reached forward and tried to grab the papers, his face white. 'You can't take them away, they're not your property.'

Mawn held them up out of his reach. 'I don't know whether

you know it or not but you could have got on to a major discovery here.'

'And what does that mean?' Venn asked.

Mawn walked slowly over to the door. 'It's early days yet, but you may just have discovered a new species: *Homo non sapiens*.'

The dusty village street separated a row of dilapidated grey stone houses from a row of acacia trees alongside a shallow river. Under the trees, shaded from the bright sun, old women in black headshawls sat impassively watching a throng of early shoppers pick over the brightly-coloured piles of vegetables on their stalls.

Peters sat nervously beside a circular metal table outside a roadside café. Passers-by seemed to regard him as an interesting specimen and made him feel that he stood out like a sore thumb. At nearby tables, knots of men sat talking quietly around clusters of tall glass beer mugs. He began to imagine that they were discussing him. Which of them were police? It was very hot and he felt out of place and unprotected.

Eventually, with a rush of relief, he saw a dumpy figure dressed in black threading its way through the crowds around the stalls. The figure resolved into a short, overweight Chinese dressed like a Methodist minister. He wore a shapeless black suit with high lapels and a silk shirt buttoned tight around his neck. On his head was a yellow straw panama with the brim turned up. Underneath the hat, there was a broad grin of recognition. The figure hurried towards Peters, hand outstretched.

'Sheldon, my friend.' Chen-wa's handshake was warm and cordial. 'What the hell you come to this place for?'

Peters laughed: 'I heard you'd become a nationalized Albanian!'

'Have to be kidding. I'm just – just – hell I haven't talked English for years. I'm just a missionary. Try to make them civilized here. So far only goddamn result is they smash up all machines we give them.'

Peters looked up at a waiter studying them. 'What are you going to drink, Arnold?'

The Chinese scientist made a face: 'No, no. Just lemon water – everything else here rots your guts.'

Peters gave the order and the waiter sniffed and drifted away with a sullen reluctance that demonstrated his indifference to both foreigners and official allies.

'Shouldn't you be a bit careful?'

Chen-wa laughed aloud: 'You ever heard them trying speak English – can't speak their own bloody language.' Peters noticed the Chinese give a long casual look around the other tables before continuing. 'Anyway – too late start licking – posteriors now. Taste must be acquired when young. Now what do you want – you don't come for the holiday. You are going to make television here?'

Peters hesitated, Chen-wa continued: 'Well, I tell you, there's something bad here, so I want to talk too. Now, you start.'

'What does the name Gelder mean to you?'

'Gelder. That's the name of – Oh, shit, forget the words.'

'You remember some of them,' Peters grinned. 'Consortium – the Gelder Consortium is that it?'

'Right. That the name! They make new water reactor – package deal – sell one to these idiots. Bloody fool thing to do – can't make own electric razors work – they bugger up clockwork and blame Gelder. Sun does not shine from Gelder's arse I tell you.'

'Arnold.' Peters leaned forward. 'What's really happened to the Pukë nuclear reactor?'

'Yes, okay, we go for a walk.' Chen-wa stood up and Peters, catching on, followed suit. The waiter, who had been chatting to two men by the door, picked up Chen-wa's lemon juice and rushed forward anxiously.

They walked alongside the river until they were clear of the market and the main village square. The bank was deserted except for a chattering group of children trying to net fish from beneath the overhanging bank.

Chen-wa's manner changed: 'Sheldon. I tell you what happen – then you go home and make big crappy TV programme and their ambassador sees it in London and I get put on the next Concorde to Peking.'

'I'm not here for that, Arnold,' Peters replied. 'You've got to believe me – nothing public.'

'Then why do you come?'

Peters stopped by the bank watching green fronds of weed undulating in the flowing water. He gave Chen-wa a summary of Mawn's dinosaur theory and finally told him about the sinister aftermath of his TV programme. The Chinese listened in silence then, as if making up his mind, began to speak in a rush:

'Now I tell you why I want to talk with you. Yes, the Pukë reactor did go up – a big smash up. These people, they keep everything secret, even from me. They ask us to come from China to give advice how to make it work and then don't tell us all information. Yes, whole reactor's gone – they had to take down station brick by brick then cover it up with thousand tons of bloody concrete – like a gravestone – be there for ever. I started radiation health department, when we begin, my job to see silly buggers don't get killed by radiation. Well I had a big worry about some of the people in the control room. I watched them during start-up before pile went critical. They make mistakes like their heads don't work properly. Then we had melt-down. Ten men killed.'

'How was that?' Peters asked.

'Some radiation – some just smashed.'

'What about the people in the control room? Couldn't they have been exposed to radiation? I mean couldn't that have accounted for their odd behaviour?'

Chen-wa shook his head violently. 'No, no, they all have radiation check – badges I measure them myself – ordinary level, nothing dangerous.'

'Then what's the problem. I don't see?'

'Sheldon. I go to many places. Your Englishman, Mawn, is it? He's not only man to study this dinosaur effect. In Moscow, they have same. In Peking too a little, but it's not bloody machines Sheldon, I don't think it is machines.'

'Then what is it?'

Chen-wa fished in the pocket of his suit and pulled out a small flat wooden box about two inches long, he held it up to Sheldon.

'These are microscope slides – they come from the brain of dead man at Pukë – one who made silly mistakes.'

'I still don't see.'

'These made by the pathologist in hospital. He says the man's brain all rotten.'

'So he could have had some disease – brain tumour or something?'

'No, Sheldon. Last year I went to conference in Odessa – heard a talk by a Russian about a new – don't know what you call it – brain condition.'

'There are hundreds, surely – I'm not a doctor – but there must be many different changes.'

'This Albanian pathologist – mostly bloody fool – he made a new name. I remember. This dead man from Pukë has "Betz-cell atrophy".'

'That's nothing remarkable, surely?'

'The Betz-cells are thinking cells, Sheldon.' He tapped his forehead with the box. 'The little buggers that do the thinking.' He gave the box to Peters. 'Anyway you take these to London. Take them to Dr Kingston at Institute of Pathology. He was at Odessa – he's a very big brain man – let him see.'

Peters put the box away in his pocket. Then, with a sudden change of mood, Chen-wa bent down, picked up a pebble, threw it into the river and called out excitedly: 'See, we have same fish in Canton.'

Peters became aware of two men who had appeared round the corner of the winding river path.

Six

The flat was in partial darkness with only a small pool of light over in one corner of the lounge where Mawn was still hard at work. Marcia entered, threw her coat over a chair, went over and put a hand on his shoulder: 'Isn't it about time you gave it a rest?'

He looked up, squinting at the light. 'What did little Venn do to you?'

'Don't be bitchy! He's getting quite cooperative, now you've told him he's got a discovery!'

Mawn smiled appreciatively at her changed attitude to Venn. 'You know I've been thinking about all this. We've found this effect – supposing it's generalized – groups of people losing intelligence – it's horrifying. Earlier on you had a go at my dinosaur effect, all right, that's not the whole answer. The two things together make an absolutely lethal mixture.'

Marcia was staring into space. Mawn tapped her gently on the arm and she jumped. 'Did you hear me?' She nodded. 'I did – I'm thinking – go on.'

Mawn continued: 'Assuming this localized loss of IQ effect is more or less widespread – well we agreed, didn't we – that the people who are affected are likely to cover up their ineptitude. Now, supposing some of these people are operating machines which are faulty in terms of my theory?' He looked at Marcia waiting for her reply.

'There would be twice as much chance of a mistake, I guess.'

'Exactly. It's difficult enough already when a mistake is made by a computer to decide who made it, the machine or the man operating it.'

'Now hold on. They do have special 'operator check' systems in some of them – machine checks operator, right? I remember that from one of my father's plants.'

'Yes, but that's not very general yet. In any case, who checks the check system?'

Marcia's face was pale: 'What on earth can we do?'

'Find out why!'

Peters awoke in a cold sweat. There had been a terror-stricken dream. He had found himself about to appear in front of a vast audience on a television programme without the slightest idea of the content. Dimly he had seen the faces of Marcia and Alex Mawn warning him not to take part. There had been danger everywhere. He opened his eyes. Above him the conical roof of the hut looked like the spokes of a wheel. Even that image held a sense of menace. He fumbled beside him on the floor mat for his cigarette pack. His fingers touched the telegram. It had read: 'Essential you arrive Rome meet camera crew Friday or shall make other arrangements. David.' Curt and to the point, it was an obvious 'or else' warning from David Danvers, the Assistant Head of current affairs at BBC.

Uncharacteristically, he reached into a holdall for a small silver brandy flask and took a heavy gulp. Everything he thought about seemed to be a source of anxiety. The previous evening he had given Chen-wa's slides and a long explanatory letter to a returning holidaymaker to take back to Marcia. He had described Chen-wa's report and about Gelder.

Gelder! The previous night there had been '*une spectacle*' – a mixture of amateur theatricals and party games so beloved by the French on holiday. Gelder had taken part enthusiastically, organizing the English contingent in the slippery pole fight – even giving a comic version of a TV commercial. Not the picture of a man under stress. Peters imagined the pressure that the Albanians must have brought to bear on him. First contract with a western firm, then a major accident and breakdown. They were probably trying to throw everything in the book at him – to reclaim some of their money – anything. He wondered who it was that Gelder met on his daily trips to the island. Probably not technical. He guessed that it must be some sort of haggle with a political, probably a fairly senior, man responsible for finance. He began to review the evidence. It amounted to very little. A few unofficial words from a scientist – a couple of slides.

He poured a second, larger brandy. Early morning boozing at fifty – beginning of the end! David had stipulated Friday. One more day! The brandy warmed his limbs. One more day. Take the camera, the telephoto lens, get one good picture of Gelder and the man he was meeting. Then get back to London and try to identify the man.

He glanced at his watch. Six a.m., plenty of time to get out to the island first, hide the boat and wait. He began to weigh up the risks, imagining a chase between his own boat and the Albanian coastal patrols. The brandy still held his courage together. He decided to use a more powerful boat belonging to Sergio.

Sergio Bracci was a minor Italian film star who had turned up at the camp in his ocean-going launch, a massively powerful craft powered by twin turbo-charged diesels. Bracci had lent him a spare set of keys as a goodwill gesture in the hope that Peters would be able to get him more English publicity. Thinking about the performance of the boat resolved Peters's last qualms.

He kept the throttles three-quarters closed as he nosed the craft through the blue-green waters of the bay. The heavy throbbing of the engines was overlain by the high-pitched whine of the exhaust turbo-chargers. He looked over at the sleeping village huts partly obscured in a light early morning mist.

Once clear of the headland, he pushed the throttle quadrant fully open. The response was immediate. The note of the engines became an aggressive thunder and the turbo-chargers' note changed to a thin strident scream. The bows lifted and the padded seat rest pushed hard against his back. He watched the speed indicator moving up. Ten, fifteen, twenty-five knots. At each side he could see a green wall of water curving away from the hull to join behind him in a boiling turbulent wake. Gradually his anxieties gave way to a sheer sensual enjoyment of speed.

The water was completely calm and it seemed only a few minutes before the familiar shape of the island appeared out of the mist. He throttled back and coasted slowly around the island twice, scanning the shoreline with binoculars. There were no boats, no people. Finally he selected a miniature bay over-hung with trees, away from the jetty he had previously seen.

As he nosed the boat carefully in towards the gently-sloping shoreline, he found that the overhanging branches made an almost perfect camouflage. Finally, he had a quick look for the high water level marked by a dark line of weeds on the sand and moored the boat fore and aft to overhanging branches leaving a sufficient slack on each line to avoid grounding the boat. He looked at his watch: seven-thirty. Judging by the time of the previous meeting it gave him a minimum of two hours.

He began to explore the island.

It was bigger than it had first appeared and he probed carefully through the overgrown remains of old vegetable gardens.

The ruins of the monastery had several rooms marking the old refectory and dormitories.

In the main chapel there were bunches of old flower garlands arranged at the base of a rough stone altar. Then he found the first signs of recent occupation.. Around an old stone tomb with a badly-eroded sword carved on its lid, there were several cigarette ends which showed none of the damp, brown staining of age. On the top of the tomb there was one grey cylindrical fragment of ash, its shape still unaltered. He uncurled one stubbed cigarette. Its brand name was English.

He found a vantage point up worn stone steps inside the bell tower. It was a small chamber with an open window space looking down on to the landing jetty. Through a hole in the wall of the chamber on the opposite side, there was a clear view over most of the remainder of the island. Above him, leading to the bell chamber, there was another series of steps, but there were several missing and one side of the wall abutting them was entirely missing and open to the air.

The sun was well up and the air was growing hot. He took off his jacket, checked the camera and settled down to wait.

The sun and the brandy began to have their effect. He dozed.

Awakening with a jerk of panic, he glanced at his watch. Nine-fifteen! He raised himself cautiously to the stone ledge of the window. A fishing boat similar to the one of the previous day was already moored about fifty yards off-shore. Alongside the jetty was Gelder's red boat.

Through the binoculars he could see two men on the foredeck of the fishing boat. With a shock he saw that one of them was dressed in some sort of uniform. He was holding a short machine-pistol casually in one hand. Above the wheelhouse a small radar scanner was rotating slowly.

Hands trembling, he brought up the camera and rested the long telephoto lens on the sill and wound the scene into focus.

He pressed the exposure button. There was no answering click and, swearing to himself, he cocked the shutter and pointed the lens for a second time. The sweat on his hands made his fingers slip on the shutter button.

A shadow moved over the sill. He spun round. Partly shutting off the bright sunlight the figure of a man stood blocking the door to the chamber. Behind him the head and shoulders of a second man were coming into view.

He felt an agonizing blow on his wrist and the camera flew out of his hand, clattering against the stone wall. The man stepped out of the sun and leapt forward pulling Peters up by his hair and slamming him back against the wall. Both men were dark and one had a full moustache. Their eyes were quite impersonal.

The second man picked up the camera and the first twisted Peters's arm up behind his back and jerked him over towards the stairs.

For Peters, the next few minutes passed like the images of a silent film. He made no attempt to say anything, knowing instinctively that it was useless. The pain from his wrist made him feel sick.

Outside, in the long grass surrounding the building, he caught a brief glimpse of a short neatly-dressed man in a light brown suit. One of his captors went over to the man in the suit and talked quietly for a few seconds. He returned and the two led him off down the slope towards the olive trees. Suddenly, with a surge of hope, he realized that they were taking him towards his own boat. It had been moved closer in-shore.

He realized dully that they must have known about it from the moment of his arrival. Somewhere in the back of his mind he remembered Marcia laughing about James Bond.

The second man was standing in the water near his boat. The first grabbed him by his injured wrist and flung him down the short slope leading to the water's edge. Peters screamed, stumbled and fell face downwards into the water. Gasping for breath he staggered to his feet and waded through the shallow water towards the shore almost blinded by pain. The second man was holding a short-barrelled machine-gun and with it he gestured angrily towards the boat. Peters stood swaying in the water, trying to understand through a haze of pain. The man gestured again.

Peters wearily turned round and waded back to the boat and, with one hand, clumsily dragged himself over the side, flopping down into the cockpit. Sick with pain he looked over at the two men standing on the shore. The man with the machine-gun started to walk back up the hill in the direction of the monastery and the other settled down near the water's edge, putting a revolver on a stone beside him. He lit a cigarette and leaned back on one elbow squinting up at the sun.

Peters watched the man with the machine-gun disappear over the brow of the hill and then started to look around the cockpit. Clipped into a bracket beside him was a lever-operated powder-projecting fire extinguisher. The lever was locked by a split pin fitted with a ring. When the pin was pulled, the lever could be depressed releasing a high pressure stream of fire blanketing powder.

Under the protection of the cockpit side he slowly worked the pin free and then, millimetre by millimetre, eased the red cylindrical shape out of its mounting clips to avoid the click of the clips on release.

The man on the shore flicked the cigarette away and lay back on both elbows.

Peters raised the nozzle of the extinguisher on to the edge of the cockpit, aimed it and with all his force leant forwards on the lever. There was a loud explosive hiss and a cone of powder jetted out and struck the man full in the face. He screamed and clawed at his eyes. Peters flung the extinguisher overboard, jammed the ignition key over and pressed the starter. The two motors fired at once. He cast off the single rope holding the stern to a rock, slammed the gear lever forward and opened the throttle wide. The boat leapt forward as he pulled the wheel hard over to head for open sea.

The man on the beach was holding his face and writhing in agony as the boat gathered speed. Above him the man with the machine-gun ran back into view. He stopped, pulled back the cocking lever, took aim and fired a long burst.

In the boat Peters, as if in a dream, watched the instrument panel in front of him shatter into fragments. Then he felt a series of tremendous blows across his back. There was no pain.

The man on the hill let the gun fall to his side as he watched the boat curve away from the straight line of its wake. The curve became tighter and, with engines bellowing, the boat began to circle round and round like a stricken insect.

Finally there was a heavy thumping explosion and a ball of flame ballooned out of the cockpit. There were a series of smaller explosions and then clouds of black oily smoke billowed up. The motors stopped and flames licked up through the rising smoke pall. Suddenly, the flames snapped out as the hull of the boat lurched over to one side and was gone.

The smoke drifted slowly away, leaving only the brightly-coloured rings of oil and a few scattered pieces of debris.

On the other side of the island Brian Gelder, deep in some of the toughest negotiations he had ever experienced, raised his head and asked the other man the cause of the explosion.

The man spread his hands: 'We have bad neighbours, they come to fish in our waters with dynamite, blow the fish to the surface, scoop them up and run for it. Sometimes they blow themselves up in the process. Is all very bad ecology, no?' The man smiled, shrugged and the meeting continued.

Seven

Marcia sat curled on the settee looking at the disaster area of the flat. It was two weeks since Peters's departure for Yugoslavia and in that time the whole appearance of the room had changed. The skilfully-blended colours and the chromium and glass coffee tables were still there. The spot-lighted award statuette still basked in its alcove, but the studied stage-set arrangements had totally disappeared. All the rugs had been swept to one side and the glass surface of one of the coffee tables was covered in scrawled felt-pen notes. There were papers everywhere. Hung around the neck of one of the statues there was a long, perforated computer tape stretching like a clothes line half-way across the room where its other end was taped to the frame of a Hockney original. There were thick piles of computer print-out paper – one of them held down by a small Henry Moore sculpture. About a third of the floor area was covered with photo-copied off-prints from scientific journals, each one had a scrawled assessment on its front cover. One was labelled: 'good data, lousy interpretation', another 'ignore – pretentious crap'.

Marcia began to work out how she could get it back into some sort of shape before Peters's return. He was fastidious and each 'prop' had its own special position. She began to worry about him. It was ten days and, apart from one hurried phone call from Dubrovnik, there had been nothing more. She looked around the disordered flat. Mawn had obviously been there all the week-end while she had been away in Kent with friends.

The doorbell rang and Marcia instinctively pulled off her headscarf and shook her hair loose before going to the door.

It was a stranger. A man in his early twenties, sandy hair, a friendly round face, grey suit and white collar setting off a recently-acquired tan.

'Miss Scott?'

Marcia nodded. The man took a thick brown envelope out of his inside pocket. 'Sheldon Peters asked me to give you this.'

'Thanks.' Marcia took the envelope. 'Say, I've just made fresh coffee, you look as if you could use some.'

He glanced at his watch. 'Thanks all the same but I'm late for the office already.' He smiled and turned to go.

'Thanks again.' She closed the door, went to the kitchen and emptied the contents of the envelope on to the table. There was a thick, tightly-folded letter and, wrapped in a wad of folded corrugated cardboard, four glass microscope slides with paper labels. She squinted at the writing on the top slide and could just read: 'Klin. Patholog. Broca area 4 H & E'. She opened the letter and began to read. About two minutes later, she heard a key in the front door.

Mawn almost sleep-walked back into the living-room and flopped into a chair. He leaned forward automatically and picked up a pile of photostats from the floor and began to read, already lost to his surroundings.

Marcia called out from the kitchen: 'There's coffee if you want it.' Mawn grunted in reply. After a few minutes Marcia appeared with a tray of coffee and the letter.

'I'm back in case you hadn't noticed.' She put the tray down. Mawn looked up irritably at the interruption.

'Eh?'

She poured out a cup and slid it over the table towards him. 'You look half dead, come on, have some of this. Oh, by the way, there's a letter from Sheld. A little guy from the Yugoslavia place brought it by hand.'

Mawn's tiredness dropped away. 'What did he say?'

Marcia frowned: 'You'd better read it.'

The letter gave a concise account of Peters's experiences in Yugoslavia including an almost verbatim record of his conversation with Chen-wa in Albania. Mawn threw the letter down with a great shout.

'Exactly what we wanted! Where did you put them?'

'What?'

'The slides, the slides!'

'In the kitchen.'

'This could be the most important link we've got. Listen, you've a totally inexplicable IQ loss in your subjects here. No cause, nothing.' He picked up the letter. 'And now this man . . .' He looked down at the letter. '. . . Chen-wa tells Sheldon . . .' He started to read from the letter: '. . . that he watched people at the Pukë reactor make silly mistakes with their hands, and . . . one of them got killed and his brain showed some physical damage . . . and the Albanian doctor gave it a name – Betz-cell atrophy. Also that the Russians and the Chinese have admitted to the same sort of physical brain damage!'

'But Alex, you can't begin to prove the link between damaged brains in one place and poor mental performance in another.'

'All right . . .' He tapped the letter. '. . . but Sheldon says here that one of the people the Chinaman actually saw make a mistake had these physical brain changes.'

'Yes, but good heavens, one case isn't a series – you can't generalize from it.'

'How many of your cases showed poor manual dexterity in the non-verbal tests?'

'A high proportion, you know that.'

'Right! The first thing we have to do is this – get those slides over to this man.' He glanced at the letter. 'Professor Kingston at the Institute of Pathology and see whether they've had any cases of this – Betz-cell atrophy – and secondly, if they have, whether they've got a register and third, whether any of the people with your IQ loss are on their register.'

'That means they'd be dead.'

'Yes, yes! Can you find out whether any of the subjects you've tested have died?'

'Easily. We've got full extraction on all our data.'

'So we can find out whether any of your affected subjects have died and if they have, whether they've got damaged brains!'

Marcia sat back: 'It's the other part I don't like.'

'How's that?'

'All this playing around with cameras on the Albanian border for God's sake!'

'It's obvious,' Mawn pointed to the letter. 'He didn't feel that was conclusive without identifying Gelder's associates. I've got to agree.'

'It's easy for you – you're not there. All this talk of evidence – what for – a court case? Why hasn't there been another phone call from Sheldon?'

Mawn picked up the phone on the floor: 'Point taken. I'll ring his office at the BBC.'

The first call set off a long series of abortive attempts to trace Peters's whereabouts. Yes, he had got to Yugoslavia – no, he hadn't reached Rome . . . Finally, Mawn picked up the dialling code booklet and had just started to note down the code for

Dubrovnik when the phone rang. The voice was hushed, female and too carefully enunciated:

'Hello, you were asking for Mr Sheldon Peters's whereabouts?'

'Yes,' Mawn was irritated. 'Who is that, please?'

'This is Mr Danvers's secretary.' The hushed tones spaced the words carefully. 'Is that Dr Mawn?'

'Yes. Will you please get on with it. What's happened?'

He could have been speaking to a computer for all the effect he had. The voice continued: 'And is Miss Scott there?'

'Yes. Where's Peters?'

There was a pause, the voice became a little more hushed: 'I'm afraid he's been killed.'

'Killed!' Mawn looked over at Marcia. 'You're sure?'

'Quite sure. The next of kin have already been informed. It will be on the six-o'clock news.'

'How, for God's sake?'

'I'm sorry, I cannot give you any more details at the moment.' The computer-like tone hesitated for a moment and then, with perfect timing, continued: 'Mr Danvers asks that you suspend your activities on the "Nightstyle" programme until he has had a chance to get in touch with you.'

Mawn slowly put the phone down. 'I suppose you got the gist of that?' he said over his shoulder. 'Sheldon's dead.'

Marcia didn't answer and he turned and saw her face. It was white and stricken. With sudden contrition he went over to her: 'I'm sorry, I didn't realize you . . .' he wanted to say 'cared so much' but couldn't get the words out.

Later, they took stock of their situation. The phone call from Danvers's secretary almost certainly meant that the TV programme was now cancelled. But what had happened? Mawn felt an increasing sense of guilt over Peters's death. First his assistant, now Peters. He, Mawn, was the only linking factor. Both had died as a result of his first statement on TV. Peters, especially, had shown great courage. How had he been killed?

Marcia shook him out of his fantasies. 'You can't take his death on yourself. Shel knew exactly what he was getting into, playing spies in sensitive areas. He wanted a scoop – a really big sensation to re-establish himself. I guess he over-reached himself, that's all.'

Mawn looked at her, troubled. She met his gaze for a moment, then looked away. 'I loved the guy, everyone who knew him did, but there's a little more than that. Sheldon was homosexual, he'd been married but it didn't stick. He had a friend, a good friend for many years, almost a marriage. He died last year.'

Mawn shook his head, confused: 'I didn't know.'

'Of course not,' Marcia's tone was sharp. 'No one outside his close friends knew. It was an entirely private thing and he kept it that way.' Her tone softened again. 'There could have been some kind of death wish tied up in this trip.' She rubbed her brow: 'Now, can we please get back to business. What do we do now?'

Mawn looked at her for a moment and then followed her lead. 'OK. What do we do, well we lack crucial evidence. We both believe your work is right, but we must get some more hard data. We've got to re-test some of your subjects and very quickly. There's no one else down the road to get help from now. We're on our own. If we're right, then the consequences are terrifying. Man staggering about the place with a net loss of ability – we could go back to the dark ages.

'So, if we publish now, every other scientist in the field will take our stuff, rip it up and jump on the bits – that's the way it is. Their job is disproof, if we're wrong anywhere along the line, they'll crucify us.'

Marcia was giving him her full attention. Her hands folded in her lap, her eyes bright again.

'Look, it's not a nice tidy academic problem. It's messy and we're going to get more attacks. We'll get no accolades, but if we're convinced of our status as human beings, then we have to act.'

'But how?'

'We've got to get an investigation going on a global scale. We've got to look at every accident and disaster, every untoward happening where people have been in control of machinery. Train drivers, airline pilots, surgeons, tanker captains, everything. We've got to get their mental abilities measured and recorded, so that we can get some action . . .'

Mawn was now completely oblivious of her presence. He left his chair and paced the room creating images with his hands.

'Somehow you and I have got to find a weak spot. Some danger area. We can't tackle it globally ourselves. There must be this hazard area – a piece of technology which is the least stable. Somewhere there is one potential volcano. The most obvious is the war machine, but that isn't going to get off first base. There's no use going to the Pentagon or the Defence Ministry and saying, give up your missiles because the operators are stupid. We'd be laughed out into the street. Our only hope is to identify the most likely place and to use it as an example . . .'

Marcia interrupted his torrent of words: 'Why can't we just let it happen – once – then people would see and they'd stop it.'

'We can't. It could be a major disaster involving millions of people. The third world war will almost certainly be started by accident. Just think of it, you've got one man on the DEW line radar trying desperately to hide his mental inability and he makes a wrong decision. We'd never even know why we all died!

'Now take this pressurized water reactor Gelder is building up in the Orkneys,' Mawn continued. 'England's first private enterprise nuclear power station. Private enterprise means cost cutting, cost cutting means lower safety margins, lower safety margins plus incompetent operators equals an accident just waiting to happen. How many of your subjects were nuclear engineers and how many of them are working in the Orkneys already? We've got to find out.'

Catching his enthusiasm she leant forward and grasped both his hands: 'Yes, we could do it. We could maybe get it delayed and then show they had faulty people working there.' She looked at her watch suddenly. 'Look Alex, that reminds me, I've got to go and meet Sheldon's mother to see if I can help.'

'That reminds me,' Mawn said. 'I'd better move out, hadn't I?'

'No, it'll be all right, his mother's a very nice old lady, I'm sure she won't mind. I'll fix it with her.' She turned quickly and was gone.

After she had gone, he began to think over the basis of his own dinosaur effect and set it against the evidence Marcia had accumulated about the loss of IQ in her experimental subjects. Why groups of people only? The puzzle fascinated him. Localized samples of middle-grade engineers, executives and professionals showing a group loss of intelligence. He began to play with ideas, inventing complex social games in office blocks where intelligence was recognized by seniors as a disadvantage.

One by one the ideas foundered and he became gradually more and more depressed. He searched his mind for the cause. Marcia's face kept on recurring. He remembered the image of her holding his hands in a curiously childlike way. In love with her? No! Like her? Yes. Attracted – definitely. He realized he had become dependent on her company, he recalled her nervous smile which almost seemed to embarrass her. She moved beautifully, a natural grace and ease. He wondered what she felt about him. For the first time for years he studied himself in a mirror. The image he saw disquieted him, almost as though an older man had taken over his psyche and was mocking him. Something would have to be done tomorrow.

At about eleven o'clock the next morning, Mawn made his way back to the flat from the University library. Stopping in front of a shop window he gazed at his reflection. Again, the long, matted hair and untrimmed beard suddenly repelled him and he remembered the overheard sarcasm of a colleague: 'Must take Mawn hours each morning to get himself that untidy.'

On impulse, he turned into a nearby barber shop and mumbled something about a need for a trim. As he watched in the mirror he wondered whether a hidden Dorian Gray image would emerge, but the result was not so unpleasantly revealing as he had feared.

At the front door Marcia stood for a moment not recognizing him. Then laughed out aloud: 'You didn't tell me you had a younger brother!'

Half an hour later, Mawn put the phone down. 'That's peculiar. You remember we assumed they would cancel the programme?'

'Yes, of course.'

'Well, that was Danvers, they're going to do it with a new presenter.'

'I'd have thought it was a heaven-sent opportunity for them to cancel.'

'So would I. We must have a friend somewhere!'

'When is it?'

'Live on Sunday fortnight. He wanted me to go in and discuss it now but I said we were too busy and I'd like to think it over and let him know. Apparently they've got a new presenter – Simon Joyce. Do you know him by the way?'

'Yes, slimy, devious and a hundred per cent on the make.'

'Anyway, the idea is for probably three people to have a go at me about the dinosaur effect. They haven't decided who yet.'

'Are you going to accept?'

'Why not? My facts are straight – nothing to worry about.'

She looked at her watch. 'We're due at "Management Personnel" in about half an hour, they said we could have free run of their data files for an hour this afternoon.'

'Very trusting of them!'

'Oh, no, they get plenty in return. I told you we did a sort of deal with them over the IQ tests – they get free capability assessment of their applicants and we get guinea-pigs.'

A torrent of punch cards poured down the chutes of the machine in a steady, unending blur. Every few seconds, with a loud click, a single card jerked sideways out of the main stream and fluttered down a second chute on to a growing pile in a tray. Marcia and Mawn sat watching the controlled frenzy of activity, totally fascinated by the uncanny speed of the process.

Finally, the girl operator pressed a button on the console in front of her, the flood ceased and the whirring died away. Marcia leaned forward eagerly and picked up the pile of extracted cards and began to count:

". . . sixty-eight, sixty-nine, seventy . . .' She put the last card down, '. . . seventy-one. Seventy-one nuclear engineers we have tested at least once.'

'That's more than I had expected,' Mawn said.

'Not really. This agency deals with a fairly narrow range of personnel that's why we chose them in the first place. They'd already more or less selected – for their own reasons – the sort of people we were interested in.'

Mawn picked up the cards and began to study the holes punched around the edges, comparing the position of the holes with a printed list of names on the table in front of him, ticking them off on the list in turn. Finally he put the the pencil down. 'You told me first of all that groups of people, in a single place, showed a high percentage of intelligence loss!'

'Right.'

'So how is it that nuclear engineers were all in one place when you tested them?'

'They weren't,' she began to tick off the points on her fingers. 'You see, we also looked at other groups – not just according to where they worked, but what they did for a living.'

'I didn't realize . . .'

'Yes you did, you saw our analysis, back in the flat.'

'It still doesn't answer my question,' Mawn persisted.

'Yes it does. Our main problem is to explain loss of ability in groups in one place, like maybe they're all blowing their minds on pot in the basement after hours – or something like that – but if you take any other artificially-selected groups, like occupation or age or salary level, they're not in one place, but you're bound to find a few of the affected people among them aren't you?'

Mawn picked up the list. 'So you've tested seventy-one nuclear engineers?'

'Yes.'

'And according to this,' he tapped the list, 'eighteen showed some loss of IQ – either on one test or two.'

'Yes.'

'So how many of the eighteen are currently working at the Grim-Ness station?' He began to gather up the papers, looking over at the sulky girl re-setting the punch-card machine. 'I think we've rather overstayed our welcome – let's get back.' Marcia looked at him, her eyes twinkling: 'I'll have you majoring in psychology yet.'

'Naylor P., Baird D., Durrell F., Elleston F., Westcott B., Haskell R., six of them.' Mawn put the list down on the coffee table. 'Six people probably concealing a loss of ability while they are commissioning England's first private enterprise reactor where the safety margins are already absolutely minimal.'

Marcia was sitting on the rug propped up on large cushions. 'Alex, are you sure we're not setting up our own private vendetta?'

Mawn looked up: 'If we get our facts right, does it matter what our motivations are?'

'All I meant was – it might push us too far, too soon.'

'It won't do that, there are too many things we haven't got. For instance, it depends what that pathologist Kingston says when he's had a look at the slides, but in the meantime, the Gelder nuclear station at Grim-Ness is the good bet. If you like, it's a microcosm of the whole situation. We won't get anyone to listen to us if we say there's a global effect and people have got to stop doing practically everything, but if we could show the presence of affected people in the nuclear station, then we'd have a case.'

'I'm not convinced,' Marcia replied. 'Just because six affected men are working up there it doesn't mean anything terrible is bound to happen. I mean – if the station starts up and nothing goes wrong we're going to look like a couple of complete goofs and then we'll have lost the chance to convince anyone how widespread the effect really is.'

'Not a bit of it. So far, the English Electricity Board have got an excellent safety record with their gas-cooled reactors – but this is as different as chalk from cheese. It's a private consortium, building a privately-funded reactor. They're already in cut-throat competition with the Japanese and the Americans. They're all chasing methods of paring down costs and so we've got a cut-price reactor about to start up, partly operated by people who very likely can't do their job adequately. No, we've got to bring it right out in the open – we've nothing to lose now.

'Almost a year ago I had a visit from Gelder's Chief Health Physicist – John Barfield. It was all under the counter – but the gist of it all was that the previous Gelder stations – one in Japan and the other in Dortmund were absolutely riddled with faults, even during building. Barfield apparently tried to reason with them at the time but he just got the same old line – "it wouldn't be economic".

'But even Gelder can't ignore this double hazard. The Grim-Ness station is due to start up in December so, between now and then, we've got to stop it!'

Gelder surveyed the two men over the top of the brandy balloon. Bellamy, his round shiny head reddened from the cognac, was rolling a cigar anxiously in his fingers. Caird appeared even more sallow and repressed; he had drunk only mineral water throughout the lunch.

The noise of the traffic outside in St James's only just filtered through the drawn curtains into the dark velvet and leather atmosphere of the club morning-room.

Bellamy spoke urgently: 'I tell you, we're already getting the first results of this guy's campaign. There are a mass of rumours circulating round Wall Street – Is our gear cheap-jack? Is it really unreliable like Mawn says? We're losing a hell of a lot of potential contracts – people are just diverting to the Japs. We've got to nail him somehow!'

'Hasn't he got any convenient skeletons?' Caird asked mildly.

'Hey, wait a minute,' Bellamy protested. 'Remember what happened to that chemical firm when they tried to hobble Nader – cost them three-quarters of a million bucks.'

Gelder sniffed the glass. 'You can forget all about that, we have to do something far more effective. This man is very, very bad news and he has to be completely halted.'

The two men looked at Gelder, startled. 'And don't worry,' Gelder continued evenly, 'nothing like that. You can't get friend Mawn on women or little boys, we've got to try much harder. Now I've been doing some research. I got in touch with one of Mawn's fellow academics who isn't exactly in love with him and I've also traced the employee I told you about the last time we met. Between the two of them, I think they can achieve exactly what we want.'

Eight

During the two days before the television show, Mawn and Marcia worked solidly at their data for presentation, the outlines of the flat slowly submerging in a sea of papers and files.

Mawn had made an uneasy agreement with the producer of the programme. The show was to follow on the first in which he had originally defined the dinosaur effect. He had already been told that the industries he had attacked would be given screen time to refute his allegations and Mawn had countered with the statement that he had new and important material which would help to develop this theory. The producer had then said that the programme was not to be a further platform for his views but rather to enable him to defend his first statements.

The programme, as usual, was to go out live on the Sunday.

Marcia leaned back in her chair and threw the pencil down. 'How did you get all this, or is that an academic secret?'

'Not at all,' Mawn said. 'Over the past few years I've had a lot of people coming to me from various firms, offering data. They're mostly disgruntled employees with a grudge, so I ignore them.' He pointed at the papers. 'But that stuff came from John Barfield a couple of days back.'

'He was taking a big risk, wasn't he? What does he get out of it?'

'A clear conscience for one. You see he used to be in medical physics at the MRC, then Gelder bought him up to head his new health physics department. It was a sort of con. Health physics is obviously essential if you build nuclear reactors, but he was also a public showpiece to allay Union protests about health hazards and so on.'

'Do you trust him?'

'John? Yes, completely. The reason he came to me first of all some months back is that basically he's a very concerned environmentalist, he didn't come for money or anything like that. He found that most of the nuclear stations the Gelder consortium had built kept on having breakdowns and accidents. He compiled the history of each one and then went to the board and made suggestions about safety.'

'And they took no notice?'

'Not only that, they told him to lay off. You see, his problem is that he burnt his boats academically by joining Gelder, he's got a big family and so on, so finally he came round to see me with the whole lot and said, in essence, "Do what you like with it – but don't tell them I told you".'

'Won't they get on to him?'

'No, there are lots of people with access to those figures.'

Marcia picked up a file and pointed to a row of figures: 'That's a bit much!'

Mawn looked up. 'What?'

'One of Barfield's estimates.' She checked with a second list on the table in front of her. 'According to him, one of the computers in the Dortmund reactor spent seventy per cent of its time out of commission with faults.'

'Not unusual with the NALA computer system. Anyhow, we checked his stuff through when we first got it. All we've got to do now is to boil it down into simple terms to convince the great viewing public. Look Marcia, if you've got any doubts at all, now's the time.'

She hesitated: 'Won't they take action for slander or something – they must have pretty big legal brains behind them?'

'They daren't. We're just pointing out the facts of what they're doing and it's up to them to answer. We've got an opportunity to reach over twelve million people. It's the best possible forum we could have. I can bring out all the stuff about your IQ loss and show this is not confined to this country.'

'Providing Simon Joyce doesn't try and screw you up – he's quite good with the needle.'

'That's a minor risk.'

'Oh, incidentally, I'm having some folk in to watch you. You don't mind?'

Mawn smiled: 'What, here?'

'Oh, yes, I often used to set parties up for Sheldon here.'

'I'll try and make it if I can. They want to have a final word on a late night chat show afterwards. So I'll make my way to their – entertainment suite – as they call it, and drink enough scotch to make my enemies interesting!'

Simon Joyce sat in one corner of the studio ante-room with the floor manager, tensely examining his teleprompt copy. He appeared not to notice his four guests.

Mawn sat sprawled in a plastic shell chair, suffering the attentions of a make-up girl, patting away at the shine on his forehead with a powder puff. From the open door leading to the studio, there was a confused jumble of noise. Two men were sweatily pushing a new desk section into position in front of a battery of cameras; another in shirt sleeves, wearing headphones, picked up an empty water flask from the desk and shook it furiously at a harassed girl who hurried away to fill it.

Mawn listened for his own heartbeat and discovered that it was scarcely above normal. He patted his jacket pocket, feeling for his notes and began to study his three adversaries.

Geoffrey Twining, Science Editor of the *Daily Chronicle* – potential ally. Professor Seager, Head of Computing Science at King's University. High table manner, but a professional character assassin. William Sampson, Secretary, Nuclear Inspectorate, Department of Trade and Industry. Neutral probably. Would defend his own masters.

The man in the headphones poked his head round the door and smiled. 'Ready gentlemen, thank you.'

Mawn settled awkwardly into his seat under the harsh glare of the spotlight. The other three were either carefully studying the dais or gazing away into the blackness beyond the lights.

Simon Joyce peered into the square aperture of the teleprompter, comparing the inch-high letters with his notes on the dais in front of him.

The title music began . . .

Marcia circulated among her guests. There were about fifteen altogether, mostly dressed in the carefully-arranged informality of the show business world. Richard Lodge stood out among the neck scarves and jeans in his Civil Service grey. His Spanish wife, Alicia, wore a dark blue velvet evening gown.

Howard Venn had just arrived straight off the plane from Lisbon and was talking to Lodge, using the special brand of authoritative enthusiasm he reserved for people who wielded power and money. His pretty, vacant, wife stood behind him, carefully holding on to a fixed smile of what she hoped looked like intelligent interest. Lodge was nodding sagely as Venn expounded.

None of the guests gave any outward indication that the gathering was a posthumous tribute to Peters. No one mentioned him and kept carefully to the strident in-group gossip reserved for such occasions. During the half-hour preceding the programme, Marcia told as many as possible the facts behind her work with Mawn since she realized that they could be helpful in various spheres of influence.

She looked at her watch with a prickling sense of anticipation and turned on the thirty-inch wall projection TV set. The guests began to settle on the floor around the screen, drinks in hands.

The title music faded and the programme began.

To Marcia's relief, Mawn spoke simply and effectively, making his points in a careful and lucid sequence with a minimum of gesture or theatricality.

As he finished, Simon Joyce came back into frame, summing up the purpose of the programme and introduced the three men who were to discuss Mawn's theory.

Marcia quickly circulated, filling glasses and trying to sense the guests' reaction to the programme.

Geoffrey Twining was first. He kept strictly to the points Mawn had made and offered carefully limited challenges which Mawn was able to both put down and to expand. Although he appeared to attack, it was clear that he was only offering pawns for sacrifice.

Marcia drew a deep breath. If the other two were as easy – she crossed her fingers.

Professor Seager took off his spectacles and carefully folded them away in the breast pocket of his suit.

'I hope you'll forgive me saying so, but a great deal of what Doctor Mawn has said worries me intensely.'

'Could you say why, Professor?' Joyce said.

'Yes.' He folded both hands demurely in front of him. 'A very clear allegation has been made. Doctor Mawn says that the whole basis of our advanced technology is in some way in jeopardy from inherently faulty machines. He has moreover invented a most seductive name for the idea – the dinosaur effect! So if we deal with the more objective aspects of what I really must label as a piece of irresponsible science fiction . . .'

'There's nothing fictional about the data I gave!' Mawn protested. 'The sources are absolutely unimpeachable, I assure you . . .'

Joyce interrupted Mawn firmly: 'I think we must give the others a chance.'

Mawn subsided and Professor Seager continued: 'Yes – ah – it has been suggested that . . .' he looked down at his notepad, '. . . the overall error rate of the NALA computer system was seventeen per cent.' He turned to Mawn. 'That is what you said, isn't it?'

Mawn nodded.

'And that independent tests of the emergency core cooling system in the Kyoto reactor showed an irrecoverable core temperature rise of fifteen hundred degrees before operation. Is that right?'

Again Mawn nodded: 'Correct.'

'You then pointed out that X-ray tests of the pressure vessel in the Dortmund reactor showed an average two per cent failure – that is to say, two inches out of every hundred inches welded showed a fault of some kind – sealing or improper penetration of the weld, I think you said?'

'Within the limits I gave, yes.'

‘And quite apart from your previous television allegations, you also seriously suggest that radiation levels in the cooling circuits were four per cent over the permitted maximum.’ Seager opened a folder. ‘Now I have been in touch with the Gelder Consortium and they have been kind enough to open their entire research data to myself and my colleagues.’ He looked down at the file. ‘The overall error rate of their computer systems on test was two point four per cent whereas you allege seventeen.’ He turned a page. ‘Their core cooling system showed a theoretical rise of only four hundred and twenty degrees and you say fifteen hundred! As to their radiation monitoring in the primary cooling circuits – they are . . .’ he looked down at the folder, ‘. . . in fact below the design maximum which was Oh point Oh five R. Now clearly, anyone is entitled to argue about statistical details but Doctor Mawn’s figures show such a complete departure from mine that I can only assume he has been wrongly informed . . .’ He pushed his glasses back up his nose. ‘And the fact that he is unable – or perhaps unwilling – to declare their origin, merely gives me further cause for anxiety.’

‘My figures can be verified,’ Mawn began, but his voice faltered. ‘They were in fact produced by the company themselves . . .’

Joyce turned to the fourth guest. ‘Mr Sampson, you represent the Nuclear Inspectorate, would you care to comment?’

‘Indeed I would. I’d like to start by pointing out that there are two forms of nuclear power station in this country. There are those operated by the Central Electricity Generating Board and those being built privately – in this case by the Gelder Consortium. Now in both cases, and I really must emphasize this, the strictest control is exercised by my department over all safety measures built into these stations, both State-run and private. Now in this case my own department’s figures agree very well with Professor Seager’s. I don’t know where Doctor Mawn got his figures, but as far as I can see they are completely without any foundation whatever.’

Joyce turned: ‘Doctor Mawn, any comments?’

‘Well, we disagree.’ Mawn’s voice had dropped. ‘All figures are subject to doubt, it depends on their origin. But, in fact, the situation is much more serious than I proposed. A colleague and I have been able to find evidence that not only are the new stations themselves faulty, but many of the operators are showing signs of decreasing ability. Some aspects of their behaviour and intelligence are showing a definite fall. So, far from being discouraged I feel that . . .'

'Oh, really!' Seager interrupted. 'Not only have your own figures been shown to be entirely and completely wrong, but now you're trying to invent some totally new effect to cover your mistake. I really must say this; the whole economic future of our country depends on abundant – and non-polluting – energy. And instead, we have heard a completely baseless attack on the very heart of one of our most important assets – nuclear power. Doctor Mawn's data could be the result of an honest mistake, he may well have been misinformed, or he could have fabricated the entire case. The law prevents me from stating my own preference!'

Simon Joyce turned to camera; 'Well, a vexed issue! That's all we have time for tonight, so . . .' He nodded to each one in turn: 'Mr Sampson, Mr Twining, Professor Seager, Doctor Mawn, thank you very much . . .'

It was Richard Lodge who leant over and turned off the set as Marcia sat, too stunned to move. There was a long tense silence followed by an explosive burst of loud conversation. Everyone seemed to get up at once and move towards the drink trolley.

The next hour was one of the longest in Marcia's life. They all acted as if the party itself was the reason they were there and the programme itself was a peripheral event. Only Mrs Venn, with her usual lack of comprehension, commented that Mawn looked better with his beard trimmed.

Marcia's mind refused to think about the debacle, to reason out what had gone wrong. Gradually, as she moved around desperately trying to find small talk, she began to reassess the whole basis of their work together.

As soon as they decently could, the guests began to drift away, each pleading baby-sitting problems or an early start the next morning. Venn couldn't resist an exit line: 'Please give

Doctor Mawn my condolences and tell him he's welcome to our facilities – if they're any further use to him.'

The last to leave was Richard Lodge. While his wife started to restore the flat to some resemblance of order, he gently touched Marcia on the shoulder: 'I wouldn't take it too hard if I were Mawn, main thing is to get priorities right. I'm quite sure your work has not been wasted.'

For about an hour she sat quietly in a chair without stirring. Finally she heard the front door. He stood looking down at her, she studied the glass she was holding, then slowly got up putting the glass down. 'Alex, for God's sake, what happened?'

He shook his head, his voice flat, toneless: 'I've no idea, no idea at all.'

Long after Marcia had gone home to her apartment, Mawn sat in Peters's long black armchair staring into space. Even the familiar bite of the whisky failed to blunt the edge of his pain. He felt an almost literal paralysis of the will, dangerously close to breaking point. In a few short weeks, the whole pattern of his life had been shattered, strand by strand. First, the destruction of the laboratory and now the final blow, the stripping away of his scientific reputation. And he had walked right into it, over-reached himself; committed professional suicide before an audience of millions. He had no further illusions about his chance of continuing his work – Marcia's stricken face had finally proved that. He had been shown up as a fantasist, a liar and cheat. Seager had done his task well – in a few short minutes, he had pricked the short-lived balloon of Mawn's public reputation and left nothing behind.

And what about Marcia and his fine words of a couple of weeks ago?

Mawn rose sluggishly to his feet and stumbled out of the flat, down the stairs and out into the deserted night street. Anything rather than stay surrounded by the ruins of their theory.

The night was clear and the wet streets still gleamed in the lamplight. Instinctively, his steps took him in the direction of the Embankment and the broad Thames river. Eventually, he reached the Embankment Gardens.

The attack was swift and unexpected. A shadow detached

itself from one of the Victorian statues and signalled. Another appeared from behind the bushes. Together they flung themselves at him.

The fight was short. Mawn kicked out at the first figure, sending him reeling back into the bushes holding the pit of his stomach. There was a brief flash of a knife as the second lunged forward. Mawn ducked and the knife swept harmlessly across his back. Then, grabbing his assailant round the legs, he lifted him bodily, upending him on to the path. The knife clattered away on the concrete as the man fell heavily on to his back. Mawn landed on top of him, jamming his shoulders back against the path. He raised his fist threateningly and the man who had been struggling violently to get free, suddenly went limp under Mawn's weight. From the darkness he could hear the footsteps of the other running away.

Mawn swung the man's head round into the light and found himself looking at a youth of about seventeen. A pale frightened face stared back at him from underneath a mane of frizzy fair hair.

A wave of pity swept through him at the thin wasted face. He bent down and pulled the youth to his feet and guided him over to an all-night coffee stall underneath the railway arch.

It was a long time before Mawn managed to convince him that he was not going to call the police. Gradually, the youth began to talk:

'Yeah, well, we just wanted bread, that's all. We'd been sleeping rough for a couple of days, both bleeding starving. We thought we'd mug the first geezer that came along the path.'

'Haven't you got a job?'

'Nah. Who'd give me a bleedin' job. I can't do nothing right can I? Tried everything. Ain't got the savvy no more. Last work I had was in a garage. Couldn't even do that right, could I? Couldn't work out what the guv'nor was on about. Me hands were going wrong. Lost it upstairs. Used to be good with me hands – onetime. Anyway, who bloody cares?'

Later, as he made his way back home, Mawn couldn't get the pinched, unhealthy face out of his mind. He had offered the youth five pounds to come to the laboratory to be tested, but he had stopped talking at once, suspecting a trap.

'. . . ain't got the savvy, no more.' The words echoed. Where would he end up if he were affected? How many more were there? In the dark streets he saw nightmare figures of a moronic populace loping into the shadows like wolves in a forest. He thought back over the television show and no longer felt any reaction. What the hell does it matter, faced with this! There was just one thing to do; to go on. Self-pity was a luxury he couldn't afford. The streets were just beginning to lighten as he reached the front door of the flat.

Marcia woke late, feeling heavy limbed and stupid. The slightest movement seemed to be a disproportionate effort. The humiliation and embarrassment of the party washed over her in waves; guarded comments and averted eyes. She began to long for the ease and comfort of her parents' home in the States and plotted the journey home in her mind's eye, realizing with a surge of pleasure that she could be packed and on a jet in a matter of hours. She looked around at the impersonal furnishings of the flat she had rented and began to visualize her own room at home.

He had been torn to bits, no point in trying to avoid it. All his figures had been hopelessly wrong – at least those he'd been given by Barfield. She played briefly with the notion that Barfield had been primed with false data by Gelder, but then dismissed it, remembering the data had been doubly checked.

She thought back over his whole approach to the IQ effect and began to suspect that he was himself faulty in his scientific approach and method. She remembered the words of one of her teachers: 'If a man wants to talk about his work before publication, the work is almost certainly incomplete and very probably wrong.' With a flush of embarrassment she remembered how Mawn's approach had originally fascinated her. A man driven by internal compulsions without any reference to his external image. She pictured Venn in the same situation. How he would have cringed: image and no substance.

He had suffered the worst attack possible for a scientist – a loss of credibility – a clear accusation of charlatanry. And in public. A public who would certainly have included many of his peers. He would never be forgiven.

There was a loud knock at the front door. She got out of bed and quickly flung on a housecoat and slippers. Fighting down a swirl of vertigo, she stumbled into the hall and opened the door. Alex Mawn stood quite still, a half-smile flickering across his face.

'Alex – I didn't know what to say last night. I just felt so bloody. Come on in.'

He followed her in and sat down. 'There was nothing to say was there? I mean I got kicked in the balls and that's that.'

'But your figures, Alex. You were all wrong!'

'I've had time to think about that now. I got them from John Barfield, right?'

She nodded.

'Whatever else he is I think he's straight. He was desperately worried about the situation, so what advantage would there be for him to give me phoney data? To change Barfield round must have really taken some pressure!'

'What?'

'It's a bit more likely as of ten minutes ago as a matter of fact.'

She looked puzzled.

'I phoned him at home – talked to his wife. Apparently he's not available – on some sort of trip – she was most unforthcoming.'

'What will you do? Didn't last night mean anything to you at all?'

'I had a long night.' He spoke quietly, looking straight at her. 'I had this happen once before. I gave a lecture at a meeting in Milan – a perfectly ordinary mistake – it happens to everybody in research sooner or later – I made a stupid error in a paper I read and this American got up in the audience afterwards and absolutely walked all over me. He pointed out that not only was I wrong, but my work had been published before by someone else. I simply hadn't done my homework – he was right, and I was wrong. I died all the deaths.'

'But it was all wrong!'

'Last night was different. After the Milan business I came home and I literally hid. I thought I was washed up – getting stupid – all that. But last night – I don't know – I haven't worked it all out yet – but somehow I know we've been got at. All that work we did in Venn's lab – you did it with me, after all – that was perfectly valid . . .'

She looked puzzled. 'You don't doubt the statistical methods we used do you?'

'No, at least I don't think so.'

'I'll put it another way. You're still sure that the localized IQ loss is genuine, aren't you?'

'A hundred per cent – yes.'

'Well, let me tell you another thing. All my instincts at the moment are to go back to Plymouth, shut myself up in my lab and get on with some nice pure academic problem in computer logic. I'm good at it, I enjoy it and it's fun. I tried that before and it didn't work. I've opened the laboratory door now and had a bloody good look at the stinking technological mess we're all in. I met one of the victims last night.'

'How's that?'

'Never mind, I'll tell you later. But listen, if what we've found is really generalized – on a global scale – it's quite irrelevant whether we've got machines which work or don't work if there is a species of man evolving who is mentally unable to operate them.'

'But, Alex – no one's going to listen now.'

'Right – my credibility's about as low as it could be. That's why we've got to get us there.'

'Where?'

'The Orkneys for God's sake! You're right, no one's going to listen until we've got cast iron evidence. So, what I suggest is this. You go round now to Venn's emporium, swipe one of those portable intelligence meters – all the other gear too – test cards – the lot. Then come back here and we'll get off. Don't forget there are six people right inside that nuclear power station who are almost certainly covering up for the fact that they're not up to their job. They start it up in December so if we can retest them in time and either show they're still affected, or better still that they've got a progressive decline in ability then we've got just a chance of getting it put off: nothing more!'

'That won't be enough to convince anyone now.'

'Have you got any other suggestions?'

'We could find some new way of presenting the material we've already got.'

'And have it filed in the basement of a ministry? At best we'd get a reluctant Royal Commission. Then there'd be a five-year wait followed by half an hour's discussion time in the House and then nothing. Marcia, if this is as widespread as we think it is, we've got to find some immediate way of getting it recognized. I accept all your caveats – six people – one place – that's no basis for any scientific paper – I know that. In a way it's almost a piece of theatre. But we're not going to publish a paper!'

'But what action can we take?'

'Get sufficient evidence, there's no other way.'

'How?'

'Get to those six people.'

'How would we get into the station?'

'Look Marcia, you believe in your findings?'

'Of course.'

'Well, are you going to risk not doing anything. If man's brains are going addled and we fail to convince people, we'll never be able to look ourselves in the face again, never!'

'Alex, I'm not used to this sort of pressure.'

'If it's global, and it's progressive, it's the end of man, Marcia. It's a hundred per cent certain somebody will touch the wrong trigger. We have got to go up there and convince them they've got dangerous people in their station. Will you do it, Marcia?'

For a full half-minute, she sat quite still on the edge of her chair, then looked up. 'There's nothing else we can do.'

Nine

Mawn sensed the springy resilience of the compacted grass and heather under his feet. He stood near the top of a rounded hillock looking down over the huge empty expanse of Scapa Flow. The hills of Hoy just showed as dark craggy outlines over the horizon to the west. Below the water, he imagined the bulbous hulks of the scuttled warships rusting away in the gloom.

As he sat down and stretched out in the golden light of the autumn sunshine the debacle of the television show, the sophisticated backbiting of the scientific community in London, dissolved away in the clear cold air of the Islands.

The plane to Orkney from London had flown through a continuous streaming overcast. And now over four hundred miles nearer to the Arctic circle, the air was scintillating and fresh. The sea was a deep mediterranean blue and there was no sound except for the light hiss of the wind through the grass. Out of the wind the sun was hot but as he stood up in the cold air blowing straight from the ice packs to the north, he was grateful for the protection of a thick woollen sweater and overboots. The chill of the wind evoked long-buried memories of his days in the Arctic. Expeditions into howling sub-zero blizzards to set up apparatus. He thought through the long soft years at Plymouth which had followed. The easy life, two lectures a week and an occasional research project to make the annual report look sufficiently fat.

None of his critics from the faculty would have recognized him. The incipient paunch had already begun to recede. The lines on his face had tautened and his stride was firmer.

At the top, he pulled cold air gratefully into his chest to regain his breath, and slowly scanned the great empty circle of sea, islands and sky.

To the north lay the low, bare hills of the largest Orkney Island, called by the inhabitants 'the mainland'. From the tip of the island where he stood – South Ronaldsay – stretched one of the four Churchill barriers running north and connecting all the islands together with a main road stretching across the shallows. He followed the path of the road to Burray, incongruously set on a piled jumble of white sugar-cube concrete blocks. A long articulated lorry had just turned off the barrier road on to the Islands and was lurching ponderously towards the main gate of the Grim-Ness nuclear power station. He could just hear the sound of its engine.

The station was totally alien to its surroundings. Set next to the coast, surrounded by neatly laid out fields of pasture and kale, it looked unreal. More like a projection of a space city. Most of the buildings were low-lying and exactly rectangular. The whole complex was surrounded by a high wire fence. From his standpoint he could see the tessellated glass roof of the great turbine hall lying next to the windowless grey building housing the switching gear. On the far side of the compound, there were clusters of smaller buildings connected by a branched concrete path which stood starkly pale against the surrounding green.

Dominating the whole complex was the giant white cubicle reactor hall reflecting brilliantly in the sunshine, sitting like an enormous iceberg among the low surrounding buildings, sinister and silent. There were no signs of external activity except for a thin plume of steam escaping from the top of one building.

Beyond the station he could make out the ragged line of the cliff edge and beyond that, the white caps of the waves breaking silently on the rock-strewn coastline beneath. Just beyond the fence to the south was the large white circle of a heliport picked out in bright concentric circles of fluorescent orange like a giant archery target. A large passenger-carrying twin rotor helicopter was parked at the edge of the landing circle and Mawn noted with surprise that both the rotors and fuselage were lashed to the ground with guy-ropes.

To Mawn, the entire scene represented the harsh clash between the artifacts of high technology and the gentle outlines of the natural world.

He looked down at his watch and, with a start, realized that it was almost time to meet Marcia in Dr Durrell's office at the station. They had previously agreed on the plane from Edinburgh that she would start the testing of the six men as soon as they arrived. She was to start with Philip Naylor, senior computer engineer in charge of intermediate systems control at the station.

The main control room of the Grim-Ness power station was in the shape of a drum. The circular wall was covered by a continuous array of complex instrument consoles, patterned with block after block of dials, paper recorders and video screens. The floor was covered from wall to wall in a dark olive-green carpet and the panels holding the instruments were finished in a matt non-reflecting coffee-brown. Overhead, shadowless illumination was provided by an eggbox array of plastic strips hiding the glare of multiple batteries of fluorescent tubes.

In the centre of the room there were four smaller consoles shaped like slightly-enlarged executive desks. Each displayed a simpler array of instruments and on one of them four vertical telephones each of a different colour hung together in a row. There were eight men in the room, seven were standing in front of the control panels around the edge of the room and the eighth, Dr Frank Durrell, sat at the desk with the four phones. He was speaking into the blue set.

'Hello, David? – Yes, Durrell – good – stand by.' He turned to one of the technicians. 'OK?' The man nodded. Durrell returned to the phone: 'Now, as you plug in each thermal sensor, give us a bleep on the tone circuit – then we can start taking baselines – just a minute.' He put his hand over the mouthpiece of the phone and turned towards a man by an instrument panel to see whether he had heard. The man nodded. 'OK – right – thank you, David.'

David Baird had been asked during his first job interview whether he had ever suffered from claustrophobia. He had answered no. There was good reason for the question.

He was working inside one of the most heavily-enclosed spaces ever designed by man. Swaddled in enveloping set of bulky white overalls, white cotton cap and overshoes, he was kneeling on the open face of the nuclear reactor core. Over his head was the vaulting inner surface of the four-inch thick steel pressure vessel – a giant metal bottle over sixty feet in diameter and a hundred feet long. Beneath him was the flat honeycombed pattern of the reactor face. Between the surface of the pressure vessel overhead and the reactor face stretched a forest of vertical metal tubes spaced just far enough apart for him to crawl between them. Two other men also in protective oversuits crouched beside him; like animals in a metal forest.

The three worked by the harsh glare of jury-rigged spotlights clamped on to tripod frames. Temporary cables ran from the lights through a three-foot hole at the centre of the pressure vessel where a section of the steel cap had been withdrawn. Over the hole the six-ton metal plug swung gently at the end of three leashes of chains leading up through the six-foot-thick concrete floor above to a gantry crane in the roof of the reactor hall a hundred and twenty feet overhead.

The air inside the reactor sphere was hot and humid. There was a strong smell of hot metal overlain by the more pungent reek of hot electrical windings.

Surrounding the three men in the pressure vessel there were the thermal shields and then finally the solid, nine-foot-thick biological shield. A concrete cube over one hundred feet in diameter and varying between seven and nine feet in thickness, totally enclosing the pressure vessel. There was only one way out of the confined space where the men knelt. Up a spidery duralumin ladder suspended across the aperture in the pressure vessel and on up a second ladder hooked to the sides of the tunnel in the concrete shield leading up through the biological shield and on to the smooth paved floor of the reactor hall above.

Hanging down through the hole in the pressure vessel alongside the long festoons of cables was a long corrugated flexible tube capped by a square-grilled box. In the box were multilayers of sticky glass fibre filters. Through the grille came a weak supply of fresh air with all the dust and particles removed. Baird and his two colleagues were working through the long, painstaking process of instrument calibration.

Inside the lifeless reactor core, batteries of 'sensing' devices were being inserted between the uranium fuel rods, to give continuous information about the state of the core. Its temperature, how fast the process of fission was proceeding and what temperature differences existed between the cooling water at the centre of the honeycomb and the high temperature water leaving the core on its way to the steam-generating heat exchangers.

Each sensor in fact transmitted its information to the computer and to the control room by means of electrical signals. This meant that Baird and his colleagues could test each sensor by artificially injecting an electric current into the wires leading to the control room as if it were an actual signal from the sensor inside the core. The engineers in the control room could then compare the readings they received with a list of baseline values supplied by the manufacturers on instrument dials in the control room.

Baird picked up the phone beside him and punched a number into the touchtone buttons. While he waited for an answering signal from the control room, he disconnected a red wire from a terminal marked B and a green wire from a terminal marked B2 and attached two clipped leads from a small portable oscilloscope to the terminals. On a small notepad clipped to his oversuit he wrote in one box of a squared-off test chart 'B sensor matrix calibration'. A light blinked on the phone set. He picked it up and spoke: 'I've got prods on B matrix outlet – do you read? – over.'

He switched on the oscillograph which immediately displayed an illuminated shower of waveforms rushing across its light yellow screen. 'Am putting saw-tooth form at RMS of four point five volts.'

An engineer in the control room watched a needle move slowly across the scale of an instrument dial. The dial was labelled: 'B, fuel pin temp'. The needle stopped at four point one. He spoke into the phone: 'It's four point one – check the level of your injection signal please.'

Inside the reactor sphere, Baird covered his eyes against the glare of the lights and studied the screen of the oscillograph. He was sweating profusely and his hands were shaking as he fumbled with a control on the face of the instrument. The peaks of the waves on the screen wobbled and then rose higher. He spoke into the 'phone: 'How's that now? – is it up? – Yes? – OK.' He put the phone down, unplugged the oscillograph and ticked off the entry in the notepad in a column headed: 'test complete'. Finally, with clumsy shaking fingers, he reconnected the red wire to the terminal marked B2 and the green wire to the terminal B.

Marcia turned a knob on the Venn meter to 'score read-out' and a strip of paper covered in rows of printed figures silently extruded from a slot in the side of the instrument. She tore it off, looked at it, then tucked it away in a file. She looked over at Philip Naylor sitting in the armchair. He was short, a dapper man of about thirty with exactly parted black hair and minimal side burns. Although off shift, he was still wearing a rather tightly-fitting off-the-peg charcoal-grey suit, white shirt and thin tightly-knotted association tie.

'How did I do?' The surface joviality only just hid anxiety.

'Can't tell yet,' she replied.

'How does that thing work, anyhow?'

'It's a way of getting rid of any personal bias by the operator – in other words me!' she replied. 'Means you're not influenced by any pressures I could put on you by using special words.'

'I'll never get used to that damn thing.'

She tried to speak reassuringly: 'I guess it's fairer than I'd be. Anyway, your results looked OK to me. It's very kind of you to give me more time – I know how busy you all are.'

Carol Naylor came in with a tray of coffee, reminding her husband in an over-rehearsed tone of haste that he was on shift in an hour. The conversation gradually turned towards the vagaries of the Orkney weather and the price of food in the Kirkwall shops.

As she drove away, Marcia remembered the tension she had caught between the couple sitting poised on the edges of their chairs in the fussy over-neat living-room. She began to imagine what they thought of her. An American psychologist looking inside their heads probably reporting straight back to the Station superintendent.

Their reaction had, in fact, been fairly typical of the others –

a general undercurrent of suspicion. When she had first tested them in London, they had all been between jobs. They had regarded the test as a job evaluation quiz to help them realize their full employment potential. An attitude for which the personnel agency was responsible.

Now that they had a good long-term job with the prospect of other water-reactor stations to build, the test represented a danger. Supposing they failed to measure up to scratch? There would be a secret personnel file somewhere – with all the test results. To how many people would this file be made available?

It had been only because Dr Durrell had given his approval to Marcia's request and volunteered to be retested himself that she had got the three men to cooperate. First of all Elleston and Haskell, and now Naylor.

Marcia drove the hired car uneasily. It was an almost vintage 1974 model with a well-rusted body. Ruined shock-absorbers made the ride a continuous bouncing discomfort. She passed the featureless cubes of the homing estate built by the Gelder Consortium for its employees and drove on towards the Grim-Ness station at the north-eastern tip of the Island. She had arranged to meet Mawn at the station just before their interview with Dr Frank Durrell.

She reviewed the past forty-eight hours. For Stanley Elleston and Roger Haskell, it had been their second test. Both men had showed a slight but definitely lower figure compared with her first measurements. Only one man – Philip Naylor – had been tested three times and all three results had shown a downward trend. She reflected ruefully that two points on a curve meant practically nothing and three points as in the case of Naylor would still fail to convince a sceptical critic. Although his results taken by themselves were impressive, his manual dexterity, pattern recognition and verbal skill levels had all shown a similar degree of loss.

She imagined trying to convince Lodge or his Ministers sufficiently with this flimsy evidence to make them delay the test.

Three men still remained who had already undergone two tests: Bernard Westcott – in charge of emergency core cooling,

David Baird – reactor engineer and Dr Frank Durrell – Chief Systems Designer and executive superintendent of the station. She wondered how to deal with the situation if Durrell's figures showed a progressive drop.

How do you tell a senior nuclear engineer he's getting to be incapable?

She began to work out her own reactions if someone were to tell her that her faculties were afflicted. She concluded that she would show them the door with appropriate dignity.

Mawn was already sitting in an outer office, trying uncomfortably to squeeze himself in between three secretaries clattering away at typewriters. Each one was plugged into a tape recorder. The room was overcrowded with a jumble of papers and filing cabinets.

As Marcia entered, one of the secretaries looked up, taking off her earphones: 'Miss Scott?'

Marcia smiled and nodded. The secretary spoke briefly on the desk intercom then ushered them through into Durrell's office.

Dr Frank Durrell sat behind a plain utility desk. The room was almost bare. There were neutral grey walls and a dark green Tintawn carpet. On the walls there were graphs and charts held in place by masking tape. His face was thin and the skin seemed tightly drawn back, so that his nasal bones seemed to make white pressure marks underneath the skin. His high, rather square forehead had sparse sandy hair brushed over from the side to hide the fact that he was almost bald. His eyes were small and deepset and he shared the blotchy pallor peculiar to a man of middle age who has been seriously overworking for a long period.

His voice was light and precise: 'Please come in.' He turned to Marcia: 'Miss Scott it must be – what – almost a year now isn't it?'

'Yes, over that, I think.' Marcia smiled. 'Oh, this is Doctor Mawn – he's very interested in our work.'

Durrell got up and shook Mawn's hand. 'Ah, yes – of course – I've heard of you.' He turned back to Marcia: 'I really must apologize – I don't want to rush you but we really are up to the eyes at the moment – commissioning for start-up is a very busy time – so could we perhaps get under way?'

'Yes, of course!' Marcia began to unpack the Venn meter and put it on the desk. There was a knock at the door and one of the secretaries poked her head round. 'Mr Gelder on the phone, sir.' Durrell gave them both a quick glance. 'Sorry – excuse me for a minute.' He went out, closing the door. Mawn began to help Marcia arrange the pile of slides to be inserted into the meter. After a few minutes Durrell came back, leaving the door open behind him. His face was flushed: 'I really am most terribly sorry but something's come up. I shan't be able to give you any time this afternoon.'

'Can we make it another time?' Marcia began.

'Well, no I don't . . . I can't really see any prospect just at the moment. Commissioning a new station runs to very tight limits.'

'Next week?'

Durrell began to move towards the door. 'Not much of a chance, I'm afraid. You see, we're under very considerable pressure – private and political – to come in on time so – as much as I'd like to – I think we'll have to call this off for the moment – so sorry – goodbye.' He held out his hand to Mawn. As Mawn put his own forward, Durrell's seemed momentarily to miss contact.

Marcia slammed the car door: 'The archetypal bum's rush!'

'The word of God came down – Gelder!'

'There are two more.'

'You've got to be kidding! Westcott's office is just down the corridor from Durrell's – I saw it on the way in. No, we're rumbled!'

'There's still . . .' She looked down at a list, '. . . David Baird – he lives down at the estate near Philip Naylor's home. If he's off shift maybe we can catch him before they do. Come on, we've got to get something before we go back!'

Philip Naylor sat by the side of a white polythene laundry basket watching a cascading stream of perforated blue tape curl into piles inside. The computer tape punch was shirring and clattering – spewing the blue ribbon off into the basket in an unending serpentine stream. The small discs punched out of the tape showered downwards like a continuous rain of blue confetti collecting in a square glass box clipped underneath the punch head. As the blue tape flowed into the basket it piled up on top of another length of similar tape coloured in a light green.

On a table beside him was a works check sheet on a clipboard. The sheet read: 'iterative loops – error function check.' Running lengths of tape through his fingers, he compared the code punched into it with the machine code on the check sheet. All around him were the tall, grey-painted units of the computer complex. The air was vibrating with a thrumming subdued thunder from air conditioning fans sucking heat away from the intricate meshes of circuitry inside the units. On one, two tape spools were stopping and starting in a jerky sequence, on another, a square panel of neon indicators was flickering in an incomprehensible fast sequence.

In one nine foot length of the blue tape, the punching machine had made two errors – both of which had been spotted by Naylor. The errors consisted of two spaces where an irregular row of holes should have appeared.

Comparing the tape for a third time with the check sheet, Naylor marked the position of the error on the tape with a pencil then picked up a hand punch specially made to fit the pattern on the tape and by depressing a lever made the holes missed by the machine. At least that's what he intended.

When a computer is used to monitor information, it has to be fed with pre-set values to act as a baseline so it can compare any information coming in with the figures it has already memorized. A computer often makes mistakes, but when it does, it brings in its own internal check-system and will register an error to its human operator so the mistake can be rectified.

In a nuclear power station this procedure is not considered to be free of hazards so many of the information channels connecting the core of the reactor to the computer and the control room are nearly always duplicated and sometimes triplicated.

This is known as the 'jury' system because the human operator can select any two out of three values and so get a majority verdict on any particular measurement as it comes in. The instructions on the check sheet were written on the firm assumption that each person working in a nuclear power station is fully tested for any colour blindness.

Philip Naylor had passed the test. He had intended to hand punch the blue tape. In fact, he picked up the green tape from the basket and punched in the correcting holes.

Agnes Baird was a warmly-attractive woman with a naturally frank and open manner.

After a second pot of tea and home-baked shortbread, concern for her husband finally broke through her reserve. Her voice had a light Welsh lilt: 'I'll have to be a bit quick, he's due back off shift in a bit.'

'What did you first notice?' Marcia asked.

'Well, I'm not sure really, like, I think it was his car. He's got this vintage bug, you see . . .'

'Yes, I noticed,' Mawn interrupted. 'A 1961 XK 120 – saw it in the garage. Must have taken years to restore – a real beauty.'

'Well, it was,' she continued. 'But he keeps on hitting things – not big bangs mind – just scrapes here and there, you know.'

'Did you ask him about it?' Marcia asked.

'I tried to, but he almost bit my head off – left it after that, I can tell you.'

'Anything else you've noticed?' Mawn said.

She got up and walked over to the window. 'See for yourself.' She pointed to a series of black tyre scuff marks on the yellow stone wall near the front gate.

'Apart from the car, I meant.'

'Oh, yes there is. David takes this *Scientific American.* It's a magazine. They all read it up there at the station. Well, in the back of it there is a regular feature I think it's called Mathematical Game.'

'Yes, I know it,' Mawn said. 'By Martin Gardner – very difficult, some of them.'

'Yes, that's the one. Well, he used to do those regular – used to pride himself. Now he just gets angry when he tries them, says the writer – Gardner is it? – makes mistakes all the time. Tell you the truth, he can't do them any more!'

'Anything else?' said Marcia.

Agnes Baird thought for a minute. 'Well, yes, matter of fact there is, the other morning – it was funny really – he's a bow-tie fanatic – it's a joke with all his mates – well he was standing in front of the mirror fumbling with it, cursing away he was. In the end I had to do it for him, almost like a baby.'

As David Baird wearily climbed up the duralumin ladder out of the pressure vessel, three hundred feet away from him in the computer room, the baseline values he had transmitted from the reactor core were flowing into the spinning memory drums of the computer.

As each burst of coded information finished its headlong rush into the machine, the error check circuits compared each coded figure with one already stored. By changing the levels on his oscilloscope rather than assuming that the sensor he was testing was at fault and by reconnecting the red and green cables the wrong way round, Baird had caused the computer to store faulty information about a heat sensor in the B matrix of the core.

Finally, by repunching the green tape instead of the blue tape, Philip Naylor had ensured that the faulty data produced by Baird would not be picked up by the error check circuits in the computer.

The Grim-Ness pressurized water reactor was contracting a disease – before birth.

Ten

'Dressing Apraxia!'

'What the hell's that?' Mawn shouted in Marcia's ear to make himself heard over the roar of the plane's piston engines.

'If somebody's got brain damage – one of the early signs is interference with motor skills, Apraxia's one example. In the early stages the patient won't show any obvious general loss of control, they just lose specific skills. To give you an idea, if you ask a patient who's got it to touch a book lying on a table, he'd more than likely touch the table instead of the book. It's the idea of the movement that gets messed up, not the actual movements of the limbs.'

Mawn tugged at his lower lip. 'So if you ask a man to operate, say, three separate controls?'

'They might not even be the right ones – exactly.'

'Try convincing the Minister of that!'

The cabin of the small Trilander aircraft tilted and there was the soft bump of the flaps as they extended. Mawn looked out of the window: 'Forth bridge, we'll be down in a few minutes.'

Marcia studied the papers on her knee: 'Alex, we haven't got much, honest to God! Naylor is the best. Three tests and a uniform progressive drop. Elleston and Haskell – well OK – they show a drop in level compared with the first test, but not much. All that remains is hearsay reporting from Baird's wife. We can't go to Richard Lodge with that – he'll crucify us.'

Mawn banged the armrest. 'What about all the other results you and Venn have got? I don't care how slim it looks, we've got to get them to postpone start-up till these people can be replaced. What the hell else can we do, it's too late to do anything else, much too late!'

November 25

Richard Lodge closed the folder on the desk in front of him, got up and walked over to the window. Outside, the rush-hour traffic in Whitehall was beginning to build up in the November gloom and in the centre of the road, the Cenotaph reflected the sickly yellow of the street lights. There was a light fog.

'What do you think?' Mawn asked.

Lodge turned: 'This is not going to be easy.'

'Don't you accept it?' Marcia asked.

'It's not that – I'm not qualified to assess its merit scientifically.' He walked back to the desk and picked up the folder as if weighing its content. 'The gist of what you're saying is that a whole section of the population is showing a loss of intelligence and some of these – afflicted – people are staffing the station at Grim-Ness.'

'Very much more than that,' Mawn said. 'We're saying that they're mostly in key positions and the reactor is due to start up in just twelve days. We hold this to be an *impossibly* dangerous situation. Cut-price reactors are bad enough but . . .'

Lodge studied him calmly: 'But the DTI records show no more than the usual run of technical faults. I checked with their Chief Inspector yesterday morning. By law they have to monitor *all* stages of commissioning.'

'But they don't know about this material of ours do they?' Marcia intervened.

Lodge put the report down. 'No, they don't. But what you've failed to show here, is that these people can't do their *job* safely. You may very well be right. It's feasible I suppose – their abilities could have been marginally affected – I don't know by what – a virus or some such. But you *haven't* proved their incompetence within the limits of their job.'

'Well, we were more or less thrown out before we'd finished . . .' Mawn began.

'That's beside the point, I'm afraid.' Lodge continued evenly, 'I think in fact this whole effect you've discovered is profoundly important but it's not enough for me to go to the Minister and say effectively: "stop the commissioning of the station." There's far too much bound up in this politically. The Government has already had its whiskers singed in the House: private enterprise taking over the public sector – you know the sort of thing. If they were to delay it now the opposition would throw the book at them, and say: "why wasn't it done by a State corporation in the first place?" '

Mawn stood up: 'So you'll do nothing?' He was pale with anger.

'I didn't say so, no.' He paused for a moment. 'Doctor – forgive me – I'm going to be very direct. That business on the television – it really didn't do your credibility any good.'

'I'm well aware,' Mawn's voice was quiet, level, 'but I think I may have been set up for it!'

Lodge shrugged: 'I only know what I know. The fact of the matter is if I take this report in to the Minister – the first thing he's going to say is – throw it away. And then, if I'm lucky and he's had a good lunch, I'll get him to put it out for independent check by our own people.'

'That'll take weeks,' Marcia complained.

'No it won't. As a matter of fact I've already set it up and if all goes well . . .' He opened a desk diary. 'I'll get you in to see the Minister on the twenty-eighth, that's just three days' time.' He pointed to the diary. 'There's a spare half-hour here – providing there's no sudden division in the House. It'll be in his room in the Commons.'

'I didn't realize. What can I say? Thanks again.' Mawn sat down again.

For several minutes Lodge sat playing with a gold propelling pencil, doodling on the blotting pad in front of him. Finally he put the pencil down and looked up. 'What I'm going to say to you must be regarded as privileged information – do you accept that?' He looked from one to the other. They both nodded slowly. 'It may sound rather vague – but the whole area is highly sensitive, particularly from the international point of view, and I can only talk in general terms at this stage.' He pointed to their report.

'What's in there bears a striking similarity to some data collected elsewhere.' He looked at Marcia. 'You mentioned some medical – er – pathological evidence?'

'Yes,' she replied. 'We shall be going to see someone at the Pathology Institute. He rang us this morning.'

Lodge rose and looked at his watch: 'I'll give the Minister a short memo on this and get it vetted as soon as possible. And we'll meet again at – er – 10.30 on the twenty-eighth at the Minister's room in the Commons. Perhaps you ought to be there by 10.15.' He sighed and started to usher them towards the door. 'And now I'm afraid I have to preside over tea and buns with some ladies from Rochdale who've been planting "trees for a green city" or some such.'

Mawn stopped at the door: 'I'm sorry we've been unable to convince you.'

Lodge spread his hands deprecatingly and smiled: 'I have masters, remember.'

Mawn persisted: 'Do you happen to remember your visit to Marcia's lab?'

Marcia glanced up at Mawn warningly, but he looked right past her.

'Indeed – yes. I enjoyed your – er – frank discussion with Dr Venn.' There was a faint edge in Lodge's voice almost as though he was anticipating Mawn's next words.

'I didn't mean that. I watched you do the joystick test. You found it extremely difficult, didn't you?' Mawn waved Marcia ahead of him and closed the door as he went out.

Lodge slumped back against the edge of the desk then raised his hands in front of his eyes, clenching and unclenching his fingers, then slowly and deliberately reached out for a gilt ash-tray. Just before his fingers touched the edge, his hand suddenly overshot with a jerk, upsetting an inkstand. He watched the black pool spread slowly out over the walnut desk top.

At Grim-Ness, the wind had swung to the north-west, bringing with it a low scudding overcast. The colour of the water had changed to a steely grey and whitecaps showed far out on to Scapa Flow. Curtains of stinging cold rain were sweeping across the station, sending huddled workers scurrying quickly into the shelter of the low squat buildings.

In the Reactor Hall, the pressure vessel had been finally sealed off and the hexagonal concrete floor slabs replaced. The giant seventy-foot fuel loading tower had been wheeled away to one end of the cathedral-like expanse of the hall.

No one would set foot inside the reactor again for a minimum period of two-and-a-half years. In twelve days, start-up was to begin and the core would gradually heat up as the atoms of its enriched uranium fuel rods began to split. Within hours of start-up, any man left inside the sphere would die from an overwhelmingly lethal dose of radiation.

Professor James Kingston was in full flight along the main corridor of the Institute of Pathology. Behind him Marcia and Mawn hurried along in tow trying to keep up with his headlong rush.

James Kingston's enthusiasm meant that he never had enough time. He enjoyed his job as consultant neuropathologist to such a degree that a colleague once said of him: 'If that bugger ever drops dead, he'll do his own post-mortem.' A portly red-faced man of fifty-eight – his breezy extroversion while demonstrating post-mortems had got many a student over his initial revulsion for the sight of the dead.

Without slacking his pace, he pulled a gold half hunter watch out of a grey camel hair waistcoat stretched tightly over his paunch. 'Oh, God, Academic Board in half an hour, dear oh dear.'

He paused before double swing doors marked: 'PM. No admittance', he looked round and caught Marcia's hesitation. 'Quite all right, dear lady – nothing to be afraid of – all end up here sooner or later you know – might just as well get used to it.' Marcia had turned pale. His voice softened. 'It's all quite tidy now, everything's done you know – all sewn up as it were.' He turned and flung the doors wide open.

The post-mortem room was circular and about twenty feet in diameter. In the centre of the room there were three horizontal white porcelain tables with cast-in gullies. The floor was grey tiled and underneath the tables there were drain grilles set in the tiles. Partly surrounding the tables, there was a semi-circle of wooden tiered seats and between the tables and the wall there were glass cabinets containing shining chromium instruments and a pair of butcher's scales. On the wall a blackboard was divided into white squares labelled brains, liver, heart, kidneys.

In the squares weights had been recorded in yellow chalk. There was an almost overpowering smell of disinfectant.

On one of the porcelain tables a white cloth covered a body. Kingston waved towards the tiered seats: 'Sit you down.' He turned to a small trolley. On the top was a bundle of damp white muslin about the size of a melon.

'Now here,' he slapped the bulky shape under the white cloth. 'This is the chappie I was talking about just a moment ago.' He picked up a brown file. 'These are his clinical notes – I'll read you the relevant details.' He fumbled for a pair of gold-framed half-glasses and pushed them on to the bridge of his nose. 'Aged forty-two – male – went to his local doctor complaining of headache, slight double vision, clumsiness, inability to concentrate. Doctor sent him up to our neurology bods.' He turned over a sheaf of papers in the file. 'Let me see now – yes, that's right – Romberg sign, pupils – mm mm – yes, yes, here it is – a summary.'

He read: 'The main features of this patient suggest a mild generalized cortical atrophy. His rather marked coarse tremor is more reminiscent of the toxic variety rather than the finer type usually associated with alcohol or the addictive drugs.'

He ran his finger down the sheet. 'Blah, blah – all pathological tests – normal – that's blood, urine, so on. No history of encephalitis – glandular fever. No evidence of addiction or alcohol. Recommend in-patient examination – ventriculography EEG. Provisional diagnosis: Cerebral Atrophy of no known origin.'

He looked up at them over his glasses: 'That's a rather elegant way of saying they hadn't got the first bloody idea what was wrong with him, but his brain was ruined.' He put the folder down. Mawn gestured at the body. 'How'd he get there?'

Kingston beamed: 'Extraordinarily obliging of him – some sort of lathe operator – turret lathe, I think they call it. Anyway, a piece flew off it – went straight through his chest. I'll show you.' He moved to withdraw the white sheet.

'Oh no, please,' Marcia gasped.

Kingston looked up in surprise: 'What? Oh!' His face fell.

'Most unusual really, came out under the right scapula – still, never mind, not essential I suppose.' He put the cloth back regretfully and moved to the muslin bundle and started to unwrap it.

'Exhibit A.' Inside the muslin was a brain, cut transversely into half-inch slices and put together in sequence. Kingston began to lay the slices out in order on the stainless steel surface of the trolley. He picked up a long pair of forceps and pointed. 'First of all, it's . . .' He looked over at the blackboard. '. . . er thirty grammes under weight, there was quite a lot of separation from the skull, a little dilation of the ventricles – here and a few areas of calcification in the occipital cortex – here.' He stroked the surface of one of the smaller slices, there was a slight grating sound. He looked up at Marcia and Mawn. Marcia had surmounted her revulsion and was leaning forward on her elbows looking down as she spoke.

'So it's generalized – not any one specific area?'

'Oh, quite! We've been doing a lot of microscopy on previous cases – this one's only had frozen sections so far, but I'm sure it'll be similar. Net result is a sort of cross between senile cortical atrophy – multiple sclerosis – although there's not much demyelinization – and encephalitis. Point is though – those slides you sent me – Albania wasn't it? – they're absolutely identical, no question about it, no question at all.'

'Yes, but that's only one case,' Mawn said.

'Oh, dear me no. We've collected thirty-two already. At the last European Pathology Congress in Vienna there were over a dozen papers on the same thing. Nobody's absolutely agreed a name yet – "chronic Betz-cell atrophy" seems to be the favourite at the moment.'

'What's it due to?' Marcia asked.

Kingston shook his head. 'No idea, practically everything's already been suggested – virus – bacteria – toxins. You name it, some imbecile's written a paper on it.'

'Is there anything consistent about the clinical picture?' Mawn asked.

'You wouldn't really expect that,' Kingston continued. 'It's generalized in the brain – microscope appearances are consistent but the area of brain affected isn't. Most common sign seems to be Apraxia, thus the motor areas are involved.'

Marcia turned suddenly to Mawn. 'David Baird – you remember his wife – the bow tie?' Mawn nodded. Kingston looked up, a little irritated at the interruption to his dissertation. 'As I was saying, Apraxia and then Colour Agnosia.'

'What's that?' Mawn asked.

'It's a condition where people can't *identify* colours properly – but they can pass colour vision tests . . .'

Mawn leant back: 'Good God almighty!'

'Quite so. Patients are quite unable to associate colours with objects – it's a known sign of brain damage – only way they can associate colours with objects is to do it by rote memory. Remember one patient I saw – fascinating – somebody showed him a colour print of a London bus – all bright red, you know. Chappie spent a long time looking at it then said it would be a sea-blue – er blood-red – tomato-orange. Typical sort of reaction apparently.'

Mawn gripped the rail in front of him: 'Could a person affected like this pass a colour vision test?'

'Oh, Lord, yes, probably a bit slow at it but they'd do it all right – in the end.'

In the road outside the Pathology Institute Marcia drew up her coat collar against the fog. Suddenly she put her arm through Mawn's and pulled close to him. Mawn looked at her in surprise. Her face was drawn.

'Alex, when Howard and I started all this, we did the test on ourselves.'

'Yes?'

'Well, we were both inside normal limits.'

He smiled. 'You probably fiddled it.'

'No, Alex. I'm serious. My results could have changed too. And what about you?'

Marcia tore the score sheet off the Venn tester, her hand shaking as she totted up the figures printed on it.

'Well?' asked Mawn.

'It's all right. Effectively the same as when I first did it.'

Mawn took the score sheet and looked at it: 'Good, so if we're both unaffected, *why* are we unaffected, that's what defeats me. We don't work among any particular group – we're not shut up in an office. Somewhere in *us* Marcia is maybe the answer. Something in our lifestyle – something we eat, some behaviour pattern. The answer's got to be in us.'

Mawn threw down the letter in disgust: 'My God – what a lot of double talk!'

'What's happened?' Marcia called out from the living-room.

He picked up the letter and walked through. 'I'll read it, it's from a Mr Tom Thorpe, Executive Secretary of the Nuclear Power Workers' Union. You remember I went to see them a couple of days ago.'

'I thought they were impressed.'

'One of them was, or he seemed to be. Listen, I'll read it to you: Dear Professor Mawn. In reference to your visit on blah blah – for which we thank etc . . . My executive have now given the matter etc etc . . . and have concluded that the matter which you brought to our attention does not require any present action on behalf of our members. You will, I hope, appreciate our side of the problem. At the present time, our negotiations with the Government regarding annual wage and salary increases have reached a delicate stage and thus, if we were to suggest that some of our rank and file members were affected in the way that you have suggested, this would, of course, seriously disturb the progress of the talks.

'In general terms, we are always interested to receive any information regarding potential industrial hazards to our members and we are grateful to you for bringing this matter to our attention. Your obedient servant – my arse! They're going to do absolutely bloody nothing, sit tight and screw more money out of the Government.'

'What did you expect?'

'Some sort of responsibility. It is the same old cloth cap attitude – where there's muck there's brass. For muck read danger in this case.' He looked at his watch. 'Come on, we're due in the presence in half an hour, better get moving. Have you ever met him by the way? I don't normally mix with Ministers.'

'Campbell Baxter?' Marcia replied. 'Yes, he came to one of our do's here. Sheldon . . .' her voice broke off, '. . . talked to him on the programme. He's fortyish, very beautiful – made a million by the time he was thirty . . .'

'As a man I meant.'

'He's a complete pro. Only reason he does what he does is because he wants to be Prime Minister, I guess. General sort of whizz-kid reputation. He's annoyed all the scientific community by trying to resurrect the old Rothschild Report.'

'What? Putting all research on a sort of consumer-customer basis?'

'That's it. Lot of my girl friends say he's very sexy but he doesn't turn me on.'

Mawn started to pack his briefcase with papers. 'Anything else?'

'He's quick on his feet – nimble but not deep.'

Mawn closed the case. 'I'll ring for a cab.'

At Grim-Ness, the two-year process of commissioning was almost complete. Each meshwork of electrical controls, every hydraulic and steam circuit, every pipe junction, switch and warning light had received double and triple checks and were slowly being linked together in a functional whole. First one system was run in isolation, then connected to its fellow. As a fault developed a halt was called and the particular system in which the fault occurred isolated until it was again in perfect order. Slowly, over the months, hundreds of miles of electrical cables were linked with steam valves, core controls and turbines until an inexorably growing sense of activity and life spread through the whole complex.

As if in sympathy with the growing sense of pulsing activity, the workers began to work for longer hours. Some volunteered to work double shifts, where before they were more likely to have complained about any need for overtime.

The interior of the steel pressure vessel was silent. Specially filtered, distilled and purified water had now been pumped in between the tall bundles of fuel rods to fill the primary coolant circuit. Between each rod bundle, long boron steel control rods were in the full 'down' position. Each rod was shaped like a six-pointed star in cross section and fitted between the rods absorbing neutrons and preventing any rise of temperature. The temperature in the core was an even twenty-three degrees centigrade, comfortable room temperature. Outside, the barometer was falling and a freezing wind curled off the heaving North Sea, booming and moaning around the alien shapes of the station.

The atmosphere in the Minister's corridor of the House of Commons is more than enough to inhibit the most determined of visitors. Mawn and Marcia had been conducted by a dour-faced steward past a series of uniformed police constables along stairways and softly carpeted corridors. Overhead were carved stone archways and every few yards a sombre-suited figure would pad by carrying sheaves of papers with an expression that suggested he was about to make a decision affecting millions. The names neatly painted on each door that they passed all belonged to public figures. Neither spoke during the journey.

Campbell Baxter's manner was instantly charming and relaxed. He leant back in an easy chair, one leg dangling over the arm. Mawn had just finished outlining their investigation at Grim-Ness station and Marcia had tried to give an encapsulated version of the pathological findings made by Professor Kingston. Richard Lodge sat uneasily on a hard chair holding a brief-case on his knees like a shield in front of his stomach.

Baxter got up abruptly and walked around behind his desk and sat down. For a moment he sat doodling with a pencil and then spoke: 'What you've just told me is in fact extremely important and I dare say . . .' he gestured at Lodge, '. . . that Richard's told you there is an acute international interest in this general area at the moment but my task now is relatively simple. You're asking me to take a specific course of action about a specific case. And what you've said in effect is that we should delay the start-up at Grim-Ness because some of the staff there are affected by this – IQ loss effect – of yours.'

'It's absolutely essential.' Mawn was vehement. 'It represents a double hazard. It's the first privately licensed reactor in this country and that means safety margins are bound to be cut because of cost . . .'

'Oh, not at all,' Baxter replied. 'That's a problem we're well aware of. You must realize that the Department of Trade and Industry has been in there right from the start. Every single phase of construction has been independently checked by its inspectors. They're satisfied, so I must accept their findings.'

'Yes, but pressurized water reactors are more hazardous in the first place,' Mawn continued. 'And not only that, no emergency core cooling system has ever been tested in practice . . .'

'Doctor Mawn all this may very well be true – it's certainly a point of view. We all agonized about the whole affair in point of fact, and this must remain between these walls, more than one member of the Cabinet was totally opposed to it. But we must have energy. If your own environmental lobby is right, we're running out of fossil fuels so what else is there to be done? Nuclear power. Of course there's a trade-off – high risk, high gain – we all admit that – at least in private, but we can't do otherwise if our economy is to be competitive. You environmentalists talk about an energy crisis – well this is the answer surely?'

'But we've given you evidence about a further danger,' Marcia spoke nervously.

'Miss Scott.' Baxter's smile had begun to dilute. 'What I have to make a decision about is whether or not to delay the start-up. Now, I think Mr Lodge and I have considered every single aspect of your report and I have to tell you that I simply can't do it.'

'My God!' Mawn cried. 'What else do you need?'

'Doctor, this is a crucial stage in nuclear power development in this country. My department has poured money into the project, far too much probably, the consortium which is building it is already stretched to the limit financially. If I was to delay this now, quite frankly I think it would put our nuclear programme back five years, we simply can't afford it and if you'll forgive me saying so, your report is not without its critics.'

'What do you mean?' Mawn demanded.

Baxter picked up a typescript. 'I submitted the whole of your material to referees for their opinion, since, of course, I'm not qualified to assess its value scientifically.'

'Could I know who they were?' Marcia asked.

'I believe it's the custom to submit scientific papers for independent and anonymous assessment before publication?'

'Of course,' Mawn said.

'Well then, I don't think it'll help matters if I tell you who they are. One is a medical statistician and the other holds a chair in psychology.' He paused for a moment looking down at the script. 'In point of fact, I find the tone of their report quite unnecessary – I – er – sometimes think that scientists are far more unpleasant to one another than even politicians but nevertheless, I am bound to act on its content.'

'But not without defence, I hope,' Mawn began.

'If I could just read it to you,' Baxter continued and began to turn the pages. 'This is their summary, the first part is just a précis of your statistics:

'You have asked us to assess this report as to its scientific merit. We find that the presentation and methodology is in general adequate. There seem to be no important deviations from what one might regard as being the proper method for this type of study. Indeed, the phenomenon which the authors allege they have observed would – if true – be of the most extraordinary interest. However, we are bound to point out that both the premises and the interpretations given by the authors are quite misleading. There is, of course, a long and well-known literature dealing with IQ levels in man. From time to time reports appear alleging that mankind is becoming debased because the relatively unintelligent have larger families and thus the overall intelligence is bound to diminish in the long run.

'The factors governing the measurement of intelligence and general ability are very highly complex. Relative word skills, dyslexic factors, the bias of testers all play a highly significant role. To assert, as the authors have done, that they have provided evidence of group loss of intelligence on the basis of the data they provide, is in our view both mischievous and irresponsible. It is well known that in any group where the individual members are related, very complex behavioural patterns emerge. In one firm where they carried out their tests for example, we have managed to establish that the entire work force knew very well that the finances of the firm were in a highly parlous state and that many of the individuals tested were under considerable threat of redundancy. How the authors failed to take the anxiety generated by this sort of circumstances into account is quite beyond comprehension. There may very well be an interesting effect buried somewhere in this data, but we are of the opinion that the authors have entirely failed to expose its true nature.

'In conclusion, we feel bound to remark that this type of paper is a good example of contemporary pseudo-science. It is regrettably true that more and more reports appearing in journals of previously reliable status are taking on the tones of advocacy rather than properly defined argument. In our view, the contents should be set aside until such time as the observations reported can be exposed to repetition by other scientific workers.'

He put the report down. 'Well, there it is. As I said, I regret its tone but I must accept its findings.' He rose and walked towards the oak-panelled door looking at his watch. 'And now I'm afraid you must excuse me, I have a meeting . . .'

'So you'll do nothing further?' Mawn grated.

'I'm not able to, there are insufficient grounds.' He opened the door and called over to a rather severe dark-haired woman seated at a window desk. 'Jane, I wonder if you'd find a steward, Doctor Mawn and Miss Scott are just going.' He turned, holding out his hand. 'Thank you very much for coming to see me. I'm sorry we couldn't do more.' He shook hands and went back into his room, closing the door behind him.

Lodge looked up as he re-entered. 'We'd better send a copy of their stuff to Bordheim.'

'Yes, do that Richard would you.' Baxter flopped down into

the chair. 'One way of keeping them quiet might be to invite them up with you for start-up at Grim-Ness. Could you bear it?'

'Yes, surely. The RAF have laid on transport, there's plenty of room.'

'Richard, what do you make of Mawn?'

Lodge paused for a moment. 'He seems sincere. I would wish he wasn't quite so polemic.'

'Exactly. What people like that don't seem to realize is we're on the side of the environment. They're just so completely unrealistic. If we let them do things their way, we'd have complete chaos. I suggest you keep a very tight rein on him.'

Eleven

December 3

At Grim-Ness the four-inch steel pressure vessel had been successfully tested to levels almost twice as high as its operating pressure. The one-hundred foot long emergency power gallery with its bubbling array of lead-acid batteries was connected to massive diesel generators for final charging and each fuel rod in the reactor was finally logged for position, temperature and zero neutron flux.

The process which every construction worker, scientist and engineer had been consistently imagining for almost four years was about to begin: 'start-up'.

High over the top of the reactor core in the neck of the bottle shaped pressure vessel servo-motors began to turn gear trains, slowly withdrawing the long boron steel rods from the reactor core below. First the rods around the edge of the core were withdrawn, centimetre by centimetre, then others towards the centre also began to lift. Neutrons, previously absorbed by the rods in their lowered position, began to strike into the nuclei of other nearby atoms of uranium, releasing secondary neutron showers. As atomic fission accelerated, the temperature in the reactor began to rise.

Anxious engineers in the control room sat around an illuminated wall plan of the reactor face. As each rod rose so did its position appear on dials alongside its marked position on the wall plan.

The dials showed that the rods of B matrix were in correct position.

Temperatures, neutron flux levels and reactor periods were recorded as within normal and predicted limits. Finally, at the end of almost three days of tense comparison and measurement, Dr Frank Durrell called a temporary halt before the final rise to operating level and criticality.

Patiently, he examined each log of events provided by each section leader. Philip Naylor was one of the last to present his data from the computer room. Durrell found in it no cause for comment and signed it and passed it back to Naylor.

Outside, the zone of low pressure which had brought the snow and wind had shifted away to the east over the North Sea towards Sweden.

To the west of the Hebrides a second region of low pressure was moving sluggishly eastwards and squeezed in between the two lay a transitory ridge of high pressure. As the air cooled, a temperature inversion developed causing a layer of still air to remain stationary overhead. A light covering of snow gave the brutal functional outlines of the station the appearance of a white demonstration model standing out against a lead-grey sky. The air was heavy and completely still and, as men walked from one building to another, the loudest sound to be heard was the dry squeaking of the snow under their feet.

The RAF Sycamore helicopter approached from the south-west, hovered for a moment over the circular landing pad and then slowly began its ungainly descent. About twenty feet away from the ground snow began to pick up in a central vortex and then to fly away from the pad exposing the concentric orange circles on the concrete.

The turbines sang down to silence and the rotors slowed and bowed downwards. An oval door in the side of the fuselage moved inwards and sideways and a uniformed RAF sergeant jumped down, hooking a short aluminium ladder over the edge of the door aperture. Marcia clambered down, the freezing air striking her face like a blow, tautening her skin into a mask and catching the breath in her throat.

As the party led by Lodge and Mawn made their way to a waiting minibus, a pale northern sun briefly appeared through a gap in the clouds. It was as though a spotlight had been turned on in a diamond mine. Every surface of the station sparkled and glittered with a million tiny points of light on the hoar frost. Almost as quickly, the sun was eclipsed by a lowering bank of dense black cloud.

'Not exactly ideal conditions!' Mawn said.

Lodge smiled: 'You're determined something's going to happen, aren't you – even if you have to drop gelignite in the core!'

Mawn turned, his face sombre: 'I don't think it's a subject for humour.'

The aircrew of the helicopter trudged past carrying holdalls, one turned and grinned at Marcia. Lodge's manner just hid impatience: 'I'd just like to point out, that we don't do this for every Jeremiah.'

'I've tried to make my point,' Mawn continued. 'I think there's a definite and measurable danger and I shall do everything I can to point it out to the people in charge.'

Lodge's voice hardened: 'I'd remind you that I'm personally accountable for you while you're here and I'd take any such move very unkindly indeed.'

Marcia stamped her feet. 'I've lost a toe already, could we get inside, please?'

Neither man heard her. Mawn's voice carried no hint of apology: 'You can have my assurance – if you like – that anything I say will be in your presence so you can take it down and use it in evidence, all right?'

Lodge stepped into the minibus, speaking over his shoulder: 'Very well.'

Inside the perimeter fence, the minibus crunched over the snow between the jumbles of contractors' huts, disassembled cranes and piles of steel scaffolding, finally drawing up alongside the entrance to the main reactor hall. There, they were met by Bernard Westcott who did his best not to react to the presence of Mawn and Marcia and instead led the party straight in to a lift and then up to the nerve centre of the station on the third floor; the great circular control room.

As the lift juddered up through its shaft set in the massive concrete wall of the Reactor Hall, each one of them was awed into silence by a deep rumbling vibration of distant machinery. The building seemed to have a pulse of its own.

A group of six men in white full-length coats stood in front of the vertical plan of the reactor face. Yellow lights winked at intersections on the hexagonal pattern and instrument dials alongside each light registered the condition of each separate fuel rod assembly.

At the central desk control Dr Frank Durrell leant forward, studying a cascade of coloured figures sweeping down the face of a monitor screen in front of him. Brian Gelder stood behind him looking over his shoulder. Durrell turned and spoke to a technician: 'All flux levels tally, do you confirm?'

The technician threaded a long squared paper roll through his fingers: 'Power density's inside limits. Yes, confirm.'

Durrell picked up the blue hand phone and depressed a switch. He spoke to David Baird two hundred feet away in the rod control room. Baird sat in front of a small scale version of the reactor face plan on the wall of the main control room. The pattern of lights on it was identical.

His desk was surrounded by the tall blocks of a computer. His position was thirty-five feet away from the reactor core from which he was separated by four inches of steel, two inches of stainless steel thermal shielding and the nine-foot thick concrete of the biological shields.

Durrell's voice came through on distort: 'David, leave this line open on the speakers. Will you check, please?'

Baird depressed a key on a switch panel, and spoke into a perforated grille: 'All right, can you hear?' As he spoke he attempted to hang up the phone but missed the receiver rest. Durrell spoke into a similar grille: 'Yes, I've got you – quite clear. Power density has been even for seventeen minutes, so we'll go on.' As he spoke, Durrell turned over the pages of an operating manual on the desk in front of him, then depressed four more switches and spoke into the grille: 'Durrell here. Are you getting me, Philip?' Naylor's voice came through clearly: 'Yes, go ahead.'

'We'll keep open now.' He looked down at the manual and read out: 'Rods five and seven A matrix, thirteen and fifteen B matrix, twenty-one twenty-three C matrix, all to positions C minus eighteen – confirm please?' Baird's voice came back through the speaker and parrotted Durrell's instruction.

In the reactor core, the rods moved up three centimetres in their narrowly fitting channels between the fuel can bundles.

In the Control Room, a soft repeating electronic chime began to sound and single red lights on four separate consoles began to flash in unison with the tone. Walking with a carefully assumed slouch, a technician detached himself from the group near the reactor plan and spoke into a microphone: 'Computer error function levels are not getting on the board.' Philip Naylor's voice crackled from an overhead speaker: 'Sorry.' There was a pause then the chime and the red flashing lights stopped abruptly. A technician turned to Durrell: 'Clearance.' Durrell nodded and turned back to his microphone: 'Move to C minus seventeen.'

In fuel can assembly four in the B matrix of the reactor core, the external temperature of the can was 610 degrees and the temperature of the uranium fuel pellets inside the can was 3,020 degrees. The instruments in the control room monitoring the B matrix registered 580 and 2,070 degrees respectively.

Read-out screens in the thrumming computer room showed no deviation from the standard values already stored and Naylor wrote neatly in a log chart on the desk beside him: 'error loops clear'.

Dr Durrell was the first to catch sight of the visitors as they entered the room led by Westcott.

After the introductions were over, Gelder quickly drew Lodge aside. He spoke vehemently: 'Richard, what's that bloody man doing here?'

'He's merely a spectator,' Lodge murmured.

'I warn you, if he so much as speaks one word out of turn I'll have him slung off the station altogether.'

'I don't think you need to be so militant,' Lodge replied, evenly. 'And if I may say so, he is after all my responsibility. Just as I represent the Minister in any decision regarding the future of your stations.'

There was a silence. Finally, Gelder spoke with a sudden shift of mood: 'I'm glad you reminded me. I'll do my best to be pleasant of course – but keep in mind what I said, Richard.'

The machining of the cans which enclose the uranium fuel in a nuclear reactor is a matter of very high precision. After the long process of cutting the spiral fluting on their surface, each rod is rotated slowly around central depressions at each end. A meter with a movable foot is placed against the centre of the can and any movement of the needle as the rod is rotated indicates that the rod is not perfectly straight. All the cans in assembly four of B matrix in the core passed the test.

The air in the board room at Grim-Ness was hazy with tobacco smoke. It was built in what Durrell privately called 'PVC Regency'. The effect was intended to convey an air of solidity and respectability couched in modern architectural terms. Rosewood wall panels were framed by extruded plastic mouldings and at intervals there were old prints of Faraday and his original apparatus set incongruously in satin aluminium frames. Bare wires protruded from the walls where wall lights were still to be fitted.

Mawn and Marcia were standing looking down through the window at the prism-shaped glass panels of the turbine hall roof far below. The corridors joining the buildings had hemispherical glass rooflights which shone through the coating of snow in the gathering northern twilight like the portholes of some immense spaceship. Underneath their feet they could just sense a faint vibration.

There was a steady buzz of conversation from a crowd of

station executives each clutching a gin and tonic. Marcia saw Gelder break away from one small group and head towards them. She turned her head quickly towards the window. 'Here it comes!' As Gelder drew near, they could both see that he was smiling and that his cheeks were flushed. Marcia spoke through clenched teeth: 'Watch out . . . he's smiling.'

'Doctor, are you being looked after?' Gelder's tone was expansive. 'And Miss Scott, have we managed to calm some of your anxieties?'

'Have you seen the weather forecast?' Mawn flushed as he asked the question, wishing it didn't sound so lame. Lodge followed Durrell and Westcott over to where they were standing.

'The weather?' Gelder's expression showed an amused contempt.

'The Met Office say a zone of low pressure's coming in from the east. There'll be some very high winds.' Gelder caught Durrell's eye and smiled as he replied: 'And what do you suppose is going to happen?'

'Well, it compounds the risk of start-up, doesn't it? You know as well as I do that these islands often get completely cut off. In point of fact the highest wind velocity ever recorded was measured just twenty miles from here . . .'

'Thanks, Doctor. You really never give in, do you?' Gelder was smiling broadly. 'First you tell us our computers are unsafe, then our staff are below par, and now the weather's going to get us.' Durrell and Westcott were grinning. 'Surely the Minister must have told you. We did all the wind-tunnel tests at Farnborough – all these buildings are safe at up to two hundred and fifty miles per hour. Quite a wind – even for these parts.'

Mawn suppressed his irritation and replied coolly: 'So you discount all our findings on your staff?'

'Not at all. It's just that your motivation doesn't exactly lie in the field of pure science.'

'And just what do you mean by that?'

'I had quite a disturbing call from the Nuclear Power Workers' Union yesterday, apparently you went to see them?'

'Yes, I did.'

Gelder looked down at his glass for a moment. 'It's very difficult for an ordinary businessman like myself to understand your motivation. According to Thorpe, you spent about an hour trying to persuade them that their work force here is in some danger . . .'

'We have quite enough evidence,' Marcia interrupted.

'Now, Miss Scott,' Gelder continued. 'Let me be perfectly clear about one thing, our labour relations up here have always been very carefully nurtured as Frank Durrell here will tell you. And one way of looking at what the Doctor did in London would be to call it deliberate and malicious interference . . .'

'Really Brian, that's going too far,' Lodge said.

'Is it really?' Gelder went on, looking straight at Mawn. 'It's very hard for me to believe your motives are just purely scientific. Now I don't know what your political affiliations are, but . . .'

He stopped, Mawn was laughing in his face. 'You'd have to do better than that. I don't suppose you'd believe in any motive unconnected with straight profit and loss figures . . .'

'And *what* about your figures?' The skin underneath Gelder's eyes had paled. 'Your scientific figures. What did your professional peers say about them? Pseudo-science wasn't it?'

'You saw that report?' Marcia gasped.

'Of course I did! I've been in almost continuous consultation with Baxter's department right from the beginning.'

Lodge turned to Mawn: 'I think I remember telling you how the law stands. Every aspect of this station had been under the strictest supervision from our inspectors?'

Mawn swung round on him: 'And have you ever tested the emergency core cooling system? Well! Has *that* been passed by your inspectors?'

'There have been model simulation tests, yes,' Lodge replied.

'Marvellous! A simulated loss of coolant accident on a *nine-inch* model reactor!' Mawn whipped round at Gelder: 'And do you remember what they showed? You know what happened in the model. Ten per cent, I repeat, ten per cent of the emergency cooling water reached the simulated core and that merely compounded the destruction of the pile. The rest simply blew out as steam through the original vent.'

A tone chimed from a speaker and a female voice spoke smoothly: 'Dr Durrell and Mr Gelder to main control, please. Dr Durrell and Mr Gelder to main control.'

Gelder turned to go. 'Get your beads out, Doctor. We reach criticality tomorrow. There's still time to make your escape of course, if you're frightened.'

Mawn and Lodge lay stretched out in deep soft armchairs after a plain meal of locally-killed beef and potatoes. Marcia had gone to bed, and both relaxed, staring into a dying log fire which had filled the room with a sweet resinous fragrance.

The 'Earl Magnus' hotel in Kirkwall was solid and Victorian. Built from local stone, the interior was overcrowded with stuffed eagles and ospreys glaring balefully out at the world from beneath glass domes. In the corner where the two men sat, a tall marquetry-inlaid grandfather tocked disapprovingly at them.

Mawn compared the comfort and nostalgia of the scene to the huge alien shapes of the Grim-Ness station away to the south. The mixture of food, wood smoke and Drambuie had lulled him into a state of indulgent euphoria and even the tweeded figure of Lodge stretched out in his chair beside him seemed a guarantee of security.

Lodge stirred, opened his eyes and slowly got to his feet, taking a slim silver watch out of his waistcoat pocket: 'Eleven. Bed I think – what about you?' Mawn nodded. 'There'll be a car here at eleven-thirty – we shan't have to hurry. I've asked for a call about nine-thirty, if that suits you?' He started to put the watch away in his pocket, but his hand jerked and trembled and the watch bounced on the end of its chain. After two more fumbling attempts, he got it back into the pocket. Mawn followed his movements. Lodge said: 'Yes, well, see you in the morning. Goodnight.'

After Lodge had left Mawn settled back, staring without expression into the glowing embers of the fire.

* * *

During the night of December third, the Grim-Ness reactor was held at 'C eight' or at a point in its operational schedule eight arbitrary stages before arriving at criticality.

From that point onwards, each man on the station began to think of the passage of time in discrete intervals which bore no relationship to hunger, the need for sleep or even the passage of night or day.

December 4. 13·20

From his desk in the Control Room, Durrell spoke quietly into the microphone grille: 'Ready to C one please – confirm.' He scanned a panel of signal lights; there were twenty altogether in four rows of five, each separately labelled: 'rod control', 'scram auto' and 'solo rod trip'. One by one they lit up, showing that each automatic safety control was fully operational. The last light to appear was labelled: 'Emergency diesel start'.

He leant forward to the grille: 'To C one.'

In the Rod Control Room David Baird moved a horizontal slide to position one. His hand trembled as he went back in his mind over all the test procedures he had carried out inside the core before it was finally sealed off. The responsibility weighed heavily. His body felt awkward and ungainly.

13·27

In the neck of the pressure vessel the control servo-motors working through gear trains withdrew the central rods three centimetres higher in their guide tubes.

Neutrons lanced through the high pressure water circulating between the bundles of fuel cans.

Baird studied the reactor chart in front of him, waiting for the signals on the illuminated hexagonal pattern to confirm that the control rods had moved to the position marked on the horizontal slide. A close observer would have noticed that his eyes were jerking with a slow rhythmic movement to the left and a rapid flick back to centre.

In the Computer Room, Philip Naylor tilted his chair and put his hands behind his head. He relaxed.

At the large wall chart of the reactor in the main control

room, Bernard Westcott copied down the readings from a group of instruments next to the wall chart.

Lodge and Sampson, the Department of Trade Inspector, sat with Marcia and Mawn in front of a block of six colour television monitors each one showing a picture of a different area of the station. Each screen showed a slight picture interference like falling snow; the inevitable consequence of proximity to high voltages and stray electrical fields.

13·32

Sampson led the visitors over to the wall chart of the reactor face and pointed to a group of lights flashing in unison on an instrument panel beside the chart.

'There you are – criticality.'

'I thought that was supposed to be a great moment,' Marcia said.

'It doesn't have any real significance,' Sampson went on. 'It's a purely theoretical point – I suppose in reality it only lasts a few millionths of a second.'

'How's that?'

'What really matters is stability as they work up the power scale afterwards. The reactor's self-sustaining and controlled, now the art is to inch its power to a working level.'

13·45

The temperature inside one fuel can in assembly four of B matrix rose to 4,020 degrees and a proportion of the uranium melted and ran out of its ceramic matrix, soaking into the surrounding alloy covering of the fuel can like molten wax into blotting paper.

Heat sensing thermo-couples near the fuel can began to feed information about the local hotspot along a pair of red and green wires through the computer, where its veracity was checked, then the information passed on into the Control Room. The information was passed as true by the computer but arrived approximately nine seconds later than planned.

13·45 + 10 seconds

In the Control Room a chiming tone sounded and a light began to flash alongside the location of can assembly four on the wall chart. Westcott looked up and called over to Durrell, 'Hot spot in four B.'

13·45 + 35 seconds
In the reactor core, the fuel can containing the molten uranium in assembly four began to bend out of line and to curve towards another adjacent bundle of fuel cans. As it did so, the local rate of atomic fission shot up and other nearby fuel cans also began to overheat.

The magnetic clutches holding the control rods of B matrix still remained energized and so the rods remained in the raised position.

13·45 + 42 seconds
Durrell whipped round in his chair: 'Why the hell hasn't it tripped – drop it!' In rod control, Baird punched the manual over-ride, magnetic clutches opened and the control rods began to fall.

13·45 + 43 seconds
The clearance between the control rod and its surrounding guide tube was designed to be 1. 2 millimetres. As the rod dropped under its own weight, it had reached a point precisely half-way down its guide tube. The local area of overheating was now increasing exponentially and the guide tube was beginning to bend out of line.

13·45 + 44 seconds
The control rod jammed just over half-way down the now distorted guide tube, thus failing to stop local fission. The metal of fuel can assembly four grew steadily hotter and began to melt.

13·45 + 47 seconds
Baird's voice yelled from the speaker: 'It's stuck, it's stuck!' Durrell swore and whipped round to Westcott, his face ashen pale. 'Prepare reactor scram!'

13·45 + 48 seconds
In the core, the overheated fuel can in assembly four burst, releasing molten uranium into the surrounding coolant water already at a temperature of 640 degrees and a pressure of 2,050 pounds per square inch. The molten metal of the fuel can and the uranium began a violent reaction with the surrounding water.

13·45 + 49 seconds
Durrell swung round to the instrument console in front of him quickly, pulling a key out of his coat pocket. Fumbling, he unlocked a square metal flap, underneath a label, 'Boron balls'; jerked open the flap exposing a flat red button two inches in diameter.

Red lights were flashing urgently over one entire section of the vertical reactor chart and a harsh alarm bell began to clang out a warning.

13·45 + 51 seconds
The reaction of the molten metals and the high pressure water produced a series of small hydrogen gas explosions, sending out shock waves into the surrounding water and dislodging other fuel cans from their carriers. As the rods began to collapse, the rate of atomic fission again rose abruptly and rods began to melt out of their supporting frames and topple towards each other.

13·45 + 56 seconds
Durrell shouted into the microphone grille in front of him: 'Scram reactor, scram, scram!'

In Rod Control, Baird threw a switch and current was abruptly shut off from the magnetic fingers holding the rods out of the reactor core. The rods fell.

13·45 + 57 seconds
In the core, the precision geometry of rod and fuel assemblies began to distort. One after another, the remaining control rods dropped down through the guide tubes and either stuck or fell out altogether.

13·45 + 58 seconds

Flashing light spread like a sparkling red tide over the whole of the reactor chart. Durrell shouted: 'ECC diesels, start!' A technician stabbed a button, the lights in the Control Room dimmed suddenly and then came back up again. From somewhere outside came a heavy rumble as the diesel engines driving the emergency core cooling pump lumbered into action.

13·45 + 60 seconds

Inside the core, the explosive reaction between the melting fuel cans and the water culminated in one long shock wave which slammed through the whole assembly, hammering against the steel shell. At a junction between the base of the pressure vessel and a four-foot diameter coolant pipe, a weld abruptly split.

13·46 + 2 seconds

In the Control Room, Westcott yelled out: 'Coolant pressure going!'

In the reactor, the super-heated water flashing into steam shrieked out through the widening gap between the coolant pipe and the pressure vessel.

Durrell, without looking up, banged down the emergency core cooling control. The noise of the diesels swelled suddenly from a muted rumble to an angry vibrating roar. The four-foot pipe blew completely off the pressure vessel and the reactor core, deprived of its coolant, began to coalesce and melt as the fuel cans collapsed in towards its centre.

Emergency cooling water, driven by the high pressure diesel pumps, jetted into the pressure vessel and immediately began to well up into the incandescent core, again flashing into steam and exploding.

The whole building suddenly shook and there was a deep echoing boom followed by the howling scream of gases escaping under pressure. Glass showered down from breaking fluorescent tubes in the ceiling of the Control Room. There was a second heavy explosion and an instrument panel sheared away from its wall mountings and fell massively forward striking one technician on the shoulder.

Durrell jabbed the button behind the unlocked plate and solenoids opened underneath hoppers full of boron steel spheres, sending them rattling down steel ducts into the heart of the disintegrating reactor.

13·46 + 10 seconds

There was a single sustained scream of agony from a loudspeaker. The horrified group standing in front of the bank of television monitors watched as one wall of the distant rod control room shook and cracked from floor to ceiling. Through the crack, a vertical curtain of steam blasted into the chamber, toppling the computer blocks surrounding Baird like a row of grandfather clocks. The steam curled around the desk, picking his body up like a leaf in wind and flinging it back against the wall. For a moment, his face froze in an expression of horror, then, pinned by a six hundred degree blast of superheated steam and gas, his white synthetic fibre coat began to melt down around the contours of his body then fly away in molten fragments under the deadly blast. His face first turned bright pink and then a suffused red. The heat boiled his eyes into white curdled lumps in their sockets. Finally, his cheeks began to split like an over-ripe peach. The screen went blank.

Marcia covered her face, weeping and Gelder ran over to the bank of screens, elbowing Mawn aside.

Durrell punched one of a row of buttons underneath the screen. A picture of the Reactor Hall came into view showing the cathedral-like building with its vast hexagonal floor pattern.

He hit another button and the main coolant pumping room came into view. 'Haskell – can you hear? Haskell!' Haskell's white-coated figure came into shot on the screen together with two other men in blue overalls. All were dwarfed by the massive ducts criss-crossing the concrete chambers. Behind him were the huge green painted hulks of the coolant pumps. 'For Christ's sake get out, we've got a melt down. Get out quick, it'll blow back, get out, for God's sake, get out!'

Behind the three men the concrete floor erupted like a volcano as one of the pumps burst like a huge grenade, flinging jagged cast iron fragments into the air like shrapnel. The room filled with clouds of roaring steam and fragments of the pumps careered and ricocheted off the walls. One of the men in overalls started to run for the door and fell, transfixed by a jagged length of copper tube. Haskell ran towards him, bent down and started to drag him towards the door, then suddenly both men were hurled into the air as the floor beneath their feet erupted. Under the hail of ragged metal like a volley from a machine-gun, the door itself began to disintegrate as the third man ran towards it.

Gelder screamed into the microphone: 'Get away – get back!'

As the man stumbled back the horrified group watched his body break up and fly apart in ragged pieces under the hail of metal.

White-faced and shaking, Marcia buried her face in Mawn's chest. Durrell had collapsed to the floor in a semi-kneeling position and Westcott was leaning up against a wall with his hand over his mouth, retching.

Gelder leant forward and punched up the camera in the Reactor Hall. All appeared to be normal, but just as he was about to select another picture Mawn grabbed his arm and pointed at the screen. Gelder looked again and started to alter the position of the camera in the Reactor Hall by two remote-control joysticks underneath the screen; it focused on the floor of the hall.

At first it seemed as if there was a fault in the picture. The hexagonal outlines of the floor appeared to be undulating. Something underneath was pushing at the steel and concrete floor. Each hexagonal segment started to break away from its neighbour, moving up and down like a series of saucepan lids on boiling pans. Then, one by one, the fifteen-ton segments began to blow away into the air as a boiling mushroom of smoke and steam blasted up into the hall like a giant geyser from the reactor core beneath. At the far end of the hall the one hundred foot charge loading machine shaped like a metal lighthouse began to tilt as the floor collapsed. As it fell, it toppled through the east wall of the building, collapsing outwards in a great cloud of glass and concrete. The control room floor under their feet shook suddenly as the massive bulk of the loader crashed to the ground.

The floor trembled as a second great cloud of steam and debris erupted through the shattered floor. Overhead they could just see through the gathering fumes that the cartwheel pattern of girders had opened outwards to the sky like gaunt fingers. On the base of the erupting clouds there was a dull flickering orange glow reflecting from beneath the floor.

Suddenly, inside the Control Room there was the harsh intermittent bark of a klaxon. The silent group around the screens jumped back in alarm. Gelder whipped round: 'What the hell . . .?'

'The doors,' Durrell explained. 'Emergency doors. They're operated automatically by radiation levels. They break up the station into a series of hermetically-sealed segments – like a submarine.'

Lodge wheeled and took a pace towards the double glass exit doors of the Control Room: 'You mean we're sealed in?'

'Each door can be opened by hand,' Durrell replied, shortly.

'Well come on then,' Gelder exclaimed. Durrell looked at him sombrely: 'You don't seem to understand – they're automatically operated by radiation.'

'So?'

'If they're closed – beyond some of them – and we can't tell which ones – there'll be radiation!'

For several minutes no one spoke. A thin trickle of dust fell from the ceiling. The room seemed to contract. Mawn stared at the block of monitoring screens, thinking, I'll even watch my own death on television.

Twelve

Gelder broke the silence, turning to Durrell: 'All right, what's the situation?'

Without replying, Durrell walked slowly over to his control

desk, opened a drawer and pulled out a rolled-up floor plan of the reactor building. He spread it out on the desk top, weighting one end of it with an ashtray. He pointed: 'We're here and the reactor's over there. In between us, there's number one boiler here. . .'

'Where're these doors?' Mawn interrupted.

'They divide up the building into sealed segments,' Durrell continued.

'And they're shut automatically by radiation sensors?'

'Yes.'

'What level?'

'Can't tell. Each sensor has a filter pad wrapped round a geiger head. Air is continually drawn through the filter and any gas or particulate contamination builds up until the geiger head trips the door mechanism.'

'But we can over-ride this!'

'Yes, each door's got a local manual control.'

'So what's the way out?'

Durrell pointed to the glass doors. 'We'd have to go through there first of all and then down the stairs, but the ground floor is probably lethal by now.'

'From radiation?'

'Yes. If the base of the pressure vessel went, it presumably blew out underneath us. There's either flood water or radiation down there – it'll be no use that way, no use at all.'

'What else?'

'There's an overhead walkway on a level with this room – it leads into the Turbine Hall.'

'If it's still there!'

Gelder had moved over to the television monitors and was trying to raise pictures from elsewhere in the stricken station. The others crowded round to watch. First the Rod Control Room came dimly into view. Through thick clouds of swirling dust, they could just make out a tumbled chaos of masonry and crushed instrument controls. Every surface was covered by a thick grey deposit. Marcia gasped as an arm came into view, protruding from a pile of shattered concrete. The arm was unattached.

Gelder panned the remote controls and the camera moved and then stuck pointing at a gaping hole in the distant wall. Through the hole they could see a flickering orange glow, and jammed up against the edge of the hole by a torn metal duct was the lower half of a torso, the booted legs protruding into the gap.

Durrell was moving quickly around the banks of instruments trying to gauge the severity of the accident, but nearly all needles were set firmly back at zero. Only one bank of indicator lights showed any activity.

December 4. 14·10

The technician injured by the falling instrument panel was sitting huddled against the wall rocking to and fro, holding his shoulder.

Gelder quickly switched from camera to camera throughout the situation. Several gave no picture, but one set in the viewing gallery overlooking the floor of the Reactor Hall was still operating. Heavy black smoke sparkling with incandescent fragments like a giant firework still gushed through the hole over the reactor, but the flickering orange glow from the burning core was dimmer. Thick swirling snow poured in through the gaping east wall and was immediately swept into the updraught over the core. A thick mushroom of billowing steam had formed above the smoke and was venting out through the torn roof.

'It's getting out,' Marcia whispered.

'It won't go very far up,' Mawn replied. 'The last met report gave us a temperature inversion overhead – there'll be a layer of still air.'

'What will that mean?'

'Depends what percentage of the core material went upwards. We can't tell. Assuming there's no wind and the temperature inversion's still in place, most particles will be carried up by the hot gases and then come down almost immediately once they're out of the updraught. We might as well assume the whole station is surrounded by a radioactive circle.' He paused suddenly aware that although he had spoken quietly, everyone was listening intently. 'What do you think, Durrell?'

'I've no means of knowing – assuming a thirty per cent loss of fission product inventory at a guess, it'll be already covering a circle maybe two and a half miles in diameter.'

'That's dust – what about radio-active gases – water vapour?'

'Depends entirely on the wind.'

'There wasn't any when we got in here.'

'I said it depends!' Durrell's voice was strident. 'I can't – I've nothing to measure it with – nothing's working.'

'Then what *are* the priorities?' Lodge asked quietly.

'To get out as quick as may be,' said Gelder.

'And walk straight into lethal radiation outside.' Mawn turned to Durrell. 'Could the cloud have got as far as Kirkwall?'

'I told you, I don't know!' Durrell turned away.

'He must,' Marcia spoke quietly. 'They've all got their families up there, Alex, they know they're all outside there somewhere.'

Durrell walked towards the door leading into the Computer Room. 'Naylor may be able to get a line out.' He pointed to the row of coloured phones on his own desk. 'Those've all had it.' Mawn and Lodge followed him out.

Gelder turned back to the monitor screens and began to search the remaining parts of the station covered by the cameras. Isolated groups of workers were trapped in the galleries and control rooms surrounding the shattered reactor. Some were lying in huddled groups, others retching from overwhelming lethal doses of radiation. Some cameras had sound and no vision and all that came over one line was an unbearable chaos of screams.

In the Computer Room, Naylor tried without success to contact the central telephone exchange. Lodge and Mawn stood behind him. Naylor spoke across to a technician who was checking resistance on the exposed telephone cables with a test lead and meter.

'Any luck?' The man shook his head helplessly. He turned back to Lodge: 'The internal's working but all the outside lines are dead.'

'Where's the exchange?' Mawn asked.

'In reception block,' Naylor replied.

Mawn strode to a wall plan of the station. He pointed: 'That's here, isn't it?' Naylor nodded. 'Well, it's next to the east side of the reactor building, that's where the loading machine took the whole wall out.'

They re-entered the Control Room as Gelder finished his survey of the building on the monitor screen. He turned: 'Any good?'

'No, nothing,' Durrell answered. 'No outside lines at all.'

Gelder pointed at the screens: 'I've been round all the cameras which are working – far as I can make out there are three main groups of survivors – can't tell yet whether they've been irradiated, the first lot are . . .'

Marcia only half listened to Gelder as he began to describe the location of the survivors. The unimaginable had really happened. She looked around at the shambles of the Control Room and shuddered as more dust sifted down from the broken light fittings. She wondered fearfully whether it was radioactive, had they already received a lethal dose from the dust hanging in the air. They might already be beyond help, their blood cells disintegrating. She saw a quick vision of the victims of Hiroshima and remembered the pathetic body scars of the survivors from the *Lucky Dragon* trawler. Rows of hospital beds. She closed her eyes against the pictures, unable to control the shaking of her legs. Gratefully she felt the comfort of Mawn's arm around her shoulders.

Three monitor screens now held steady pictures, each showing one of the three main service corridors of the reactor building.

The first, running alongside the base of the pressure vessel leading to the underground coolant ponds was completely blocked by the section of the collapsed roof. The view was almost obstructed by fumes and a torrent of water pouring in.

The second, a passageway leading from the Reactor Hall to the exterior seemed to be clear of damage.

In the third, the scene looked like the site of a mining disaster. There were about thirty men lying sprawled on the floor and propped up against the wall. It was clear that the full force of the initial explosion had fired debris in through the long row of shattered windows like a charge of grapeshot. Several bodies were almost entirely dismembered and the survivors, covered in a thick muddy layer of water and dust, huddled in a row against the wall. Several were already in the agonies of acute radiation poisoning. One with his arms wrapped around his stomach sat absolutely still, his mouth open, screaming. Another lay back, head lolled to one side, and watery vomit streaming from his open mouth.

They all jumped back involuntarily from the screens as the floor suddenly slapped violently at their feet. Somewhere far below there was a rumbling detonation, films of dust fell from the ceiling, settling over their hair and shoulders.

'What the hell was that?' Gelder asked.

Durrell ran quickly over to the monitors and switched on the picture of the Reactor Hall. Black fumes were still belching out through the vent in the floor, but the orange glow had almost disappeared. Durrell turned slowly, walked over to a chair and slumped down. For several moments he sat staring fixedly at the floor. Gelder grabbed him by the shoulder: 'What's happened?'

'I don't . . .' Durrell began. 'I can't be sure but I think . . .'

'I'll tell you what's happened!' Mawn exclaimed. 'You've had a melt-down.'

'What?' exclaimed Marcia.

'Melt-down – the China Accident!' He turned to Gelder. 'You've a little experience of this already, haven't you – remember the Pukë station in Albania?' He turned to the others. 'The glow in the fumes, it's gone! That means the whole core has melted and slumped down through the pressure vessel. Just now it'll be on its way through the biological shielding underneath the reactor – right?' Durrell sat without answering.

Lodge's voice trembled: 'You can't be certain of that.'

Mawn whipped round at him, his voice grating: 'I've no need to be sure!' He jabbed a finger at the screen. 'Somewhere down underneath that floor there's a miniature sun and it's going to go on burning down. Through the vessel – through the shielding

– out through the foundations and right down into the earth and you're not going to be able to do a damn thing about it.'

He strode over to Durrell: 'That's right, isn't it?' Durrell nodded slowly, without looking up.

'What's to be done?' Lodge asked.

'Some of your jokers call it the "China Accident". What they mean is it might melt through to China!'

Durrell was talking to himself: 'We'll have to evacuate the station. Get my staff out.'

Mawn turned to the others: 'We'd better consider the facts!'

'What the hell makes you qualified . . .' Gelder began.

'Because this situation has been in my mind for the last month. I've anticipated this – thought it out in advance. Has anyone else done the same?' He looked around. 'I thought not.' He looked around and ticked the points off on his fingers: 'Number one, we're stuck in here, we don't know what the radiation level is, but there are no breaches in the walls and the air conditioning filters have stopped so we might just be all right. Number two, between us and the outside are any number of sealed doors. Number three, the amount of air we've got inside here is strictly limited and so we either suffocate or open one of the sealed doors and let radioactive air in. There's no point in thinking any more about the core – no one's going to go down there with a bucket of water, so let's forget it and think our way out of this place. First, before we do anything else.'

Lodge gestured towards the monitor screens: 'What about all those men – they need help?'

'Well they won't get it if we don't get out. Now . . .' He swung round to Naylor who had rushed in from the Computer room. 'Have you got any suits?'

'Suits?'

'Protective suits for God's sake – have you got any?'

'Oh – yes – there are some – they're in the aid room.'

'Where's that?'

Naylor pointed at the glass exit doors: 'Through there, along to the end of the corridor, turn right and it's on . . .' He paused for a moment, '. . . just down on the left.' His face clouded.

'Something the matter?'

Naylor looked at him sombrely: 'There's one of the doors just before you get to it. It'll be shut.'

Durrell had stood up. He spoke quietly: 'There are geigers there – anti-radiation injections too.'

'Are they any use?' Marcia asked dully.

Durrell shrugged: 'Amino acids cysteine and methionine mainly – yes, they protect mice against radiation.'

'Mice! My God!' Gelder exclaimed.

Mawn turned to Durrell: 'You said these doors can be opened by hand?'

'Yes. There's a large wheel, it over-rides the automatic solenoids.'

'Is there any indicator on this side – the safe side of the door?'

'We don't even know if it's safe this side ...'

'Don't be so bloody academic. Is there or isn't there any indicator showing how much radiation there is on the *far* side?'

'No, just a warning light which goes on over a certain level.'

'Right, so much for that!'

'What do you mean?' Gelder asked.

Mawn ignored him and turned to Naylor: 'How many suits are there?'

Naylor thought for a moment: 'Should be at least a dozen.'

'How heavy are they? What I mean is, could one man carry the lot?'

'No, two could, probably.'

Gelder was studying the plan of the building, his poise had returned: 'As far as I can make out from the scale of this, the aid room is about a hundred feet or so past the sealed door – shouldn't take long to get there and back.' He turned back to Mawn, there was a thin smile on his face: 'How do you rate the chances, Doctor? A forty yard dash.'

Durrell glanced at Naylor: 'I think we'd better make the first venture – we know the building pretty well.'

'No,' Gelder spoke crisply and decisively: 'This station is wholly my responsibility.'

'You'll need help,' Mawn said.

'I prefer not to risk the lives of the staff here,' Gelder said, coldly.

'Risk!' Mawn flared. 'Your own negligence has already killed more than half of them.'

There was a shocked hush then a storm of protest.

'This is not the time . . .' began Lodge, but Mawn cut in again. 'Not the time to strike attitudes, either.' He thrust a finger at Gelder: 'I'm not having our lives jeopardized by super hero here.' He grasped Naylor by the lapels: 'Take that coat off!' Naylor pulled back. 'Take it off man.' Without waiting, Mawn took hold of the white coat cover and pulled it down roughly over Naylor's arms then began to tear it into four squares about two feet across. He looked up at Durrell: 'Get yours off too, and tear it the same way – quick!'

'Will you tell us what . . .' Lodge attempted to put dignity and authority into his voice to hide the tremor. 'We must know what you're doing.'

Without looking up, Mawn went on: 'We don't know what radioactive crap there is out in the corridor and we certainly don't know what there is beyond the door. So we're going to make our own protective suits.' He began to fasten a piece of torn coat around the soles of his shoes, tying the four corners. He looked up at Gelder, gesturing at Durrell who was having difficulty tearing the white rayon cloth.

'Just copy what I do. It's the best we can hope for at the moment. Cover ourselves as completely as possible – head to foot – then go out there – get the suits – come back, dump all these bits of cloth *outside* the glass doors then come back in with the suits. OK?'

'Makes sense,' Gelder said.

'Go and get some more coats. For God's sake *move* some of you.'

Naylor ran back into the Computer Room and returned after a few moments with a crumpled polythene sheet and several lengths of punched computer tape. He dropped them on the floor beside Mawn. Mawn had finished tying the cloth round his shoes and was tucking his trouser legs into his socks. He looked up at Gelder: 'Cover the whole of your body surface as best you can, no gaps.' He pointed at his shoes bound with the pieces of torn coat. 'Cover your feet like that.' As he talked he tore the polythene into two ragged halves and pulled it down over his head like a hood, then around his shoulders. He pointed to the lengths of computer tape and said to Marcia: 'Now bind this sheet around me, wrap me up like a parcel.' Marcia picked up a length, hooked it round his neck and began to walk round and round him binding the sheet close to his body. Mawn pulled the edge of the sheet down round the edges of his face like the hood of an anorak. He gestured to Gelder: 'Somebody help him do the same.' Durrell and Lodge picked up the other half of the polythene and draped it over Gelder's head.

'What's this supposed to do?' Gelder asked impatiently.

Mawn replied: 'If there's radioactive dust in the air between here and the suit room it should stay on the outside of all this.'

'I'll buy that,' Gelder said. 'One thing. Why not one man – two journeys rather than two men and one journey – puts only one man at risk surely?'

'No time,' replied Mawn. 'Two may get it done quicker.'

Gelder shrugged down into the polythene without replying. Finally, each man was almost totally swathed in a baggy mass of polythene and torn workcoats, wrapped incongruously in bright blue computer tape held in position with sticky tape. Each man had makeshift fingerless covers bound over his hands.

Mawn turned stiffly to Durrell: 'Two handkerchiefs.' Marcia fumbled in her handbag and brought out a small folded white triangle. Mawn brushed it aside: 'For God's sake – come on, come on – two handkerchiefs.' Durrell took one out of his trouser pocket, Lodge produced an elegant silk square from the breast pocket of his tweeds. 'Now wet them.'

'What?' Marcia said.

'*Wet* them! Then wrap them round our faces, the wet fibres should absorb most of the suspended particles in the air. I'm not getting a lungful for anyone.' He rounded on Westcott: 'Water! We need water.'

'I – there's none here. The loos are along the corridor.' He pointed to the glass doors.

Gelder smiled: 'Why not piss on them?'

Naylor held out a plastic cup: 'No need, there's some cold coffee here.'

Marcia crumpled up the handkerchiefs, poured half the coffee into each bundle and squeezed until the cloths were evenly stained brown. Then she gave one to Naylor and wrapped the other round Mawn's nose and mouth knotting it behind his neck. Mawn nodded his thanks, and had a quick last look at the building plan. He beckoned Gelder over and trudged clumsily towards the glass doors. Both men walked out into the long corridor.

As the doors swung to behind them they were both immediately aware of the chilling cold biting into the wet cloth bound round their faces. Ahead of them, two panes of a window had been blown in by the blast and snow was driving through the jagged holes forming a pool of half-melted slush on the green linoleum floor underneath. Mawn shuffled quickly ahead. His voice indistinct behind the cloth: 'Move. Don't hang about – longer we're out here, the more we're at risk.'

Both men broke into an awkward shuffling run, eventually reaching a T-junction at the end of the corridor. They turned right and saw that about twenty feet ahead the corridor expanded into a chamber about twelve feet wide and fifteen high.

Shutting off the far end of the chamber was a massive steel wall covered by parallel rows of electrical conduits and air trunking. In the centre of the wall was a thick steel door surrounded by heavy lever bar locks. To the left hand side of the door there was a handwheel shaped like a cast iron version of a car steering wheel and over the wheel a single red light flashed reading: 'Danger. Radiation. Do not proceed.'

Mawn immediately started to inspect the boxes of control gear bolted to the wall by the side of the wheel. With his finger he traced electrical conduits from one unit to another. Gelder crouched beside him: 'Why the holdup?'

Mawn spoke without looking round: 'I want to make sure it doesn't slam shut behind us.' He quickly unscrewed a fly nut, pulled open the cast iron cover of one box and pulled out a fuse. There was the loud click of a relay and the red light went out.

'Be a sound way of getting rid of me wouldn't it?'

Mawn turned slowly, his eyes staring over the mask: 'I need you alive, friend.'

Gelder's eyes narrowed. It was impossible to tell whether he was smiling. 'In that case I don't mind your walking behind.' Mawn turned back and spun the wheel. The lever bolts slowly began to retract inwards towards the centre of the door. He grabbed the handle with one hand and, bracing himself with the other against the surrounding steel wall, began to pull the door open until he could just peer into the gap. The two men braced themselves for what the corridor might reveal. Under their feet the floor trembled, there was a distant heavy rumble. The whole steel wall in front of them vibrated and the door swung open under its own weight.

Ahead of them the corridor was dimly lit by a string of flickering emergency lights. The linoleum floor was covered in a thick layer of white dust and one section of the wall had collapsed inwards leaving a vertical gap stretching between floor and ceiling. The debris only partially obstructed the way ahead.

'Is it radioactive?' Gelder demanded.

'How the hell do I know?'

'What I meant was, is it gas or dust?'

'If it's gas we've already breathed it, so we're dead. When we get moving, hold your breath as long as possible.' He stepped through and started to uncoil a fire hose, fumbling through the rough covers bound over his hands.

'If the dust is radioactive we can get rid of it like this.' He turned the polished brass valve attached to the hose. 'Hope to God there's some pressure.' He gestured at the tap. 'I'll go forward, you turn the tap wide open.' As Mawn knelt with the hose nozzle pointing ahead of him, Gelder wrenched the valve open. There was an agonizing pause, then abruptly the flattened hose coils writhed and tautened. The nozzle in Mawn's hand kicked like a gun and spat out a stream of water and air.

First, Mawn directed the nozzle at the ceiling, then along each wall and finally over the floor until the whole corridor was running with a muddy whitish paste. Mawn yelled above the noise of the water: 'Turn it off!' Gelder screwed the valve shut and the splashing jet curved downwards and stopped. Mawn flung the hose down and beckoned urgently to Gelder. 'Now move. Don't touch the walls or anything else, just keep on going like hell – never mind if your feet get wet.' He got up and began to run down the corridor. Gelder followed. They passed two doors and came to the third marked: "Emergency Aid". Gelder rushed forward and wrenched at the handle. It was locked. He stood back and flung himself at the door, rebounding back. Mawn pushed him away, looked at the door for a moment then raised his leg and kicked forward with all the weight of his body behind the blow. Once, twice and three times, then there was a splintering sound and the door flew open, the barrel lock clattering ahead of them into the room.

Mawn stepped in, switched on the light and pulled the door to behind them, jamming a metal chair against the handle to keep it shut.

Gelder looked around: 'No windows – no grilles, good.'

Mawn took a pistol shaped geiger counter down from a row of similar instruments on a shelf above him and clicked a switch on its side. He swept the nozzle around the room. There was no sound. He moved a knob on the top and pointed it around the room for a second time. A speaker set inside its barrel immediately gave out a series of irregular clicks which altered in rate as he pointed the nozzle in different directions. He looked down at a swinging needle. 'Not bad – not bad.'

Gelder visibly relaxed. Mawn began to run the instrument over Gelder's protective covering. The rate of clicking shot up until it became a rising continuous note.

'Christ almighty!' Mawn exclaimed. He began to run the instrument over his own arms and legs – again the clicking rate rose to the level of a continuous note. 'We're both saturated in the bloody stuff. Get it off, come on.' He began to strip off the tape and the polythene, finally removing the cloth round his shoes.

'I thought you said we'd keep it on till we got back . . .' Gelder began.

'We've collected too much on the way here. Now – do it carefully, don't raise any dust as you get it off. Just move quietly, no jerking.' Slowly the men broke the binding tapes and eased themselves out of the makeshift covers.

Hanging along one wall, like a series of puppet dolls waiting for animation, was a row of white plastic oversuits. At the top end of each one was a transparent head piece like a space helmet with two white gauze filters in the position of the ears. The arms and legs were closed by diagonal zips and there were gloves hanging from the wrist bands by single cords.

Mawn took one of the suits off its hook, opened the central zip and as quickly as possible eased into the shiny plastic. Gelder followed suit, his voice muffled through the transparent cylindrical headpiece: 'You mentioned stuff for injection?'

Mawn searched quickly along the rows of steel shelving, finally picking out a wooden box labelled: 'Cystathone Parenteral'. He spoke without looking round: 'Get as many of the suits as you can carry.' Gelder began to unhook each one, draping it over his arm. Mawn put the box down on a table and gathered the remainder, rolling them up into as small a bundle as possible.

Gelder paused by the door: 'What about covers?'

'Not enough time,' Mawn replied. 'Just bundle them up like this, come on.'

Both men made their way cautiously back along the passage to the Control Room. Each moving awkwardly and staggering under the weight of their burden.

At the door, the occupants crowded behind the glass panels watching their lumbering approach. Mawn gestured them back then opened the door and eased himself through, Gelder following.

Marcia ran forward, but Mawn gestured fiercely: 'Get back, we almost certainly got some dust on the outside of these things on the way back.' He threw his bundle of suits down on the floor. 'Before you get into those we might just as well take the anti-radiation stuff.'

Durrell had already opened the box and was laying out a row of small plastic tubes about the size of a cigarette. At one end of each tube there was a sheathed hypodermic needle. From the box he had also taken a small bottle of spirit and a tin full of small lint swabs. His voice sounded firmer: 'I've only seen this demonstrated once.' He removed his tie, then his shirt. 'You have to give it into a muscle – they said the safest one was this.' He pointed to the outer surface of his upper arm. 'Right here.' He described his action. 'First you shake a little spirit on to the swab like that, then rub the skin – like so – then you pull off the needle cover and then . . .' He poised the needle over his arm. 'You shove it in like – ah!' He jerked his hand down and the needle disappeared into his arm up to the end of the tube. 'Then you squeeze the tube flat until all the contents have gone in. Then pull it out and wipe your skin again with the swab. Right?'

He looked round to see all had been watching. He gestured at the box. 'You can all do the same – anyone has any trouble I'll do it for them.'

Gelder unzipped the front of his suit, pulled it down over one shoulder, picked up one of the ampoules and stabbed it straight through his shirt into his arm, squeezed the tube flat, pulled it out and threw it away into the corner of the room. Durrell started to protest, but Gelder waved him to silence: 'Just let's get out!'

Mawn had lain the suits out flat on the floor. One by one, they injected themselves and got into the suits leaving the transparent head-pieces hinged back.

Durrell beckoned them over to the station plan, it was now heavily scored in red pencil markings. He used a pencil as a pointer. 'Some of the circuits – here and here, have packed in, but we can still get the Reactor Hall ventilation control and the corridor – here.' He glanced up at Mawn and Gelder. 'Since you both went off, Elleston up on the sixth floor told us he saw about twenty or so people get away in one of the lorries from the transport pool. They went north.' He looked at his watch, 'They should be in Kirkwall by now.'

'So if we're relatively safe here,' Lodge said. 'Why move? – seems to me the best thing we can do is to sit tight surely.'

Durrell paused before continuing: 'There is one other thing, I'm afraid.'

'What?' Mawn demanded.

'Westcott here, has brought up another possibility. You see, the core is burning down through the foundations . . .'

'We know that, so what?' Gelder spoke impatiently.

'At a probable rate of two hundred feet in every twenty-four hours,' Mawn put in. 'At least that was an estimate made back in 1972.'

'Yes,' Durrell continued. 'Well, the simple point is this. As Mawn says, if we say the temperature of the core is around 3,000 degrees Fahrenheit, then this figure is probably right.'

'Get to the point, for God's sake,' Gelder exclaimed.

'When the site was first prospected, the designers found a gloupy . . .'

'A what?' Mawn asked.

'They're common on these islands,' Durrell continued. 'It's a long natural tunnel – a cave with a blow hole really. We made use of it to carry the turbine cooling water out to sea. It saved about a hundred feet of concrete ducting . . .'

'Where is it?' Mawn's voice was flat, hard.

'That's it, you see,' Durrell went on. 'There's a tunnel from the condensers in the Turbine Hall here . . .' He pointed to the plan. 'Which runs just to one side of the reactor building – here – and connects up with the gloupy under the cliff and then on by tunnel out to sea about three hundred feet out in the sound – here.'

'How far down is it?' Gelder demanded.

'It averages about twenty feet,' Westcott replied. 'The tunnel isn't directly below the reactor, but we can't be sure which direction the core will take as it burns down.'

'It'll be a trade-off, won't it?' Mawn interrupted. 'The core will fall under its own weight, but it'll also take the path of least resistance or lowest melting point . . .' The floor under their feet trembled, there was a distant explosion. '. . . so, if the core bursts through into the tunnel and the tunnel is full of water . . .'

'Which it is,' Durrell put in.

'. . . then we could have a situation like an undersea volcano – Krakatoa for example.'

'God almighty!' Gelder exclaimed.

'It's pure guesswork,' Mawn continued. 'But the water could flash into steam and it depends entirely whether it can escape quickly enough back through the tunnel into the turbine condensers or out to sea through the tunnel . . .'

'It won't do that,' Westcott intervened. 'The tunnel out to sea is already full of water – so you've got several hundred feet of tunnel blocked by a water plug. It'll go up all right, Christ! How long? Twenty feet – two hours and a bit.'

'And we're already over an hour in,' Gelder said.

'So that means we've got to get clear absolutely now,' Mawn exclaimed.

Gelder turned to Durrell: 'Frank, there's little we can do for your people now – I think they probably know it. Even if we could get them out – we'd all be irradiated . . .'

Durrell looked at him blankly and Gelder stood silently aside as he moved over to the monitor screen. One by one he contacted the isolated groups of men trapped in different parts of the shattering building.

The men in the corridor had reached a stage of drunken euphoria. Durrell repeated his warning to them and urged them to get out and away from the building but one of them staggered towards the camera, his face distorted by its closeness to the lens. He was holding an empty whisky bottle. When he spoke his words were slurred: 'Hallo there, Dr Durrell. How are ye – bloody cold down here, I'll tell ye.' He waved the bottle unsteadily at the camera. 'Ye might bring a wee bit more of this when ye come down, the lads could do with some more – aye, it's cold.' He shivered and retched. 'You might have a few words wi' ma wife would ye – we're awful sick down here – awful sick.' He trembled and his face distorted with an impotent fury. 'Tell yon laddie, when we get out of here there'll be a reckoning wi' you bastards – you got us into this.' He lurched forward and swung the bottle towards the camera. The watchers in the Control Room jumped back involuntarily and then the screen flashed once and went blank.

For several moments no one moved, then Durrell leant forward and switched through to Elleston, on the sixth floor. His face was almost invisible behind a zig-zag interference pattern on the screen. His voice was clear and urgent: 'We've just seen one of the lorries come back in again – what the hell's going on?' Durrell spoke urgently into the microphone: 'You must get out, the core's gone down and we think it may hit the turbine coolant – you've got to get out quick . . .'

Elleston's voice was almost facetious: 'Oh, it's far too cold outside, we're quite snug in here . . .'

Durrell shouted: 'For God's sake, listen to me, you've got to make your way out – go down by the fire stairs near the goods lift . . .'

Elleston's voice was now totally devoid of expression: 'Dr Durrell, we've done a few measurements.' They could just see him wave a pistol shaped radiation meter behind the swirling interference on the screen. 'We've all had over a thousand R. Leave us be – just leave us be – we've all had it – whatever you do – so don't bother – there's no use . . .'

Thirteen

Durrell stared at the screen for several moments then reached forward and switched it off. Gelder broke the mood, moving towards the door and one by one, the others followed, shuffling awkwardly in the bulky restriction of the protective suits. In the corridor all they could hear was the harsh sibilance of their breathing inside the helmets.

As they turned to the left at the T-junction, the string of emergency lights dimmed and then flickered out. Westcott switched on a hand lantern and moved ahead, probing the way with the cone of light. At the far end of the corridor there was a faint light from a window. They all crowded around.

A wide courtyard lay between the reactor building and the Turbine Hall and facing them was the service block, workshops and staff canteen. They could see that part of the glass roof of the service block had collapsed inwards under the cartwheel shape of the girders from the roof of the Reactor Hall. Smoke curled out of the gaping hole and from the other end of the building bright orange tongues of flame billowed out of a shattered window. From the roof of the Reactor Hall, clouds of black smoke were curling down over the courtyard and mingling with the driving snow. Durrell peered out: 'God, that's all we need, there's a wind.'

'What direction?' Mawn asked.

'Too many buildings about – can't tell, maybe south-east.'

Durrell turned to Gelder: 'Your helicopter pilot, did he say where he'd be?'

'Said something about watching from a colour set,' Gelder replied.

Durrell pointed to the service block: 'In that case, he'll probably be in the staff room over there.'

'Can we reach it?' Marcia asked.

Westcott gestured down the corridor: 'Down there's an overhead walkway across to the Turbine Hall, then we can go through the workshops and lorry pool, then there's a short bit of open ground to the service block.' Mawn and Gelder had already begun to move off, as he spoke, the others followed in a shuffling jog-trot. Gelder reached the archway leading out on to the walkway, then stopped dead. The others gathering behind him.

In the deepening twilight, they could just see that the floor sagged and the girders forming its structure were twisted. All the glass had been blown out of the windows and snow was pouring through the shattered structure. The ground was three storeys below.

Mawn eased forward, past Gelder and began to inch his way out on to the sloping floor. There was a sudden groaning sound and the whole sagging structure jerked downwards and then stopped abruptly, flinging him off balance. Unsteady and awkward in his suit, he slowly got to his feet and, holding on to the bent and distorted girders for support, eased forward. Finally he made the far side and stood in the archway leading into the Turbine Hall. He shouted back, his voice muffled by the helmet: 'Come over one at a time, keep to the edge!'

One by one, with the care and delicacy of acrobats on a high wire, they felt their way over the roadway beneath and on into the Turbine Hall. The entire building was deserted and snow was pouring steadily through the broken roof. The galleries and giant pipes were already covered in a blanket of snow, only the massive hulks of the turbines, still hot from their previous operation, showed through like black whales in an arctic sea.

They moved on through a door leading out of the echoing cathedral-like building. Beyond it was a concrete staircase where emergency lights were still lit. After they were all safely inside, Westcott held the pistol shaped geiger counter ahead of him. During the long walk from the Control Room they had all got accustomed to its regular clicking warning. Now the noise had almost stopped. Naylor put the counter on the floor, unzipped his helmet and hinged it back over his head. 'The level's down – we can have a breather.' Gratefully the others unzipped their helmets; their faces shiny with sweat.

Men in overalls were waiting at the bottom of the staircase. Inside the workshop the leading man, Jack Duffy explained, above the clamour of a small generator, what had happened to them:

'We took off in some trucks from the pool. Did what we could, sealed off the heater inlets and taped up the windows. But it was bloody awful, mon. It's snowing tae thick to see and the geigers went right off the scale up near the Churchill barriers.

'We were getting plastered with this wet snow, it was all grey coloured. The other two went on over the barriers – bloody suicide if you ask me. We turned back – put the lorry next door. I'll tell ye, we took a reading on some of the snow on the outside of the lorry when we got in. It's pumping out hard gamma – we would na' have stood a chance.'

'What about yourselves?' Durrell asked.

'Aye, we could've already copped it, our clothing's all right – canna tell how much we breathed in though. What about your people?'

Durrell began to explain the situation and Gelder turned to Mawn: 'Let's get the chopper pilot!' Naylor nodded, picked up the counter and led them across the shop floor between banks of lathes and milling machines towards the exit door. He turned: 'It'll be a quick dash across open ground, go like the devil.' He pulled his transparent helmet back over his head and Mawn and Gelder followed suit.

Naylor pulled the door ajar: 'Quick now!'

Outside, the wind plastered the swirling snow over their helmets, almost blinding them as they dashed over towards the entrance door of the service block.

Inside, the air was thick with acrid smoke which went straight in through the filters on their helmets. They could hear the rapid clicking of the counter slow down as the door swung to behind them. Gelder started to undo the neck zip of his helmet, but Naylor shook his head violently, warning him not to and opened the door leading into the canteen.

The scene was like a Goya etching of war. In the dimness, the huge black girders from the Reactor Hall roof hung down through a gaping hole in the ceiling and, underneath, the rows of metal framed tables and chairs lay crushed like toys underneath a twisted mass of concrete and steel. Over every surface there was a thick layer of greyish dust.

At one end of the shattered room, the body of a middle-aged woman in pink kitchen uniform was pinned against the wall behind the serving counter, half buried in a broken pile of cups and plates which had cascaded down off the shelves behind her.

One man lay with his legs trapped underneath a large jagged piece of concrete. There was no gap between the concrete and the floor. Another had been impaled on the leg of an unturned table. He was still moving feebly, trying ineffectually to prise himself off a metal leg protruding from his groin. Other bodies were scattered around the floor and the three men silently moved from one to the other searching for signs of life. Finally, Gelder shouted and beckoned to Naylor. He pointed grimly at a pair of flying boots protruding from a pile of debris: a dark glistening pool of blood had formed around them. He shrugged hopelessly and turned away.

Mawn was bending down beside one man lying curled up against the wall. He was bleeding from a ragged wound in his thigh, his face putty-coloured in the flickering yellow light. Mawn quickly took off his belt and pulled it tight around the upper part of his thigh. The man opened his mouth to scream. The two men crouched down beside Mawn and raised the wounded man to a sitting position.

Gelder and Naylor put their hands under the man's armpits and gently raised him to a standing position holding his legs just clear of the ground. Mawn and Gelder took the weight of his body and started towards the door.

In the workshop people were beginning to filter in from other parts of the building, many of them wounded. As the three entered Durrell rushed over: 'Did you find him?'

Gelder slipped his helmet back over his head and eased the wounded man down on to the top of a steel workbench. 'Yes, we found him.'

Mawn crouched beside Marcia who was binding makeshift rags around the head of a technician lying slumped against the pillar of a drilling machine. She looked up and smiled wanly. Mawn pulled her briefly towards him, holding her head against his shoulder.

The air in the workshop was cooling down rapidly. A jury-rigged air heater had run out of fuel and the news of the melting reactor core and its proximity to the turbine cooling duct had spread a growing air of depression. Even the group from the Control Room were affected by the claustrophobic conditions. Outside, the wind thumped angrily against the walls.

Gelder was helping Durrell to carry a wounded technician over to a line of men propped against one wall. Mawn watched him. The finding of the dead helicopter pilot had seemed to alter him. At first he had been almost theatrically in command of himself, but now he moved automatically, his actions clumsy and awkward. Perhaps, he thought, he had looked forward to a quick flight over to the mainland to organize a massive rescue operation, turning defeat into a personal triumph.

Marcia had moved over to another wounded man. He felt a sudden wave of affection towards her slight, angular figure.

'Mawn!' Durrell beckoned him over to a small group standing round a small scale map of the Orkney islands spread out on a bench. Durrell pointed a screwdriver in a circle around the island of South Ronaldsay. 'Far as we can see there'll probably be a very high radiation level here. One thing we can assume, the wind is, in fact, in the south-east, so whatever solid material blew out of the reactor it will almost certainly have come down on the Churchill barriers – so we can't go that way.'

'Since we've already been irradiated,' Mawn said.

'Right. There's a small blizzard outside and if the snow is hot then it's bound to stick to these suits.'

'Is there no one else who can fly the helicopter?' It was Lodge who had spoken. He was standing on the edge of the group. He appeared withdrawn and his lips trembled as he spoke.

Gelder looked around, a small flicker of hope in his eyes, then shrugged: 'I can drive a plane, not a chopper.'

'Forget it!' Durrell snapped. 'It's doubtful if it could fly in these conditions anyway. No, we've only one way now.' He pointed with the screwdriver. 'Down here – the B9044 – then south on to the A961 to Burwick.'

'South!' exclaimed Gelder. 'There's nothing down there.'

Durrell gazed at him sombrely: 'Frankly, Mr Gelder, unless we can get to expert medical help in the next forty-eight hours or so . . . God help us! You see we must have had . . . well, quite a dose already.'

'How does it show?' Marcia asked.

'Nausea, vomiting, cramps, sometimes a headache early on anyway, then . . .'

'There's no point in this,' Lodge said irritably, 'we're bound to get more radiation if we go out into the open.' His voice was high, edgy. Mawn looked at him. All the calm urbanity of the Civil Servant had cracked away. Mawn looked at his watch: 'We've maybe half an hour before the core burns down to the coolant ducts, so let's cut out the debate and get on with it. Now, Durrell, you said there's a road to the south?'

'Yes, the B9 . . .'

'Right, we take that.'

Westcott began to protest: 'You've seen what it's like outside – it's snowing like hell. I'll stay in here.'

Mawn looked across at him incredulously: 'It was *you* who told us about the gloupy wasn't it?'

Westcott just stared back at him, his lips trembling and Mawn realized he was only just under control. He turned to Durrell: 'What do you think?'

Durrell hesitated, his face a grey mask of defeat, then shook his head hopelessly: 'We've no chance here, no chance at all.'

'Then for God's sake let's move!' Mawn strode to a group of technicians clustered nervously around Jack Duffy. 'What transport have you got?'

Duffy looked up at him, his breath reeked of whisky, his eyes were watery. He gestured towards the door leading to the transport pool. 'There's a couple out there besides the one I drove back. That one's useless, be plastered in the stuff, would'na suggest you use that.'

Mawn's voice dropped a little: 'Then what?'

'We stop ourselves up in here and wait. They're bound to have heard the explosion up at Kirkwall, besides the other two lorries'll be there by now.'

Mawn's voice rose: 'Haven't you got it into your thick head. In about twenty minutes the reactor may hit the water tunnel and the whole building goes up.'

'Och, I dinna think so. I reckon this place'll stand it – remember we saw it go up brick on brick. No, laddie, we'll all stay here – they'll come and get us out all right, dinna ye worry.'

Mawn looked over at the pathetic row of casualties propped against the wall. 'And what about them? We need you to get the lorries going, you're a driver, you know the road . . .'

'And just who the hell d'ye think ye are – giving us orders – you hav'na been out there, I *have*.' He gestured with a whisky bottle. 'I'm telling you it's plain bloody suicide.'

Mawn looked over at the others. The men behind Duffy

looked apathetic, defeated. Duffy's face was clouded with drunken resentment: 'If ye want tae go you can sodding well go by yourself.' He staggered away. Mawn turned after him and grabbed him by the shoulder, he realized he had to win the argument and win it quickly. He reached forward, snatched the whisky bottle from Duffy's grasp and flung it away to shatter against the far wall.

There was a moment's shocked silence then Duffy reacted. 'You sodding bastard. I'll bloody kill ye.' He rushed at Mawn and made a wild swing at his jaw. Mawn hit him once, heavily square in the stomach, Duffy dropped to his knees half-stunned and gasping for breath. Mawn looked quickly around but the others were reluctant to come forward. He strode forward, grasped the other whisky bottle and sent it to join the first.

'Some of you give him a hand. The rest wrap up the casualties as best you can – anything you can find, rags, coats, just get them covered – it'll keep the worst of the dust off them. Move!'

The men hesitated for a moment then began to shuffle away. He called after them: 'And tie some wet rags over their faces, leave it so that they can breathe – but only through the cloth.'

Mawn walked to Marcia who was looking down helplessly at a girl of about eighteen lying motionless on the floor: 'She's dead is she?' His bluntness made her swing round. 'We can't take them all.'

'What?'

He gestured at the other casualties: 'Some of them are very bad, they're bleeding a hell of a lot and they're shocked, if we start mucking them around on lorries – it's going to be bloody cold outside and it'll more likely kill them than if we leave them here.'

'You can't leave them,' she blazed. 'What about the core?'

'It's one or the other.' He looked at his watch. 'Look, we may only have about twenty minutes, choose the ones who look as if they're going to make it.'

'What about the others?' she said helplessly.

Mawn held her shoulders tightly. 'Look, Marcia, there's *no* choice, *none* at all.' Her face was thin and white with the cold but her eyes were dark and outraged. She shook her head: 'I'll stay here with them.'

'Then I'll have to carry you out of here.' For a moment there was silence, then Naylor touched him on the shoulder: 'Ready to go now.' Marcia looked from one man to the other, then slowly got to her feet. She looked down at her hands covered in a mixture of dirt and blood then slowly followed them over to the door to the transport pool.

'We've got about twenty into the lorries,' Naylor said.

In the doorway Mawn looked back for the last time. In the flickering yellow light of the emergency bulbs the row of silent figures propped against the wall looked like figures in an ancient tomb. He closed the door behind him.

The vehicle bay was a furore of activity. Lit by harsh head-lamps, two lorries and a Volkswagen minibus already had their engines running. Under Durrell's instructions each vehicle was being sealed. Polythene sheeting had been draped over the tarpaulin covers and the uninjured technicians were sticking strips of masking tape over all the apertures. One man, his head inside the bonnet of a lorry had disconnected the corrugated heater and was stuffing rags into the open end leading to the cab.

The wounded were being carried like trussed mummies into the backs of the lorries and the air was thick with exhaust fumes. Durrell and Naylor were moving from one man to the next, running geiger counters over the surface of their clothing. Duffy shuffled over to Mawn, his drunken surliness was gone: 'Get aboard.'

Durrell nodded to Naylor who was standing by a large red-painted lever switch. He pulled it down. There was a shrill whine and the exterior doors began to swing upwards. Durrell shouted: 'Everyone inside, close your doors and stay there. Once we get out, stay close together. Duffy in the first lorry will lead off.' Duffy swung up into the cab, a technician began to lace the rear curtain of the tarpaulin cover and as the cab-door slammed the exhaust blew out a cloud of smoke and the lorry swung round and lumbered heavily out into the snow.

The second followed suit. In the back, huddled together for

warmth, Westcott and Sampson sat jerking from side to side trying to brace themselves against the tarpaulin cover and hold the casualties in place on the floor with their feet. As the lorry reached the door opening, Naylor leapt into the cab.

Gelder sat waiting at the wheel of the sealed minibus with Dr Durrell by his side. Mawn, Marcia and Lodge sat in the back. Their helmets glinted in the reflected glare from the headlamps. Gelder let in the clutch and drove out into the open. Immediately thick flakes of snow began to build up on the screen. He switched on the wipers and the rhythmical whirring of the motor seemed almost reassuring. Mawn switched on the interior light and held up his watch.

'It's time!'

'Switch the bloody thing off, I can't see a thing,' Gelder rapped out impatiently peering ahead into the dark. Just ahead they could make out the red tail lights of the second lorry. As the van jerked and bounced over the piled up snow they all imagined the incandescent core forging its way down through the rock beneath them.

Gelder stood suddenly on the brakes and the van slithered to a halt. He quickly backed away until the headlights picked out a snow-covered body lying in the centre of the roadway. Durrell moved to open the door, Gelder leant over and pulled him back violently. 'Keep the door shut!'

'It looks like Gillian, my secretary . . . I must get out . . .'

Without replying Gelder jerked the gear lever and with its wheels spinning, the van swung around the body and straightened up. He floored the accelerator, peering furiously ahead through the screen. 'I've lost them!' He wrenched the wheel and drifted around the first bend of the exit road. The tail swung wide and there was a loud metallic clang as it bounced off a concrete marker post.

'For God's sake take it easy!' Lodge yelled from the rear seat.

For answer, Gelder hinged his helmet back: 'I can't see in this damned thing.'

'Look out!' Durrell yelled.

Again Gelder spun the wheel, the van skidded broadside

and banged up against a great pile of masonry from the Reactor Hall. One window cracked under the impact.

Ahead they could just make out the giant bulk of the loading machine lying like a gigantic nine-pin where it had smashed out through the wall of the Reactor Hall. Lodge picked himself off the floor. He stared fixedly ahead, mouthing words to himself.

'The main gate's through there,' Durrell's voice rang out.

'No, look!' Marcia pointed towards the boundary fence.

The first two lorries had halted by the perimeter fence and the squat figure of Duffy was knotting a thick rope over the top of one of the concrete posts. To their horror they saw that he had no protective suit.

'I'll get out,' Durrell moved to open the door but Gelder stopped him and pointed.

Duffy had moved quickly round to the back of his lorry and crawled underneath to tie the other end of the rope around the rear axle casing. As they watched he slid out, feet first, and jumped back into the cab.

The engine raced and the lorry leaped forward. The rope sprang up out of the snow, jerking taut, but the post held, with the rear wheels of the lorry spinning and throwing up fans of snow. He reversed again up to the fence then lumbered forward again. Three times he repeated the manoeuvre, then jumped down and quickly started to unscrew the tyre valves of the rear tyres, air hissed out until the rear of the lorry began to sag.

Jumping back into the cab, he let the clutch in slowly until the flattened tyres started to grip and then, as the lorry crept forward he suddenly gunned the engine. The rope tautened, then there was a sharp crack and the post split about a foot from the ground. The lorry careered forward, pulling down about fifteen feet of the chain link fencing.

Reversing again, Duffy turned the lorry round in a wide circle to avoid tangling in the rope, then nosed the bonnet back towards the gap in the fence. Ahead of him was a long thirty degree snow covered slope leading down towards the Grim-Ness road running parallel with the cliffs past the station. Beyond the road, there was a ten foot border, then a low wire fence guarding the cliff edge. The lorry crunched over the remains of the fence then dipped sharply downwards on to the slope. Wheels locked, it began to toboggan down to the road. First it lurched sideways then began to swing round. As it reached the road, the rope tautened, the momentum of the lorry pulling the broken fence down over the edge of the slope behind it. The lorry lurched to a halt, its bonnet pressing up against the fence at the cliff edge. Duffy jumped out, slid on his belly under the axle and cut away the rope.

The second lorry nosed up to the edge of the slope and began to slide down. As it gathered speed the driver locked the wheels, but instead of slowing, the vehicle began to swing out of line, until it spun completely round. At the bottom it cannoned into the rear end of the stationary lorry bouncing it forwards through the cliff fence. There was a loud metallic clang as the front wheels dipped down over the edge. Duffy leapt out, but a black pool of sump oil was already welling out from underneath the engine, hissing in the snow.

Gelder put the van into gear and guided it through the gap in the torn fencing and eased the front wheels down on to the slope. Suddenly the ground seemed to jerk violently upwards.

From somewhere directly underneath them came a long deep rumbling blast of sound. The van was flung into the air and immediately began to career down the slope. There was a second booming detonation and the van gathered speed like a bobsleigh, Gelder wrestling desperately with the wheel. Totally out of control it broadsided to the bottom of the slope and slammed sideways on into the nose of the second lorry.

For a split second it remained stationary, then Gelder floored the accelerator and, weaving and twisting, the van gathered speed, swinging from side to side up the road as he fought to regain control over the ice. In the headlights the entire surface of the road in front of them began to weave and undulate as if it were made of rubber. Over the scream of the engine, apparently from the ground beneath them, came a deep juddering thunder.

'We can't leave them there. Stop!'

Durrell was pulling hysterically at the wheel but Gelder, holding on to the wheel with one hand, fought him away. Briefly Durrell gained an advantage and diverted Gelder's attention for a split second. Ahead the stalk of a concrete lamp standard appeared out of the dark.

Mawn leapt at Marcia hurling her to the floor. There was a thumping rending crash and then silence.

After a few moments, Mawn painfully picked himself off the floor by grabbing the top of the front seats. The windscreen had shattered and both Gelder and Durrell had been flung forward through the glass. Durrell's body was hanging down over the front of the van, only his hips and legs were still inside. The subterranean roar had grown suddenly deeper and the whole earth was shaking.

Silhouetted against the sky, the giant outlines of the Reactor Hall began to crumble inwards. The air was full of a grinding, shuddering vibration. Then with a shrieking howl like an enormous jet engine a giant mushroom of steam and debris fountained out of the collapsing masonry. The outlines of the remaining buildings began to waver, fragment and plunge downwards. Debris started to rain down around the van. There was a deafening clang and the van roof suddenly dented inwards. The whole vehicle was shaking violently on its wheels.

A ragged crack suddenly appeared through the snow and whipped across the road, ripping it apart. The van teetered and began to slide towards the crack. The crack suddenly widened into a fissure, steam began to boil out and on the far side, they could just see the occupants of the two lorries jumping down and running like ants from a burning nest.

The ground under the lorries tilted crazily and both men and machines began to slide and tumble towards the cliff edge. One man scrabbled desperately at the tilting road, then disappeared screaming into the fissure. Both lorries, locked firmly together, careered towards the cliff edge, balanced for a moment and then toppled over and were gone.

Gradually, the earth tremors died away and from where the station had been, there was a roaring spouting volcano of fumes blasting hundreds of feet into the air. At the top, it was already forming into a giant mushroom cloud which was already pulling away in the wind.

Mawn switched on a hand lantern and pulled Marcia to her feet: 'Are you OK?'

She started to flex her limbs feeling for injury. She nodded her head still too shocked for speech.

Mawn bent forward over the front seat. 'Let's get these two in.' He grabbed hold of Durrell's hips and began to drag the limp body back through the crumbling edges of the broken windshield. Marcia glanced over her shoulder. Lodge was hunched in a corner. His eyes were glazed and there was a long abrasion down one side of his face.

Mawn had got Durrell's body back into the front seat. His visor was broken and the circular air filter had been pushed inwards. A thick brown mass of blood covered the side of his head, running down inside the suit.

'Give me the light a minute,' Mawn called. 'Christ! the side of his head's right in. Help me get him in the back.' Marcia put the lantern down and between them they heaved and pulled the apparently lifeless body over the front seats and into the back.

Gelder's face was covered in a mask of blood. A long jagged flesh wound stretched over his forehead and on into the hair line. He was breathing in harsh jerking gasps. With difficulty they manhandled him into the passenger seat and strapped him in place with the seat belt.

Mawn climbed awkwardly into the driving seat and turned the ignition key. The starter whirred; nothing. He felt for the choke and was unable to find it. Again no response! Then remembering the Volkswagen automatic choke he floored the accelerator pedal, released it and turned the key. The engine fired immediately. He turned to Marcia, shouting over the noise of the engine: 'Do you remember the way?'

'It's the same road we used when we first came up. Down about two miles then on to the A road and along past the housing estate.' Mawn nodded, turned and started to back the car away from the lamp standard. Then he jumped out and walked round to the front to examine the damage. The lamp standard had made a long creased indentation in the front body panel and the beam from one headlight was pointing crazily up into the falling snow. He stood in the bitter wind trying to regain his breath, looking up at the great mushroom of fumes lying over the collapsed Reactor Hall. Instead of moving away to the north, there was a long plume directly over his head. He leaped back inside shouting to Marcia: 'The wind's changing, it's coming after us!'

He slammed the van into gear and wrenched it around back on to the road. Snow immediately began to pour in through the shattered windshield and every few minutes, he had to slow down and clear the perspex surface of his helmet. The skewed headlamp beam glared back off the curtain of snow so that he could only just see ahead. After a few minutes, snow began to pile up over the front of his helmet and freeze in position. Occasionally he had to stop altogether and bang the flexible plastic with his fist to crack off the impacted ice. His hands grew numb and it became acutely painful to even unbend them from the wheel. In the back, Marcia attempted to wedge the three injured men in position as the van bounced over the snow.

Gradually Mawn's senses began to dull as the cold crept in through the suit. His reactions got slower and he began to misjudge corners and twice drove off the road into drifted snow.

Lodge appeared to be asleep. His head lolled back inside the helmet, his mouth wide open. Durrell's colour had almost disappeared. All bleeding from his wounds had stopped and Gelder hung from the seat belt, his breath rasping and irregular.

As the road unwound, Mawn managed to force the agony of the cold away. Ahead was a main road sign almost obliterated by an encrustation of snow. The sight spurred him on and, misjudging, he slewed the van round, broadsiding across the road up on to the verge. He let the clutch in slowly to give the wheels a chance to bite. They started to inch forward, then the engine raced and the van spun at right angles to the road. He turned the wheel and pointed the nose down the hill.

'For God's sake what are you doing?' Marcia cried. 'We can't go back there!'

'Reverse – lower gear.' Slowly he let the clutch in and started to back the van up the hill. Gradually the wheels bit and, looking back over his shoulder through the rear window, he steered the awkward bulk of the van up towards the crest of the hill.

He shouted: 'You're in the way. I can't see!' Marcia ducked.

At the top, he turned the van around and began to coast down the other side, the engine whining in bottom gear. He peered ahead through the darkness. There was a small point of light, then another, and another. He shouted to Marcia and pointed them out and again lost his concentration for a few vital seconds. The back lashed round in a vicious spin, sending them sliding off the road backwards into a snow-covered hedge. He gunned the engine, but the wheels found no grip and spun uselessly.

Wearily Mawn tore one of the rubber floor mats off the floor and clambered awkwardly down. Straining with all his remaining strength, he tore the mat into two halves and put one half down in the snow just ahead of each rear wheel.

Inside again, he let the clutch in feeding power to the wheels slowly. Gradually the tyres moved on to the corrugated surface of the rubber and then gripped, but started to slip again as the mats shot out backwards from beneath the tyres in a spray of snow and dirt.

Jamming on the handbrake he jumped down again and replaced the mats ahead of the wheels for a second time. He leant tiredly against the van for a minute, his body leaden with cold then he looked up in sudden alarm. There was no pressure of wind on his suit. Burwick lay behind him, the road was to the north and south, they were over the brow. To the west he could just make out the small peak of Cairn Hill. On the east side, a faint gleam of ice, Lake Cleat. Full of misgiving he tramped back up the hill.

At the top, the blast of air almost took him off his feet, gusting hard from the north-east. He started to race back, slipping and falling as he slithered down the icy road to the van. He ran for the door pulling himself in, shouting to Marcia: 'It's over us. Blowing like hell!'

He let in the clutch, gradually the wheels began to grip and they regained the road. The last mile was all downhill but the van seemed almost uncontrollable, swinging from side to side as if trying to escape from its driver.

Finally, through the snow pouring in through the windscreen aperture, he made out first one light, then the dark grey outlines of a row of cottages. Almost dead with fatigue he found himself bringing the van to a halt on a quayside. He switched off the engine and in the silence, all the strain and fear suddenly welled up inside him and he slumped forward over the wheel.

Fourteen

Someone was shaking him by the shoulder. He looked up wearily, automatically wiping the snow off the face-piece of his helmet.

There were voices. A clamour of questions. He pushed himself away from the wheel and eased himself painfully out of the cab. A circle of faces drew back in alarm at the sight of the giant figure in its white plastic suit and helmet. For a moment he stood there swaying in the snow, then, realizing the situation, shouted: 'All of you get back! Get back inside. For Christ's sake get back.' Then, without warning, his body began to tremble, an intolerable nausea ballooned into his throat, the faces seemed to veer sideways and he pitched forward on to the snow.

Somewhere in the distance, there was somebody talking: 'Will you take a bit of this?' He opened his eyes warily. He was lying on a black wooden wall seat and a large elderly man with iron-grey hair and a craggy, blue-veined face was holding out a tumbler half full of whisky. He put his hand up to his face. 'My helmet, for God's sake!'

Marcia was standing beside him: 'It's all right Alex, I used the counter – the levels are fairly low in here. We took your suit off.' He raised his head. He was in the bar of a low-ceilinged pub. A group of men in fishermen's garb stood in a semi-circle, watching. He sat up and gulped down half the whisky.

'We've got the others out.' Marcia's voice faltered. 'Dr Durrell's dead – I couldn't do anything.'

'Aye, they're in the back room, the other one's pretty bad. Dr McBurney's been in and done what he can, but they'll be needing a hospital.'

Mawn staggered to his feet. The man moved to push him back on to the couch but Mawn shrugged him aside: 'I've got to get a phone.'

'We've already done it.'

'What about the lines to the mainland? Are they working?'

'Aye, why shouldn't they be?'

'We've got to get help!'

'I think they'll be getting it in hand already.'

'In hand?' Mawn's mind was clouded with fatigue.

'What the hell happened up there? We never wanted that bloody thing on the island in the first place.'

'Why couldna you bastards leave us alone.'

The low bar-room was beginning to fill with men and women with their children all huddled in thick overcoats against the weather. After an agonizing wait Mawn finally got a line through to London. A full rescue operation was already being mounted. A county class guided missile destroyer, the *Westmoreland,* had been diverted and was pushing through heavy seas from Rosyth with all hatches sealed. A specialist medical emergency team from the atomic weapons research establishment at Aldermaston was moving north by special train. Police throughout the north of Scotland had been alerted and were touring the towns and countryside with loud hailers telling residents to stay inside under cover.

Aircraft from Coastal Command were loading up with radiation detection equipment to overfly the radiation cloud and plot its course as it swept southwards over Scotland. National radio and television announcements had already been made.

Back in the bar he suddenly recognized Mrs Naylor and Mrs Baird in the crowd. He had a momentary, horrific recall of Baird's face splitting in the jet of steam. They were all looking at him expectantly as the grey-haired man held up his hand for silence.

Mawn began hesitantly and gave a full account of the disaster as he had seen it, telling them that the station had been entirely demolished and that they must expect the casualty rate to be heavy.

Mrs Baird began to weep.

Mrs Naylor stepped forward: 'Then how did you get out? Did you just run, leaving all the others?' Her eyes blazed. Mawn hesitated: 'Some people – there were two lorries anyway – they got to Kirkwall.' He felt an intense self-disgust at the half-truth, saw the cruel false hope in the eyes of the listening women.

'Who was in them?'

'Where can we find out?'

The questions tumbled out. Mawn clapped his hands for silence: 'Please! The ones who got across to Kirkwall should be in hospital by now.' He turned to the grey-haired man: 'I'm sorry, I don't know your name . . .'

'Furse, Jimmy Furse. I run the pub.'

'I suggest you start by ringing everyone who's got a phone and tell them to stay inside until help arrives. If they live close enough to neighbours without a phone, tell them to contact them but *without* going outside. Tell them to bang on walls, throw stones anything. But *not* to go out and to seal up all their windows and doors.'

'Some of them live away out in the hills,' Furse growled.

'I'm sorry, that's the best we can do. You'll all have to stay inside here, you can't go back to your homes because there may be fall-out from the station.' He turned to Jimmy Furse: 'What about food and heat?'

'We'll have enough food,' Furse replied grudgingly: 'There'll be compensation I suppose?'

Mawn held back a surge of anger: 'And we'll need blankets. I don't know how long we'll have to stay in here.'

A woman spoke angrily: 'You bloody scientists never do know, when it comes to it.' Mawn went on: 'There's a navy ship on its way, it should be here some time tomorrow.' He hesitated: 'Then, I'm afraid, it's very likely you'll all have to go over to the mainland . . .'

There was a tumult of protest. A fisherman stepped forward, his face suffused with anger: 'We're no leaving the isles. This is our home!'

Mawn held his hand up: 'It's too dangerous here. Nobody knows how long it will take to clear . . .'

The storm of protest grew.

'You'll ruin our village!'

'Listen please!'

'No, you listen to us!' The fisherman brandished his arms: 'We didn't want that damn power station here in the first place – you'll ruin us all, it's your doing – we'll have none of it!'

There was a chorus of assent. Mawn had to shout above the noise. 'Shut up and listen to me. Outside there's very probably a cloud of radioactive debris. The wind is now blowing from the north and it's bringing it all right down over us here. Now you can't feel it – there's no smell or anything – but it's very, very dangerous.'

'If we canna feel it, wha's the harm?' a voice demanded.

'It's radioactive.'

A woman's voice shouted: 'I dinna ken what ye mean wi' all those long words. I've a bairn staying over at Coldharbour farm. Why can I not fetch her? There's nothing but snow out there.'

Mawn pointed to the door: 'Anyone who goes out there now will almost certainly die in a very few days.' The deliberate overstatement had an immediate impact and the protesting voices slowly died away. He opened the door leading to the saloon, turning to Furse: 'They're in here are they?' Furse nodded.

Mawn switched on the light: 'And if you want to see what you'll end up as, if you go out, come and look!'

Durrell's body was on the saloon floor covered by a blanket. Gelder lay back on a wall seat, his head lolled to one side. There was vomit on his chin. The villagers crowded silently into the door opening. Mawn turned to them:

'You'll be like that.' He walked back to the door. The crowd melted back in front of him. 'Now listen please, we've got to go round this building and seal it right up. Every single crack – anywhere where air can get in – block it up – newspaper, rags, anything you can find.'

'We'll aye suffocate,' a voice complained.

'No, no you won't. Enough air will get in.'

An old man in faded dungarees spoke: 'How long will we be awa from the isles? Can ye not at least tell us that, man!'

With a shock of pity Mawn saw that he was almost blind.

'Not for long. Just until it's safe to return.'

'Then ye'll have to leave me. I canna go. I've never been off this island. I could'na find my way.'

Marcia gently took his hand, leading him away to a corner seat. Mawn drew a deep breath: 'It's bound to get very stuffy after a while so once we've got ourselves sealed in, it'll be best if you can manage to stay as still as possible. That way you won't use up so much air.'

During the following hour, every corner of the house was searched for places where the air could get in. From the loft to the cellar door, they used everything they could find to plug gaps. One man was rolling pieces of bread and squeezing the dough into the gap between two halves of a sash window. Another drove newspaper into a door crack with a screwdriver.

One elderly woman in a black shawl had rolled up a rug and was pushing it up against a gap under the front door, another was scooping earth from an indoor plant pot and forcing it into the edge of a window frame. She jerked in alarm as the wind suddenly buffeted the panes, rattling the frame.

In the saloon, Marcia was cleaning Gelder's face, trying to move him into a more comfortable position. He groaned faintly as she tugged at his shoulder. Mawn came in and moved to help her. She turned: 'I can hardly feel his pulse.'

'What about the doctor they were talking about?'

'He's off somewhere else – anyway, he's seventy-five apparently – probably hasn't a clue what's going on.'

In the bar people were beginning to settle down. Some sat leaning up against the wall, the children had been taken upstairs by Mrs Furse to rest on hastily improvized beds laid out on the bare floorboards.

Gradually, over a period of about an hour, the voices died down. One small group of fishermen sat in a silent circle facing each other on the floor quietly passing a bottle.

Mrs Baird sat in a wall seat holding a crumpled handkerchief to her lips sobbing. Mrs Naylor sat beside her, her arms round her shoulders. Someone turned out the lights and through the windows, they watched the snow swirling against the panes building into small drifts on the wooden frames. The wind howled and buffeted and there was a loud clattering sound from the roadway outside as a roof slate fell.

In the saloon, Mawn put his arm around Marcia's shoulder and led her gently back into the bar. Settling himself down on the floor up against the bar counter, he beckoned her down beside him. He took his jacket off and draped it round her shoulders. For a moment she pulled away from him, then she put her head down on his shoulder, closing her eyes. In the dim blue light from the window, Mawn could see the tears running down her cheeks. He brushed them away with his fingertips.

She opened her eyes, the tears glistening: 'All those people, Alex . . .'

'I know. There's nothing more we can do about it now.'

'Do you think they're all dead?'

He looked down at her, stroking her hair: 'The lucky ones are!'

She shuddered: 'What about us? How much have we had?'

He pulled her head down holding her against him: 'I don't know. I think we'll be all right.'

'Does it take long to kill, radiation I mean?'

'Marcia, leave it. We're all right so far. Try and sleep.'

She pulled suddenly away from him: 'You don't even seem to care?'

He paused then reached out and pulled her down against him: 'I care. Now please, one thing at a time. We've got to rest.'

She put her arm up around his neck, pulling herself closer. Mawn sat staring at the snow building up on the window sill in front of him. Then, gradually as if he had taken a powerful narcotic, a warm irresistible lassitude spread through his body. His eyes closed.

In the dream, he was trapped inside an enormous wooden crate. Light was streaming in from one side through gaps in the planks and someone outside was banging in heavy nails. The knocking grew louder. He opened his eyes. Through the window in front of him, a harsh dawn light was streaming into the bar through the condensation on the window panes. Someone was pounding on the front door. There was a shout:

'Anybody there – open up now!' The knocking began again and there was another shout: 'Come along – let's have you!'

Mawn scrambled to his feet and ran over to the door: 'Who is it?' he shouted.

'It's all right. It's the navy. You can open up, it's safe.' Mawn kicked away the carpet, slid the bolts and swung the door open.

Silhouetted against the bright early morning sun, stood a bulky figure in protective suit and helmet. Inside the helmet was a cheerful red face and a shock of curly ginger hair. Beyond the figure, about three hundred yards out to sea, the long grey shape of a naval vessel stood out against the sparkling water. On the quayside, its engine running, a Westland Wessex helicopter crouched nose down on sea floats, its rotors idling. The face spoke, peering in through the door.

'Many of you are there?' He stuck his head in, looking round at the prostrate figures now waking. 'Stone me, have a party did you?'

Inside, people were getting stiffly to their feet, rubbing their eyes and stretching.

'Can I have your attention for a minute please. My name's Petty Officer Gage. I'm off the *Westmoreland*,' he gestured over his shoulder. 'She's standing out in the bay there. Now outside, there's a chopper and we've got to get you off a bit sharpish – there's quite a bit of radiation about.'

'Have you measured levels?' Mawn asked.

The smile behind the helmet faded a little: 'If you don't mind sir, the navy's in the atomic age now, we're quite capable of taking care of things, thank you.' He looked around again. 'Anybody hurt? We'll take them first.'

Three other men in similar suits had approached.

'Yes,' Mawn replied, gesturing at the saloon bar door. 'One in there, he's got what looks like radiation sickness and a head injury. The other's dead.'

'Right then!' The figure turned to the other three in the doorway: 'Hanson, Smith and you, in there at the double. One wounded – one sleeper, leave him for last.' The three suited figures lumbered through the bar and on into the saloon. He turned to the crowd of faces surrounding him:

'Now, in a bit, we'll have you all aboard below decks, safe and sound. With a bit of naval hospitality laid on. We'll take you off ten at a time in the chopper, no time to take anything else I'm afraid, so just yourselves as you are. Get the kiddies wrapped up.'

The three men pushed their way back through the crowd carrying Gelder's limp form. As they passed the Petty Officer unhooked a pistol geiger counter from his belt and ran it quickly over Gelder's body. It clicked violently. 'Quick with this one, we'll have to put him in decontamination.'

The men struggled out towards the helicopter, their footprints showing black against the fresh carpet of snow. When they returned, Gage had already ushered nine more of the waiting islanders to the door. He spoke as if he was addressing his own men: 'Now quick as you can, double over to the chopper and get straight in, sit down and don't move.'

The islanders broke into an uneasy shambling run over the snow and crowded through the oval hatchway of the helicopter. The door slammed immediately, the aircraft stretched up on its landing struts and took off, swinging round straight out to sea towards the waiting destroyer.

Mawn and Marcia stood by the bar. They had both struggled back into their protective suits, the helmets hinged back. Next to them, Mrs Naylor and Mrs Baird had put a small month-old baby inside a protective plastic envelope supplied by one of the naval technicians. Down each side of it there were rows of press-studs and over the head portion there were a series of drawstrings around the edges of a transparent section. Both women seemed unable to understand how the fastenings worked. Marcia, seeing their difficulty, walked over to help. She had no difficulty in completing the closure. She turned back to see Mawn staring at her.

His voice rang out: 'Just a moment!'

The two women looked up nervously. He pointed at Mrs Naylor. 'Where do you come from?'

'How do you mean?'

He walked over excitedly: 'Where do you live?'

'London, why?'

He turned to Mrs Baird: 'And you?'

'Cardiff. All my life.'

Outside, the siren of the *Westmoreland* sounded twice.

'Come on, Alex,' Marcia said urgently. Mawn remained stock still.

'Marcia, where were you brought up?'

'Alex, what is this?'

'Where were you brought up?'

'Long Island – most of the time.'

'The IQ loss, Marcia! I told you we had to have the answer ourselves. We're not affected are we?'

'No.'

'*Why* not? Don't you see? Those women are affected. They couldn't manage that simple task – you could. What's the *one* thing we couldn't understand?'

'People in one place being affected, people in another unaffected.'

'Right. Which people, Marcia?' He grabbed her by the shoulders.

'And *where* did they live?'

'I don't . . .'

'Listen, you and I have lived most of our life in the country. Those two lived in cities. Try and remember, Marcia, your groups – your affected groups – *Where* were they sited?'

'I haven't got the stuff here, I can't . . .'

'Just try and give me the *location* of some of the groups that *were* affected.'

She hesitated: 'Well, there was one firm in London, another in – Birmingham, two in Manchester . . .'

'Go on!'

'. . . one in Bristol – Plymouth yes, I think there was one there . . .'

'OK now *where* were the ones which didn't show the effect?'

'There was one in the country in Breconshire, they'd moved out of Newport, another in Sussex – let's think – yes, one right out on the moors in Yorkshire. One in Devon – near Dartmoor . . .'

'Don't you see?'

'What?'

'They're all in the bloody country!' He was shaking with excitement. 'Your affected groups are all in cities, the others are in the country. It's in the cities, Marcia. Whatever it is, it's in the cities. Something's rotting people's brains in the cities.'

Fifteen

'I have already spoken with Dr Bordheim of UNESCO and he fully confirms the conclusion reached by Mawn. There is now quite overwhelming evidence to show that there has been a loss of mental ability in both men and women and that the worst affected have lived in cities for some considerable time.' The Minister, Campbell Baxter, was speaking from a high-backed Jacobean chair at the head of a long marquetry-inlaid table reflecting a rich brown glow from a chandelier overhead. On his right hand a man of about thirty with alert blue eyes and slicked-back fair hair was making notes. Five other men were present.

'It is also quite clearly global. No country with any large city is immune and so our most urgent task here will be to co-ordinate a plan of action as quickly as possible. I cannot possibly over-emphasize the gravity of this extraordinary effect. I have already been involved in the most delicate negotiations with the Trades Union Council. Their attitude, of course, is to demand recompense and safeguards for their workers who are affected. The military are also extremely nervous about the whole of our defence commitment. They are at the present time completing intelligence testing on all crew members of our deterrent fleet. I don't need to tell you the appalling consequences of any human error on board a missile submarine or, for that matter, in any defence installation. The only consolation seems to be that the Russians have the same problem.' He turned to a broadfaced man of about fifty on his left. 'Perhaps at this stage you would summarize the Orkney disaster, Mr Fordyce?'

'Yes. There are still eighty-four people unaccounted for. Of course, no one can go near the site of the station to search for bodies since the whole island of South Ronaldsay is – er – quite uninhabitable because of the ambient radiation. Over the remainder of the Orkneys there were eighteen deaths from acute radiation and seventy-four non-lethal cases. These are being treated in various Scottish general hospitals and are probably recoverable. The Pentland Firth and Scapa Flow have been closed to shipping. In fact there is a slow eastward drift in these waters and one hopes that the radioactive content will dilute sufficiently before it reaches the west coast of Sweden . . .'

'Yes.' Baxter intervened. 'The Swedes have already made some very firm claims in the United Nations General Assembly. Please continue.'

'. . . As to the Scottish mainland. It's fortunate that the north-eastern tip nearest to the disaster site is fairly sparsely populated. There were nine deaths on the mainland but the fast breeder reactor at Dounreay which, as you probably remember, has been operational for nearly three years, has had to be shut down because of radioactive deposition in the area. One hopes this will not be permanent.

'As to soil contamination, this I am afraid, is going to be the most difficult and expensive operation. We estimate that altogether some four and a half million tons of top soil is seriously contaminated and will have to be removed and stored – probably at Windscale . . .'

There was a shocked murmur.

Fordyce continued, unperturbed by the effect of his words, 'The Americans already have experience of this procedure. It is now many years since they were forced to remove many thousands of tons of top soil from Palomares in Spain after a bomber exploded and released three hydrogen bombs, so we shall be able to draw on considerable expertise there . . .'

He looked hard at the Minister.

'. . . always providing, of course, that the operation is adequately financed. Finally, we estimate that there was probably a forty per cent serial voiding of the reactor core inventory and this had inevitably led to a widespread release and – I regret to say – ingestion of both radioactive iodine, tellurium and caesium. The Medical Research Council tells me this may well affect the local incidence of various malignant conditions – particularly thyroid cancer – over the next thirty years or so. I think that covers most of it.'

Baxter nodded to him: 'Thank you, Mr Fordyce. In point of fact, I don't think we need detain you any more – thank you very much for giving us your time.'

Fordyce stood up and began to gather his papers into a briefcase.

The Minister continued. 'Now we come to the main issue of this meeting and I don't think I need emphasize its extreme urgency. The source of what the press have now called the "Brainrack". Tony, if you would summarize progress to date . . .'

The man by his side nodded, his voice had the high braying inflexion nurtured at Eton and in the guards. 'Minister, gentlemen. Thus far the field seems to be fairly open. There have been many suggestions: Dr Bordheim and his people at UNESCO seem to have got through a great deal of the more obvious investigations. We have their data to hand. The first thought was that there was some sort of virus about in the cities . . .'

Baxter intervened. 'Professor Kingston, would you care to comment on that?'

Kingston, who had just completed a sketch of a thighbone on the pad in front of him, looked up and adjusted his gold rimmed half-glasses: 'No. Practically no chance of an infectious agent – viral or bacterial. As I think my report shows – all the brain tissue changes are against it. In fact they are more consistent with some sort of chemical irritation.'

'Can you be more specific?' Baxter asked.

'Not at the moment, no. You see the brain has only about three main types of response to injury, very limited, very limited indeed.'

'Surely,' Baxter went on, 'if we know it's something in cities, in the air, ground or water, we should be thinking about carbon monoxide and lead. I know we have the new legislation phasing lead out of petrol but surely there would be enough still about – residual dust and so on – to produce this sort of thing?'

Kingston smiled tolerantly: 'We've looked. No – not a bit like lead encephalopathy. No basophilia – blood changes – no not a bit like lead.'

'And carbon monoxide?'

'Again no. There were no brain petechiae – beg pardon – small haemorrhages from capillaries – no, not carbon monoxide at all I'm afraid. By the way, I had a look at the brain of that chappie from the Orkney station – Durrell wasn't it? – extraordinarily interesting. Apparently he'd been tested by this psychologist...'

'Miss Scott, yes?'

'Well that gives us another rather pretty correlation. It's building up to the most fascinating picture. As I wrote in my report – Chronic Betz-Cell Atrophy – this new condition – it really does tie up excellently with the intelligence loss.'

'Could you outline the effects you see stemming from this, Professor?' Baxter asked.

Kingston spoke gravely: 'You have to imagine a world where a considerable proportion of folk in the cities have become less able. First of all, judging by the histological changes – the affected people will never recover. Adult brain tissue doesn't regenerate once it is damaged. I honestly fear the consequences. I don't see it as the least unlikely that our life style may change really quite sharply. In many ways, you could compare its potential to that of some of the great epidemics of the past –

the influenza which decimated Europe during the First World War would be one such example. Just consider – a high proportion of workers in factories may never be able to handle their machinery again. Decision makers . . .'

He looked around the table slowly.

'. . . may have their judgement affected. We live in a densely populated world which depends almost entirely on complex and highly developed technologies. If we can't work them reliably any more then the social upset and unrest which may result quite frankly frightens me to death.'

It was Lodge who broke the silence. His face had an unhealthy pallor and he pressed his fingertips against the surface of the table to hide the tremor: 'You say this is quite irreversible?'

'Almost certainly.'

'Is it progressive?' Lodge asked.

'I can't tell – depends whether the cause – the agent, whatever it is – is still about. If it is – yes, it will progress I suppose.'

Lodge nodded slowly and looked down.

Baxter broke in: 'This brings us to the next issue. Dr Mawn and his colleagues made considerable attempts to delay the start-up procedure on the grounds that some of the staff were affected by loss of ability. As we have just heard the post-mortem findings on the technical director, Dr Durrell, have certainly confirmed this assertion.

'To be perfectly frank, my colleagues and I were intensely suspicious of Mawn's claim. On at least one occasion – on television – his views were shown to be entirely without foundation, but I'm bound to confess that his findings are now of central importance. It was he and Miss Scott in fact who spotted the relationship of the effect to cities and this has led over the past few weeks to the general acceptance of this idea. It therefore seems that we are bound to seek his help and so I have proposed to the Cabinet that he be given a temporary position to further his own and Miss Scott's work and also to prepare a report on the situation as a whole.'

He looked around for signs of reaction, but finding none, continued:

'The Cabinet approved in general but they have also made it abundantly clear that his sphere of influence is to be strictly limited by a properly-worded brief.'

The fair-haired aide took up a newspaper from a pile in front of him, his drawl unmistakably hostile. The papers carried a large photograph of Mawn and a banner headline: 'THE BRAIN-RACK – Is mankind reverting to the ape?' Underneath Mawn's picture in a smaller type was written, 'Why was this man's warning ignored?'

'It seems fairly obvious to me that we have another public guru on our hands – a saviour as it were . . .'

Kingston's geniality disappeared: 'If you're referring to Dr Mawn, a very large number of lives would have been saved had the government taken adequate notice in the first place.' He glared at the fair-haired aide. 'God knows how you can afford to be so self-indulgently critical of the one person who had the vision and perseverance to uncover this ghastly affair. I've come to know Alex Mawn fairly well over the last few weeks. He's a difficult and shirty person in many ways, but it seems to me he's come very well out of this affair – quite apart from being half killed in the process . . .'

Baxter turned to the fair-haired man, his voice a shade more peremptory: 'Anything further, Tony?'

'No, sir.' The aide put the newspaper down on the table, his hand shaking noticeably.

Baxter glanced at the grandfather clock. 'He should be here by now.' He turned to Lodge: 'Richard, would you do the honours?'

The air in the ante-room was dry and overheated. A fierce black iron radiator under the high Georgian window clicked angrily and a wigged seventeenth-century incumbent glared down disapprovingly from an over-varnished oil painting. Mawn sat with his feet up on a Victorian chaise longue and Marcia poised uncomfortably on a high-backed wooden chair on the opposite side of the room. She was flipping the papers of a glossy magazine.

Mawn thought back over the three weeks which had passed since their rescue by the navy from the stricken island. Feeling for the still tender bruise in the fold of his left elbow, he remembered the blood transfusions, the regular blood counts.

With a start he realized that he would miss his appointment at the Westminster Hospital. The physician there had told him on arrival that his white blood cell count was down by over fifty per cent from exposure to radiation. Ruefully, he began to worry about his fertility, whether he would now be able to father a child.

He glanced over at Marcia and wondered whether she too had been rendered barren by exposure. With a surge of resentment he recalled her father, Harland Scott. How he had flown directly from America and whisked her away– into the rich surroundings of a private room in the Wigmore Clinic. Scott's attitude had first of all been effusively grateful, then had rapidly changed to a muted suspicion – had he really done enough? The two men had had no contact beyond carefully planned pleasantries. Without real envy, he looked at Marcia's suntan from the two weeks at the Marrakesh Hilton, still only just hiding the underlying pallor of anaemia.

He had looked forward eagerly to her return from North Africa, but soon after they had met at the airport they had found it difficult to talk. There had been an embarrassing strain and artificiality. It was as if, he thought, she was wanting to extricate herself, to get back to the easy Long Island life. To hide from the grating realities which their work had revealed.

The door opened and Lodge came in smiling, his hand outstretched: 'Hallo again. Nice to see you, won't you come in.' He paused. 'The Minister will make you an offer. Do think about it before you accept. Most of the shots are in your locker now . . .' He paused, realizing he had transgressed and checked himself. Mawn saw that his hand was trembling. 'Really, it's very good to see you both and looking fit again.' Before they could reply he led the way back into the Minister's room.

After the introductions, Mawn began to feel the pressure of the occasion. He wasn't at a student seminar, he was in the surroundings of power and decision. He felt a surge of anxiety. His palms were moist.

Baxter deftly gave him a precise account of their previous conversation:

'. . . and so in the circumstances, the Government thinks it right that you should be asked to head this small committee with nominees put up by yourself and our own relevant departmental heads.'

Mawn looked around the dour faces. Kingston winked at him, smiling. He remembered Lodge's comment. 'Well, thank you, Minister, but I'd like a little time to consider it if I may.'

'Of course. Oh, yes, I forgot to mention that there would be a small budget to get things started. You would be empowered to take on secretarial staff, equipment and so on. You would be in a position rather similar to a Select Committee, but in this case we can streamline matters considerably. In fact, were you to accept, we would very much like it if you could prepare a preliminary report within, say, four or five weeks. You would of course, be responsible to myself and this committee and naturally we would expect to discuss any findings you made before publication.'

A censor, Mawn thought to himself. He said: 'I'd like time to think about it.'

'Well, please let me know within perhaps two or three days,' Baxter said. 'It's very very important to get things under way.'

'Yes, I'll do that – thank you.'

'Good. Now we were talking previously about the nature of this "Brainrack" as the press have called it. Professor Kingston had reviewed the medical evidence and this seems to point against any disease process.' He turned to Kingston: 'That's so, isn't it?' Kingston nodded vigorously. 'Have you anything further to suggest Dr Mawn?'

Mawn immediately felt the relaxation of moving back into a purely scientific area of discussion.

'Yes, I have, yes. We've carried out some further breakdowns on the data we've already got. There's no doubt that it's city-based, but there are some affected people who live and work in the country, but so far – and this is by no means certain – all those in the country with the effect have at some time lived for a fairly prolonged period in a large town or city.'

'Have you had any further notions about the cause?'

'Not yet, no. If it's not bacterial or viral but it is in cities then it has to be an environmental factor. Lead from cars – carbon monoxide – noise – I just don't know.'

'I think we've already disposed of the first two,' Baxter replied. 'But I can't think it will be long before we do find out. I suppose there has never been such a systematic global effect. Almost every city in the world seems to be tearing itself apart to find the cause. However, we must get on.' His charm began to withdraw. 'It was very kind of you to come, Dr Mawn. You will let us know, won't you?'

'Yes, of course.' Mawn got to his feet, nodded to the others and was led out by Lodge.

In the ante-room Lodge's manner was hesitant: 'One thing I feel bound to say. The Minister was very anxious to clear up this business – you know – the television show. You did appear to have some facts – er – quite wrong if I may say so. Is there anything we can do about it?'

Mawn looked at him steadily: 'Yes there is. I'm going to see Brian Gelder.'

The doctor paused in front of the panelled door. 'I shouldn't stay for more than a few minutes. He's very sick. There is a depressed skull fracture as well as the aftermath of radiation sickness.'

'Is he going to be all right?' Marcia asked.

'It's very difficult to be certain at this stage, but his chances aren't as good as they might be. We were worried for a time about bone marrow aplasia but some new cells have appeared so he may recover – he just may.' He turned to go. 'Come and see me in my office before you leave.'

Mawn nodded and opened the door. The room was high and airy and Gelder lay propped up in bed. On a side table, there was a colour television set and on another a profusion of flowers, potted plants and fruit. On the table lying across the bed, there was a tape-recorder and a pile of letters. A nurse was busy adjusting an intravenous drip bottle hanging down from a vertical iron frame and an elegantly-dressed woman was seated in an armchair taking shorthand notes.

The pale skin of Gelder's face seemed stretched tautly over the bones and his eyes were deeply sunken. One hand picked nervously at the bed covers.

Mawn looked at the woman in the chair. 'Could I have a word with you – in private?'

The nurse clicked disapprovingly and the secretary started to protest, but Gelder waved them to silence and he nodded them to go. 'I'll give you a buzz.'

As the door closed behind them, Mawn turned away from the window. 'I want your help.'

Gelder's eyes mocked. 'I'll buy you a drink for getting me out of there if you like. By the way, thank you.' He pointed to a pile of newspapers. 'You seem to be doing all right without me.'

'I've been asked to prepare a report on the "Brainrack" effect.'

'Congratulations.'

'And they're to provide quite considerable powers, including the power to call witnesses.'

'I'm sure you'll do very well.'

'But before I start work, I have got to put a few things right.'

'You're driving now.' Gelder lay back smiling.

'As you're aware I've lost whatever standing I had in the scientific community,' Mawn rapped suddenly.

Gelder turned away: 'Is that why you wanted the others out?'

'You don't have to worry. I doubt whether I can prove anything.'

The mocking smile was back on Gelder's face: 'What a relief.'

'But I could make a very good attempt using the powers I've got.' Mawn caught a warning glance from Marcia. He was lying and it would only take Gelder minutes on the phone after they had gone to spot it.

'I intend making a start with George Teller!'

The smile disappeared: 'Who?'

'George Teller – industrial spy and murderer.'

Gelder's face seemed to sag slightly and Marcia felt a sudden twinge of pity. His voice faded: 'What about him?'

Mawn gripped the rail at the foot of the bed. 'You sent him to my laboratory and he caused the death of one of my assistants and the destruction of my work.'

Gelder closed his eyes and turned his head away in the pillow.

'Alex! It's not what we want,' Marcia said.

Mawn wheeled, his eyes cold: 'Leave this to me!'

'No, Alex, Barfield.'

He started to say something, then turned back to Gelder. 'She's right. This is not an emotional issue. Or I'd have broken your neck in the Power Station. How did you manage to screw up my figures in the "Nightstyle" programme?'

Gelder opened his eyes: 'Your figures! What you mean is my figures given to you illegally by one of my employees – when he was still under contract to me.'

'You got Barfield to give me false figures, either with Seager's connivance or without. It was a deliberate attempt to discredit me and hold me up to ridicule.'

Gelder shrugged weakly: 'Whatever I say or sign isn't going to make any difference with the public.'

'For God's sake. I'm not concerned with the general public!' He pointed to the pile of newspapers: 'You've seen those – according to them I'm Oppenheimer, Churchill and God rolled into one! No, that's not my concern. I've got to convince my own peers – I've got to go into Whitehall and get some sort of acute action out of the mandarins and you've got to help me. As far as I'm concerned you're guilty of manslaughter, and perhaps twice over. What do you know about Sheldon Peters's death?'

Marcia tried to pull his arm: 'Alex, that's enough, leave him.'

He pushed her away: 'From what I hear you haven't got much of a chance and frankly that doesn't really worry me at all. You're already responsible for a tremendous loss of life. Do you want to die with that on your conscience?'

Mawn's voice changed and became gentler, more pleading: 'I've got a chance of doing something about this "Brainrack" effect but I can't clear myself. I must have a statement from you before I can work effectively. Surely to God, you owe me that at least?'

Gelder lay quite still, his eyes closed. He made no response. Marcia pulled Mawn away, then bent over the bed, feeling for Gelder's pulse. 'We must get the doctor.' As they moved towards the door Gelder started to speak. His voice was weak but clear:

'I sent Teller. That was my idea. Setting up Barfield was a joint effort; two other men were involved, Ian Caird and Carl Bellamy. We made him give you false material.'

'For me to misquote in front of nine million people!' Mawn said bitterly. 'And to do the hatchet job you set up Professor Seager with the real figures.'

'He didn't need setting up. He just hates your scientific guts. We knew that, so once we'd given him the figures, that was all the ammunition he needed.'

'Wasn't he worried by them himself? Didn't he check them over?'

'I don't know.'

'Was he able to check them? Had he access to your files?'

'Yes, full access at all times.'

Mawn leaned back, his face a mask: 'Will you write this down and send it to us?'

Gelder looked up at Mawn, nodded and turned his head away: 'Now get out.'

On the way to the flat in the car, Marcia's anger boiled over: 'Did you have to do that?' Mawn shrugged and looked out of the window. He felt sick and disgusted. A small victory over the dying. Marcia started to say something, then seeing his expression, drove on in silence.

Sixteen

Mawn looked morosely around the empty flat. He was in dressing-gown and pyjamas seated in one of the black leather armchairs nursing a brandy and listening to a Bach concert on the radio. He recalled Marcia's half-hearted invitation to dine with her father. The frostiness in her voice had made him decline. He felt unaccountably depressed and got up to pour another drink. Finally he forced himself to admit that he was depressed because of her recent aloofness. He realized he was afraid of losing her. He had started to feel that fear lying in the hospital bed with nothing to do except watch the dripping blood in the transfusion set.

Irritably he got up and switched off the radio. He heard the front door click. Marcia was standing in the doorway.

'Hi,' she flung herself down in a chair, her face flushed. Here it comes, he thought, wait for it!

She avoided his eyes, hands twisting nervously: 'Can we talk, really talk?'

He waved the brandy glass expansively: 'By all means.'

She nodded at the bottle: 'And can I have some of that, before it all goes?'

He poured a full measure, her hand trembled as she took the glass.

'I'll make it easy for us shall I?' He smiled. 'You're going to tell me it's about time I moved on. Well, OK, it's getting on my wick as a matter of fact. And I don't somehow think father quite approved, did he?'

'Pardon me?'

'Big daddy! He's probably convinced you need more care and protection after all this. I'm sure he's got a rich executive lined up for you. Twenty feet of Cadillac and a gold-plated loo.'

She slammed the glass down on the table. 'You arrogant self-centred bastard! You always know exactly what I'm thinking don't you. Little rich dilettante goes running back home when the going gets hard. Just because you're a mathematical whizz-kid you know every other goddamn thing. It would never cross your mind that you're wrong would it?'

Mawn looked up at her in surprise: 'What were you going to "really talk" about?'

'I wanted to talk about you, you great oaf. You hardly speak to me, you were incredibly rude when you picked me up at the airport. What am I supposed to have done? I was all screwed up about it. I wanted to help.'

'I thought you . . .' Mawn's voice dropped away lamely.

'Thought what? After *la dolce vita* in Marrakesh I wanted the high life again. You're the most disgusting prig. Just because you're the son of a manual worker you think it gives you some special advantage. Pure working-class boy shows corrupt rich girl how to live. Christ! You give me a pain in the arse.' She turned away in disgust.

'What can I say?' Mawn began. 'I'm sorry . . .'

'Sorry, sorry! Bump into someone – *sorry*. Completely misunderstand someone – *sorry*. Mess everything up – *sorry*. It doesn't mean a damn thing. We don't have any equivalent where I come from, thank God.'

'All right! No more apologies.' Mawn's voice rang out. 'Just the simple truth. I was shit scared of losing you.'

She halted by the bedroom door: 'You can find plenty more psychologists.'

'No, you personally. In every bloody way.' He walked over to her, standing awkwardly, his hands shaking. She turned and he had a brief glimpse of large eyes full of tears, then she was crushed against him. Mawn lifted her and carried her over to the bed and as she put her arms up around his neck and pulled him down beside her, all the tension and fear swept out of him in one single flood which he was completely unable to resist. He buried himself in the gentle sweetness of her body, giving in completely to the warmth of her touch. It was as if he had never made love in his life before. Every single feeling he possessed seemed to flow directly and easily into his movements as he entered her.

For a long while he remained absolutely still, not daring to break the perfection. She was lying with her head against his shoulder, her long dark hair spread like a fan across his chest. His pulse leapt at the thought of completely and uniquely caring for one single person. In the warmth of her body he felt protected from the days that lay ahead. The sinister pattern of the Brainrack seemed almost infinitely remote.

For a long while after she had fallen asleep he stayed awake watching the light patterns of passing cars sweeping across the ceiling. He imagined the drivers unable to control their vehicles. How would they see him? The man who said their minds were going. They would probably blame him. He would become the symbol of the whole effect. He listened for a while longer to the quiet rhythm of her breathing. Tonight nothing else seemed to matter.

Over the following days, they became totally wrapped up in the ordinary routine of the flat. He felt the years slip away from him and began to talk with a compulsive enthusiasm which he had thought had gone for ever. Ideas and concepts flowed in a continuous stream.

One morning Mawn sat in front of a jumbled pile of mail trying to sort out the serious from the insane. He had got accustomed to the venom of the mad letters, the threats, the warnings of doom, the religious fanatics who usually wrote in a heavy aggressive scrawl about the judgement of God and Sodom and Gomorrah. He had been accused of putting drugs in the water supply, of being alternatively a communist agent, a fascist lackey and a revolutionary. One correspondent had even suggested that he had invented the whole effect so he could capitalize on the serial rights.

He felt her hand on his shoulder: 'We're having lunch with my father, don't forget.'

'Today?'

'Yes. The Savoy Grill.'

'Five quid to have a waiter peel your grapes!'

'All he wants is to help.'

'Why?'

'I told him all about it, what you need. You're supposed to

let the Minister have his answer today. Look, he can get you money . . .'

'Marcia, I can do things my way, without going round begging off rich industrialists.'

'No you can't. Remember what Richard Lodge said. All you'd get officially is just a little money – enough to keep you right under their thumbs. You'll never get good people if you can't pay them. Why does it matter where the money comes from?'

Mawn looked away uncomfortably: 'It's not that simple. There's bound to be strings attached.'

'Why? for Pete's sake? This Brainrack hits everyone from the large corporations to the corner drug store. Besides I guess he also wants to do this for me.' Marcia rose and walked to the window. 'You see, we haven't been too close. His last wife – well we didn't get on too well. You know, classic only-daughter reaction. I was betrayed – shut out. I behaved like a spoilt kid I guess – but that's how I felt and we split up.' Mawn leant across and filled her coffee cup. 'Well, anyway, now all this, it's changed things. Now he's crazy to do things for me. He sees it as my discovery. I'm sorry, I know that's unfair to you, but he does.'

Mawn tried to explain, fully aware of his clumsiness: 'I don't mind that and I've nothing really against your father. It is just that I live here in a flat you borrowed for me. I'm using your data, now you're asking me to take your father's money. I just can't do it.'

Marcia put an arm round his neck: 'You've got a real life-size chip up there. What the hell, he's got far too much loot, and I can't think of a better use for it!'

Mawn stiffened, then shrugged: 'I'm not sure I take you seriously as a Marxist.' He pulled her over on his lap. 'OK, we'll talk.'

She hugged close to him. 'I promise you that when this is all over I'll do anything you want. I'll even be tweedy British, polish your shoes and live in the country and . . .'

He pushed her away, smiling: 'And slop around in the mud in gum boots?'

Their embrace was broken by the sound of the mail dropping through the letter box. With it was Gelder's statement confirming what he had said at the clinic. It was carefully written to minimize legal risk but the content was clear.

The Savoy Grill was in full spate. Waiters scurried between the tables with laden silver trays, just managing with an almost balletic skill to avoid touching the diners. On a low stage an orchestra was playing nostalgic tunes from West Side Story. The lead violin was very slightly off key. Mawn stared around, objecting silently to the perfumed theatricality. He was brought back to himself by Harland Scott: 'You didn't answer my question!'

'Mm? Oh, I'm sorry.' Mawn collected his thoughts. 'For the moment I'm going to beg, borrow or steal every university laboratory I've got any contact with. There isn't time to get a new lab going. The Betz-cell atrophy is caused by some environmental factor in large cities and it's got to be only a matter of time before we find it. Since it isn't bacterial or viral it must be chemical – not genetic – no evidence – it's just got to be a chemical.'

Scott put his hand over Marcia's. 'And your work started it all.' Marcia smiled. 'Yes, but I didn't see the connection – he did.'

'What did you think of Gelder's statement?' Mawn asked.

Scott looked at him thoughtfully: 'It was a minor masterpiece. I doubt whether any attorney could make a charge stick – but it certainly convinced me.'

'It's careful not to mention Caird or Bellamy,' Marcia protested.

Scott smiled: 'Didn't need to. You're both witnesses, their names were mentioned. I know Bellamy as a matter of fact. And his boss. Guess I'll have a word or two in their ears, then shake a collection box.'

'Surely they won't move?' Marcia continued.

'They will. They know they're in over their ears.'

Mawn looked more closely at the white-haired American

who looked like a minister of the episcopal church with his gently smiling eyes and heavy sensitive lids.

'It's not only money,' said Mawn. 'I don't think they'd have agreed to Gelder's action unless they were worried about the Brainrack effect in their firms. I could use their active co-operation, access to their files.'

'You'll get it when I've done talking to them.'

Marcia turned to her father: 'Alex is due to see the Minister in about an hour's time.'

Scott beckoned a waiter, getting to his feet. 'And I've got to be on a plane. While I'm over, by the way, I'll jingle my box around Wall Street too.' He put notes down on a silver tray held by the waiter. 'And now goodbye kids. Oh! One more thing. I've opened a trust fund in your name, the current account reads at 200,000, as a starter.'

'In my name?' Mawn began.

Harland Scott bent down and kissed his daughter. 'Please yourself what you do with it.' He stroked her hair. 'Set her up in a chateau in France if you like, or get some work done: either way,' he raised his hands, 'no strings! So long now.'

Mawn sat down in the ante-room trying to stare down the fixed glance of the figure in the oil painting. As the fair-haired aide ushered him in he looked quickly at his watch and noted wryly that the waiting time had come down to seven minutes.

In the dazzle from the chandelier it appeared first of all as though the composition of the committee was the same, then he saw that his main ally, Lodge, was absent. Instead, there was the face that had been part of his worst dreams for almost two months. His mind shot back over the debacle of the television programme. Professor Seager sat doodling with a pencil, not meeting his eye.

On the left of the Minister there was a new face. The whole of its surface seemed to be hung with folds. The deeply-sunken eyes moved with an almost reptilian deliberation over Mawn as he walked to his place. He was introduced by the Minister as Doctor Max Bordheim from UNESCO. The Minister wasted no time in preamble.

'We have a full agenda so, may I begin by asking you, Dr Mawn, whether you are going to be able to accept our offer?'

'In principle, yes,' Mawn replied. 'But I would naturally like to know more about the details of operation.'

'I understand. But you do realize that time is of the essence and we must be able to establish an effective liaison between your side of things and our own efforts – mainly in the interest of accuracy.' The reference was obvious and Mawn coloured. 'So we have asked Professor Seager if he would act in this capacity. He has, as you probably know, been acting as head of one of the Rothschild groups in advising the Cabinet and I'm sure you will appreciate his expertise.'

Mawn was uncomfortably aware of all eyes turned in his direction. He was being asked to accept his public humiliator as monitor. If he accepted, he would have his hands firmly tied. If he refused, he would be judged guilty of personal chagrin and found wanting. He felt all the bitterness and anger of the past rising like a sour bile in his throat.

'Well, Doctor?'

The Minister's tone was sharp and he realized that they had all been waiting for his reply. He forced himself to speak calmly, looking directly at Seager.

'I think I can function perfectly well without any additional assistance.'

Campbell Baxter frowned: 'To be frank, I think we have to avoid anything which interferes with the work which lies before us.'

Mawn took a copy of Gelder's statement out of his briefcase, he spoke in a flat, staccato tone, as if he were deploying a mathematical argument.

'Before I go any further, I'd like to read you this statement . . .' He read out Gelder's words slowly, without any inflexion. '. . . and so you will see that doubts about my credibility can be answered, and I hope you will now consider this matter closed!' He threw the statement down on the table.

Baxter glanced over at Seager, trying to gauge his reaction. 'Well, you've obviously been subjected to a lot of injustice and

I'm very relieved to find out the truth. But I don't see how this affects Professor Seager.'

Mawn took a slim journal out of his case. He extracted a single sheet of typed paper and cleared his throat:

'This is a copy of *Nature* dated January of this year. In it is a paper by Professor Seager and a co-author. It is an analysis of operational faults in nuclear power systems. Now, when we first gave you our findings about the Brainrack effect you subjected our report to independent scrutiny. I have got an independent report on Seager's paper by an expert whose name I am perfectly willing to supply in confidence. I will just read you the final paragraph: "the arguments presented show a distinct bias towards acceptance of high risk control systems and appear both specious and speculative in the light of the fact that the statistical support for the assertions made is lacking in strength. In many cases the authors have argued from the particular to the general without sufficient reason. In my view, the work looks as though it was assembled without due regard to accuracy . . ." and so on.'

Seager started to protest. 'I really fail to see what this has to . . .' Baxter waved him to silence.

'All I was demonstrating,' Mawn continued, 'is that for every thesis there is an anti-thesis. For every original discovery there will always be an opponent to unseat it. If you examine the opponent's work, it is amenable to exactly the same degree of intellectual destruction.'

Seager coloured.

'Professor Seager has obviously selected data which suits his case and completely ignored material which would have led to the truth . . .'

'This is absolutely intolerable . . .' Seager began angrily.

'. . . Had he supported my analysis of the dangers at the Grim-Ness station instead of opposing it – for what I can only call personally vindictive reasons – the whole tragedy might never have occurred!'

The Minister picked up the journal and gave it to his aide. His eyes were cold and watchful: 'Please continue . . .'

'On the television programme I made several major points –

admittedly on material sent to me by a Gelder employee – I make no secret of that. I have also been told by Gelder that Seager had complete access to their research data. He must have seen that I had a perfectly valid case. He was given a full opportunity to examine my figures before the programme and at that stage, he could easily have come to me and tried to resolve the discrepancy, but instead, he used the occasion to mount a purely personal attack.' Mawn looked down at a transcript of the programme. 'And I quote: "Doctor Mawn's data may well be the result of an honest mistake, he may well have been misinformed or he could have fabricated the entire case. The law prevents me from stating my own preference".' Mawn paused. 'You can draw your own conclusions.'

Baxter looked down at the blotting pad. 'This certainly makes matters difficult. Perhaps I can have a word with you, Professor Seager after the meeting.'

Seager's face had now paled.

'And now, we really must continue. I was about to tell you, Doctor, that we have been able to find an initial sum of £10,000 together with temporary premises in the new wing of St Olaf's medical school. I hope you will find that acceptable?'

Mawn made an attempt at humility. 'Thanks, that will get things started.' He paused. 'But I've already been given a substantial grant from an American source.'

He watched Bordheim's smile spreading. 'So I think you'll agree this will enable me to accomplish rather more!'

Bordheim rubbed the end of his nose with a pencil, looking from one to the other. His eyes were almost closed.

'But what I most urgently need, Minister, is access to departmental reports. Mainly Department of Health – tests on school children and so on. Also data on the testing of military personnel . . .' He handed a list to the Minister who adjusted his glasses and scanned it.

'Well, several of these are certainly outside my jurisdiction, but I'll do what I can.' He rose and, without a further glance at Mawn, hurried from the room followed by his aide and Professor Seager.

Outside in the ante-room, Mawn felt a touch on his arm.

Bordheim's voice had the over emphatic use of consonants of his Swedish origin.

'Congratulations! You have made more happen than I did over two years.' The fingers tightened on his arm, drawing him away out of earshot of the others. 'We have now made over four hundred kilos of paper in Paris. Everyone argues all the time, nobody will do anything. The Americans say one thing, the Russians say nothing, the French protest, the Chinese read us little lessons; it is all impossible.

'Now, I tell you my friend, we have much data – I will give it over to you. It will be very helpful, I think. Many experiments. We started to make some ideas about the man-machine-interface, but very soon, like you, we had proved it was people. What we did not see was that it was city people. That was very good. So now must we abandon the cities? Is that what you would say?'

Mawn smiled: 'Not quite that. But we must find out exactly what it is.'

'Oh, yes, we must find out. Then maybe we find it's oxygen or water, so we all say goodbye. I have said I will send you all our information and I wish you success. And now, goodbye. I have to go back to the paper factory in Paris.' The grip on his arm relaxed, the eyelids came down and he shuffled away, chins folded against his collar.

Seventeen

Over the following eight weeks, Mawn found himself at the centre of a rapidly-spreading international octopus of communications. Max Bordheim was as good as his word and each day brought a new batch of data from the UNESCO headquarters in Paris.

One by one, the cities of the world began to turn themselves inside out to identify the cause of the brainrack. Sewers, underground tunnels and skyscraper blocks were all combed by a growing army of technical specialists. Every factory, chemical store and public institution was minutely probed for any possible source of a chemical poison.

Doctors and pathologists worked impossible hours in laboratories and post-mortem rooms slicing, examining, analysing and sifting the body tissues of people who had died from any cause in the cities.

Potential culprits were put up, examined and then discarded. No unusual levels of the heavy metals were found in the tissues of the dead. Lead, cadmium, mercury were all exonerated.

The search turned to the waterways. Already heavily polluted by the myriad of industrial effluents poured into them day by day, each river, canal and dock basin was sampled and analysed. In Europe, the Rhine – already known as Europe's majestic sewer, became a particular target for international scrutiny.

With Marcia beside him, Mawn worked at all hours wading through the mountains of data strewn around the makeshift department in St Olaf's. His students from the university at Plymouth had joined him and he had already put a dozen different departments to work investigating various possible chemicals which could have produced the brain damage.

The most horrific statistic which emerged showed that a probable thirty per cent of the total population of the world were affected. The high proportion at first seemed unlikely but demographic evidence confirmed that a probable sixty per cent of people lived in or near a major city.

The media maintained a constant barrage of questions and pressure and each day brought an article or an interview showing what the effect would be on a particular section of the populace if it proved to be irreversible: airline pilots refused to fly with crew members who had not been tested; drivers demanded that no one should be given a car driving licence until they had been proved free of the brainrack; anaesthetists suspected surgeons; generals grew ulcers over the men controlling underground missile silos; and policemen regularly refused point duty in areas of urban congestion on the grounds that some drivers might not be able to control their cars.

Apart from those in the cities who had actually been shown to have the effect, many others imagined that they had and doctors began to talk of the 'brainrack neurosis' as an entity quite separate from the real one. It became a major excuse for work absenteeism.

Mawn's picture always appeared beside the articles, but the policy of the papers and media had changed. Whereas they had begun by raising Mawn to the status of Messiah, now they were beginning to demand quicker results. How long is it going to be! When will this man tell us what's wrong? The questions became gradually more terse and hostile.

In the United Nations in New York, each country intimated that the brainrack had originated in one of their neighbour states. The developing countries felt they had a clear case in placing all responsibility on to the richer nations and taking practically no action at all.

As Mawn's load increased so did his capability. Having long despised the amateur politicians of his university campus, to his surprise, he began to take a chess-player's delight in battles with Civil Service mandarins reluctant to part with what they regarded as their own private material. There were innumerable protests from manufacturers as their products came up for detailed scrutiny by Mawn's growing army of chemists.

Then the inevitable happened and the public began to adapt to the situation: 'Sorry, can't come out tonight – got a touch of the brainrack.' It became a stock joke for public speakers – 'Well, ladies and gentlemen, speaking as one idiot to another . . .' Slowly the syndrome was integrated into everyday life as if it was of little importance. Teachers began to hold conferences to adjust school curricula. New tests based upon the original Venn pattern were devised to sort the normal from the affected.

During the early part of the investigation, Professor Kingston had been coopted by Mawn to correlate all chemical and pathological enquiries. Like Mawn, he had been sifting data flowing in from laboratories and hospitals throughout the world and, by using facilities provided by the World Health Organization, a general international agreement had been reached concerning the nature of the brain damage underlying the brainrack effect.

There was no doubt at all that it was due to a chemical and the search had been directed towards an analysis of brain tissue to see whether any abnormal substances could be identified by analysis.

One laboratory in Geneva announced that they had isolated a substance from a series of post-mortem brains. It was present only in microgram quantities and it had proved difficult to identify specifically. Eventually a similar discovery was made in a biochemical laboratory in Los Angeles and by combining the data from each institution it was possible to name it. It was called: cyclic pentane acetylide.

The public announcement of the identity of the chemical had a shattering effect.

Kingston was sitting on the edge of Mawn's desk. He was pointing to one of a series of purple stains on a long roll of squared paper.

'There's the criminal – petrol – gasoline!'

'You're absolutely sure?' Mawn asked.

'We are now. Cyclic pentane acetylide. I never would have believed it you know, never.'

'Does it have any other sources?'

'Not as far as we can see. Two chemists way back in '68 first reported it in the air. They wrote a paper showing that car exhausts give off over 180 separate chemicals. It's just one of them. Many of them are actually quite simple – hydrocarbons – ethylene and so on.'

'So it's not lead or anything!'

'No. Just a product of burning ordinary common-or-garden petrol.'

'But people in cities have been breathing it for years!'

'Exactly. You see, the brain changes are very chronic, very long term. They've been developing for years. Nobody's immune. I was doing a P-M on a kiddy of four the other day, his brain already showed change.'

'Christ!' Mawn exclaimed.

'Quite so. Brain tissue is very sensitive – particularly in the young. Actually, we've got plenty of redundant brain cells – maybe we never use them. But this acetylide, it seems to have some sort of affinity for fat, the special fats in the brain. Probably what happens is that city folk breathe it in over the years, it dissolves in the brain fats and then starts picking off brain cells over the years, one by one. Eventually, the net reserve of cells is reduced to a level where intelligence, behaviour and so on begin to be affected.'

'Self-induced idiocy from the motor car!' Mawn spoke as he walked over to a computer terminal and began punching instructions on the keys.

'What're you doing?'

'Running a frequency scan – on jobs.' He stopped hitting the keys. There was a moment's pause, then yellow digits began to tumble down the screen, finally settling to indicate a vertical row of numbers from one to ten. By the side of each number was the printed name of an occupation.

Mawn pointed at the names: 'Fits very well with what you've found. What I told the machine to do was to extract the occupations of affected people and then put them up in order of frequency. In other words, which jobs recur most often among the affected people.' He ran his finger down the screen.

'One – taxi drivers, two – traffic wardens, three – road sweepers, four – policemen with a long record of street work. It fits!'

Kingston continued: 'I said just now, it only comes from the combustion of petrol, but we can't in fact be a hundred per cent certain that the chemical is *only* a product of the internal combustion engine. There are so many new industrial processes – nobody has the slightest idea what half of them push out into the air. It could just be that one of them was producing it.'

'The same industrial process in *all* the cities of the world. That's unlikely, surely?' Mawn asked.

'I agree it's unlikely. But if it *is* petrol – my God! the implications are absolutely staggering.'

Mawn began pacing: 'We've got to be sure, that's all – we've got to be damn sure!'

'Logically, the first thing to do – and I've already set this in motion – is to take blood samples from city people and try and isolate the substance from the living.'

'And if you find it in city people's blood and not in country people?'

'Then the next step,' Kingston continued, 'would be to take a sample population – say fifty or so. Measure their blood level while they're in the city and then send them into a rural area . .'

'And see if their blood level goes down!'

'Exactly. But that still doesn't indict the motor car completely.'

'I tell you one thing that would,' Mawn continued excitedly. 'If we find this acetylide compound in the air – presuming it's a volatile . . .'

'The petro-chemists seem to think it is.'

'. . . Right. If we find it in the air and we are not absolutely sure that it's the internal combustion engine which is producing it. Then it's perfectly obvious what we have to do!'

Kingston looked at him: 'I can't stand the suspense.'

'I've got to persuade Baxter to take cars out of London – to see if the level goes down. See if it disappears.'

'How long for?'

'I don't know yet. Several days for certain. We'll need to get baselines. There'll obviously be complications – ambulances and police cars will have to run. If there's a wind there'll be contamination from other cities – but it should give us the answer. If we keep cars out of London and the acetylide level drops and if your city people lose their blood level when they go to the country – yes, that'll be enough – just enough.'

Kingston looked at Mawn over his half glasses then he began to laugh: 'My God, laddie, you're going to be popular!'

The taxi was inextricably wedged in a dense tangle of fuming stationary traffic. Ahead, a huge articulated lorry was belching a grey-blue cloud from its exhaust. A policeman trapped on a traffic island with his arms by his side looked around helplessly. Mawn glanced at his watch, paid off the driver and guided

Marcia between the shining bonnets to the pavement.

They walked quickly through Scotland Yard and on into Whitehall. Again the traffic was stationary, bumper to bumper.

In the Minister's ante-room Marcia was recovering from a helpless fit of coughing. 'It's the worst I can remember.' She coughed again. 'Good propaganda. I must remember to cough in his face.'

Lodge took them both through into the meeting room. After the formal greetings and enquiries, he turned to Mawn: 'How's the Doomsday report?'

'Two or three weeks at most,' Mawn replied.

'Splendid,' Lodge smiled. 'Poor Baxter is being hit from all sides, from the Prime Minister to the *Daily Mirror*. There's always something reassuring about a quick White Paper don't you think?'

Mawn glanced at him sharply: 'Whether it's reassuring or not depends very much on you people.'

Before Lodge could reply the Minister swept into the room followed by his aide, Bordheim and a new scientific adviser. Baxter went through the preliminaries with a terse lack of ceremony, finally turning to Mawn.

'When will your first draft be complete?'

'We've reached a problem area, I'm afraid,' Mawn replied.

'Oh!'

'We need to carry out a much more rigorous test.'

'What kind? You can hardly expect more extensive facilities, than you already have!' Baxter's voice was sharp and Marcia noticed his eyes were red-rimmed, his complexion showing the uneven pallor of prolonged overwork and pressure.

'If I can just summarize our current thinking,' Mawn continued. 'Much of the evidence singles out a hydro-carbon released by . . .'

'Yes, yes, I know all about that.' The Minister cut in irritably. 'I'm not entirely unaware of what goes on. A substance from the motor car exhaust you're saying.'

'The evidence correlates very well with the medical findings, so we need to complete the logical proof. As you know . . .' Mawn continued, '. . . there are over 180 compounds released by the internal combustion engine, some only when the choke is used – I have the reference here: Sanders and Maynard in the journal of Analytical Chemistry in . . .'

Baxter gestured angrily: 'Please, if you wouldn't mind just keeping to essentials.'

Mawn controlled his irritation: 'Right. Basically, then, we need to find out whether this particular compound is directly and solely responsible and this will naturally take some months or even years of quite concentrated research.'

'Years?' Baxter frowned.

'Several years. And should we be successful it may well take as long again for the fuel industry to devise means of removing the substance from petrol.'

The Minister looked over at Dr Kenny, his new scientific adviser.

'True. That sort of work can't be forced along too quickly.' Dr Kenny was young, open-faced and unafraid to speak his mind.

Baxter looked around the table, seeking support. His face was haggard: 'But this just isn't going to work. If this – material *is* the root cause, then the brain damage is going to continue. There'll be thousands of new cases. We must do something more immediate. We've already had the first reading of the Bill on exhaust converters. Lead content is seventy per cent down on the 1970 level. Surely we can develop effective new legislation.'

Mawn caught Bordheim's eyes levelled on his. The lids lowered a fraction, waiting.

'Minister, with respect, there is one way of immediately solving the problem – to stop the use of the motor car.'

Baxter smiled thinly: 'And throw the country into a complete state of economic confusion. We will have to be a lot more practical than that. To begin with, it would probably treble the unemployment rate . . .'

Mawn persisted: 'You haven't understood what I said, sir. I am asking you to agree to a removal of all motor vehicles from London for a period of three to four days so that we can measure atmospheric levels of the acetylide.'

The silence creaked. Baxter stared at Mawn incredulously: 'Four days – London?'

'The best time would be over the Easter holiday in ten days.'

'It's completely out of the question,' Baxter exploded. 'In any case wouldn't another city – a smaller one – do?'

'No. All our previous baseline values have been carried out here, in London. Were we to start somewhere else, we would be very considerably delayed.'

Baxter jerked to his feet and walked over to the long bay window. 'We simply haven't got the powers, it's just not possible!'

Mawn drew out a paper from the file. 'As a matter of fact you have. Under the Emergency Powers Act 1975 sub-section four . . .'

Baxter swung round: 'But that's in the event of a nuclear attack man!'

'It also covers,' he read; 'Any other contingency that is deemed to be on the scale of a national disaster.'

'For God's sake – you can't call this a national emergency!'

'With hundreds of square miles of Scotland probably uninhabitable for a generation!' Mawn rapped out. 'What else do you want? I'm sorry, but my colleagues and I see this test as crucially important. It can short circuit years of a more pedestrian enquiry. We do not feel able to publish without it.'

'Then you'll have failed to meet the brief given you by the Government,' Baxter retorted.

'I don't see it like that, and neither will the public. It could well be their view that I have been prevented from doing my job. There is, of course, another alternative. The Americans have already made it perfectly clear that they will shortly be doing a test on one of their own cities. Naturally, they haven't got my own data, but I should feel bound to let them have it, if they are able to go ahead before we do.'

Bordheim studied Mawn appreciatively.

'Of course, you realize you are now bound by the Official Secrets Act.' The fair-haired aide did his best to sound authoritative. 'Any such act would be taken very seriously, I'm afraid.'

'Good God!' Mawn burst out. 'This is nothing whatever

do with nationalities or secrets. Secrets are simply a device for protecting the incompetent. We've got a major human tragedy staring us in the face – one which is probably going to have a permanent effect on the way we live in future and you suggest that it should be pursued in secrecy!' He gestured angrily. 'Bordheim has already told me about the piddling bureaucratic mess he has had to contend with in Paris. He's been continually surrounded by vested interest, jealousies, deliberate attempts to suppress information. Unless I can pursue this enquiry right out in the open with no strings and no interference, I'd rather not do it at all. From your point of view, there's a chance to take an enormous swipe at one of the biggest problems we face.

'You all know perfectly well that the writing is on the wall for the motor car. Right back in the early seventies the Leach Report for OECD showed perfectly clearly that the car's demand for oil and petrol will far outstrip supply before the end of this century. And now we find that just ordinary petrol – not lead or carbon monoxide or any other shit the things push out – just petrol, may well have changed the whole of human evolution.

'We now have a generation of the relatively incompetent. The whole of our race is now populated by an entirely new species – *homo non sapiens*. I tell you – we've got a unique opportunity to do something and we've got to use it!'

Baxter walked slowly back to his chair at the head of the table; the aide met Mawn's gaze and then dropped his eyes.

Bordheim cleared his throat. 'It will be difficult to decide how much information you will gather by such an experiment. To me, it is of great promise. I think it should be made possible even if it should prove negative. There will be no harm in it.'

Baxter had calmed: 'But Dr Bordheim, you and Dr Mawn are in a privileged position as scientists. You only have to consider the need for experiment. If such a test happens and we take cars out of London – I shall have every lobby in the country down on my neck. Business will suffer, the tourist bureau – everyone – will find their own reason for objection. Many firms work over Easter – the Trades Unions will accuse us of all manner of sins.' He turned to Mawn. 'Should it be found possible to mount this test, you may wake up on the Tuesday to find yourself the most unpopular man in the British Isles. And that may well destroy your credibility once again.' The Minister looked across at Mawn – there was an element of threat in his tone. 'I will raise the matter at the Cabinet meeting this afternoon, but in the meantime I urge you to re-examine the whole idea with your colleagues and decide fully and clearly whether you can find an alternative method.' He rose to go, turning to his aide: 'I believe that's all?'

Later, in the secluded bar of a basement wine house near the Embankment, Lodge spelt out the Cabinet conclusion to Mawn, Marcia and Bordheim.

'In a nutshell, the word is that they will lay on the test if you are convinced there's no alternative. Baxter's had a word with the PM on the phone while you were out. To be honest I don't think they dare stop you now. Not with three by-elections pending and a working majority of twelve. But, I'm afraid you've created a considerable amount of hostility. To be frank, you have them by the short hairs but they won't let you off if you're wrong.'

Mawn lowered his pint glass wearily. 'There's nothing else I can do.' Lodge looked at him speculatively: 'Perhaps not, but there are ways of doing things – a word to me first!'

Mawn looked across at the older man: 'I'm sorry, Richard.'

'Never mind, the damage is done. So – message is, go ahead if you must, but any come-back, and believe me there may well be a massive backlash, will be laid squarely at your door. Now, I must be off.' He finished a gin and tonic and rose to go. Marcia grasped his arm:

'Richard, what could we have done?'

The tall, slightly-stooped man looked down at her: 'Civil servants aren't really allowed to have personal advice to give,' Lodge smiled.

'Please?'

'Well, I really can't say, it's a tremendous gamble isn't it? If it comes off and people actually enjoy walking about empty streets and you get some spectacular results out from it – then it could make your case, I suppose!'

'Or?'

'Or, if it rains all weekend, as it normally does, businesses lose money, people's pleasure is seriously disrupted, the test does not work out, then it could be as the Minister said.' He turned to Bordheim: 'What do you think, Max?'

'Well, yes I think you're right, Richard. It could be a very short way to the truth. But if it does not give us what we need, then the people will say: we gave this environmentalist full powers and look what he did. They will never again trust the environmentalist. They will just say he is an incompetent and not to be trusted.' He looked at Mawn: 'It is a big decision. I am glad it is not myself who has to make it!'

As the taxi rattled through the dark streets, Marcia put her hand over Mawn's but there was no response. He sat hunched in his overcoat on the far side of the seat staring out of the window.

She began to think out the details of her flight back to America on the following morning. The doctors had been severe, telling her that she should stop trying to meet the relentless schedule demanded by Mawn. She had an acute bronchitis, they had said, and her normal body defence mechanisms were failing to respond because of her still-diminished white blood cell count. She could see her reflection in the glass partition of the cab in front of her. She decided ruefully it was quite a dramatic image. Large dark eyes set in a pale taut face.

She took her hand away. Mawn made no response. She began to long for the trip. To get away. He had long since ceased to react to her as a person. Even the research they had previously enjoyed together had taken second place to the driving need to complete his work at St Olaf's. She had simply become an adjunct as he sat in his office, drawing, calculating and planning. There had been no time for any quiet periods alone. He had become increasingly short-tempered and was already falling into the trap of being unable to delegate. Every single point raised by an already grossly overworked team around him had to be personally brought for his approval. She began to worry whether he would break under the strain and realized, with a shock, that she wasn't sure if she would mind much if he did.

She pictured the long lawns leading down to the lake at her father's Long Island home. Her room looking out over the maple copse. All the nightmare would soon be behind her and life would soon return to a relaxed and tidy predictability.

Even the flat had ceased to be a refuge. From the moment they got in, he would begin dictating an endless flow of memoranda into a tape machine, often pacing the floor into the small hours of the morning. She felt totally confused. One moment the idea of a shared future seemed the most exciting thing in the world, the next made it seem too demanding and lacking in affection.

Harland Scott was waiting in the flat as they came in. He took one look at his daughter and immediately went to the phone, cancelling an arrangement he had made to attend a function at the American Embassy. Then he rang the restaurant on the ground floor and ordered a meal to be sent up.

While Marcia bathed, Mawn gave the older man a condensed account of the day's activities. Scott was friendly but noncommittal and the conversation soon drifted into an uninvolved scenario session on the long term effects of the brainrack.

After the meal, the three sat quietly stretched out in the low armchairs. Scott toyed with a cigar.

'Frankly, I would never have believed you could have gotten so far, I really got to hand it to you. Sometimes I feel I've spent a lifetime trying to dodge the time servers – you've accomplished a hell of a lot, it certainly justifies the money.'

Mawn sensed a warning behind the praise. 'Thanks.'

'You're doing the work! It makes me feel tired just sitting around watching.'

Marcia leaned over and held her father's hand: 'You know Dad told me I was getting mellow and gracious when he came over last year; which I figured was an insult.'

Scott squeezed her hand: 'Which I guess it was in terms of the dough I blew on your education. OK I take it back. If you feel like moving out of this country – I guess Bordheim isn't going to last for ever. I'm convinced you could make a hell of a lot more of his job – with the backing you've got now.' He stood up, looking down at Mawn. He seemed about to place his hand on Mawn's shoulder, then drew back. Mawn could feel Marcia's body nestling in against his.

'You've a big decision and I'm glad I'm not making it, but there are maybe a few other factors you haven't thought through yet.' Mawn looked up. 'You're taking out pretty severe odds on your experiment – you're going to have to shoulder the responsibility for immobilizing this whole city.'

'Not entirely,' Mawn protested. 'Electric trains – the tube, they'll all be running.'

'OK. But you're going to have every amateur environmentalist – all the eco-freaks – jumping on your bandwagon.' Scott poured another brandy and sniffed the glass before continuing. 'Let's assume your experiment is a good one. OK, so all the nuts get together and say, "let's completely ban the automobile", you'll get all the extremists, all the twentieth-century Luddites wandering around with sledge-hammers. Now I happen to think folks will fight like the devil to keep their autos. Take some little guy who's just saved enough money to buy his first jalopy. He's going to be mad as hell. He's going to come to you and say, what about the rich guys, they've all had their cars, now I can afford one you're going to tell me I can't have it!'

'OK. But suppose we do prove it's the automobile, something has to be done,' Marcia interjected. 'What?'

Scott spread his arms: 'The civilized way. We live in a democracy – carefully phased legislation, time to let the industry adapt. Time to develop alternative power sources – Stirling engines, alternative fuels, that kind of thing.'

Mawn's voice tightened: 'How long will that all take?'

'I can't be sure,' Scott continued, 'but industry's got to have a reasonable chance . . .'

'How long? Ten years? Seven? Five? Could it take less than five years?'

'I guess about that.'

'Five years while the industry finds out how to be reasonable! And meanwhile we go on producing wrecked brains!'

Marcia drew away at the tone of Mawn's voice.

'Hey, don't shoot the pianist,' Scott smiled.

Mawn sat forward: 'Can I ask you a straight question?'

'Go right ahead.'

'How much of your income comes from the car industry?'

Harland nodded easily: 'Quite a large slice, OK?'

'And it would take time to extract your money and invest it somewhere else?'

'I guess so.'

'So a prolonged legislation would suit your book better?'

'I've just said so.' Scott's eyes were watchful.

'And if I go too quickly, my fund dries up?'

'Alex!' Marcia drew away from him.

Scott shrugged: 'I don't recollect saying that!'

'So any decision I take won't affect the fund?'

Scott shook his head: 'Not as far as I'm concerned. I wouldn't be able to speak for any other sponsor though – especially if you start to try and force this kind of arbitrary decision on them.' He rose to his feet. 'I've got to get back – it's been a long day.' He looked over at Marcia: 'And our flight's at a God-awful hour. Don't get up, I'll find my own way out.'

At the door he turned to Marcia again: 'See you at the terminal, honey.' He nodded at Mawn: 'Be seeing you. Keep at it.' There was an ironic ring to his voice which lingered long after the door had closed. Mawn waited for the storm. But instead she wearily looked round the flat and said: 'Let's leave clearing till the morning. Mrs Best will be coming anyway.'

Later, in the darkness of the bedroom, Marcia's voice was matter-of-fact: 'You were goddamn rude to my father.'

'Yes, I suppose I was.'

'He's worked like a bat to get the fund going for you. Then you go and spit in his eye.'

'Would it help if I wrote him an apology?'

Marcia edged away from him: 'Don't be sarcastic. He was hurt a little.'

'He'll be OK.'

'No, it's you I'm worried about.'

'Oh, yes?'

'I know you're having to push everyone to get the report out – I know all that.'

'Marcia, please, I'm tired, what are you getting at?'

'You're turning into a complete obsessional. It'll affect your judgement.'

'Do you always do your analysis in bed?'

'Please, listen to me?'

'I'm listening all right!'

She paused: 'Have you decided to go ahead with the test?'

'I've another day and a bit yet.'

'Even after all you've heard. The minister, Bordheim, Richard Lodge, my father?'

He sat up on his elbow: 'And that's making you doubt it?'

'OK. I'm frightened,' Marcia replied. 'It's too – I don't know – extreme! You've won all the public goodwill you need, now you may be going to blow it all for one experiment.'

'Which you thought essential.'

'I'm not so sure now, Alex. Why London? It could be another city. There's time.'

'No, there isn't. We can prove the experiment in the same time, surely? But, it won't have the same impact,' Mawn said.

'Impact!' She sat up in bed abruptly. 'So dad was right, it isn't just an experiment – you're setting up a political ploy!'

'Both, probably.'

'Alex, for God's sake, you're not a politician – you're a scientist. You could ruin everything.' She pulled him towards her but he dragged away, his voice rough: 'All right, what about you? Are you quite sure you aren't scared that some of your father's loot isn't going to get lost? You might even have to give up a few thousand dollars of your allowance.

'No, you'd better get this straight. If I decide to go on with this and if the money dries up because people like your father are scared off, so much the better! We're going to have a massive, honest experiment that people will never forget. And it's not going to be in five years when your father gets even richer at the expense of some other polluting industry – it's going to be in ten days' time . . .'

The bedroom light glared, blinding him. She was already by

the door, white faced and shaking. 'Save it! Save it for your damn lousy public.' The tears were streaming down her cheeks. 'Nothing will stop the great Alex Mawn will it? Alexander the Great – saviour of the world. There's no point in talking to you is there? You don't give a damn about anyone else and you never will.' The door slammed behind her.

Mawn dropped back on the pillow, his thoughts racing. First there was rage at her attack, almost immediately giving way to a shuddering sense of isolation. Each person he knew seemed to be withdrawing. He got out of bed to follow her but a sense of shame at his outburst prevented him. This time he had really gone too far. He started to feel an aching sense of loss and desolation but he pushed it to the back of his mind and climbed back into bed. It was a long time before he slept.

In one dream, he was wandering, full of anxiety, through a deserted city street. A steady driving wind blew papers along the pavement. The roadway was full of debris and curled up in the gutter a figure dressed in dirty rags looked up resentfully as he passed by. It was a grotesquely transformed Marcia. Her face was the face of an old hag and her mouth twisted in an idiot, drooling grin.

The next morning he made several clumsy attempts to break through to her but he was completely out of his depth. He felt totally inept and was almost glad when she insisted he did not take her to the air terminal. He had a vague memory of a brush of cold lips and she was gone.

Eighteen

The atmosphere of the empty flat pressed in on Mawn intolerably. Each sign of her presence was an ache. He forced himself to work, but as he began to arrange the detailed plans of the test, his mind began to rebel.

Just how essential was it? How much was he deluding himself. Was it just to the greater glory of Alex Mawn? Could there be other ways of measuring the necessary atmospheric levels. Gradually the idea built up in his mind that what he had done was merely an attempt to realize a fantasy of his own. To see the city emptied of cars, to see it return to dignified human occupation and to banish the ugly cacophony of the traffic for ever.

He spent hours on the telephone ringing expert colleagues to try and settle his doubts. Jimmy Kingston was at his most friendly and pompous: 'My advice, dear boy, is to go right ahead. Don't let anyone deter you. Perfectly splendid notion.' The words seemed particularly empty and non-committal.

Holden: an elderly biochemist and one of his own teachers was next. His reply was typically guarded, careful to give approval to the need for proper measurement, but equally careful not to commit himself to the scale of the enterprise. He had finished by doubting the long term effects.

Again and again, he received only general support. Some were even openly hostile to the idea and no one seemed able to furnish him with the specific and expert support he so urgently needed. When he put the phone down for the last time, his mind was whirling and no nearer the final decision.

He began to compare the pros and cons of the test in separate columns on a sheet of paper. The result seemed overwhelmingly in favour of the test, but the nagging self-doubt remained unrelieved.

For the rest of the day he wandered morosely round the flat, picking at food. By the time the light began to fade in the big picture window of the living-room, he had drunk over half a bottle of brandy and instead of relieving his tension, it merely blunted his ability to think clearly.

When the phone rang, he violently resented its jangling intrusion. Her voice was distorted by the distance: 'Alex, it's me, yes. I'm at Kennedy. My father's waiting to ship me down to Florida.'

His depression lifted almost instantaneously. He couldn't find words: 'How are you?' Then inconsequentially: 'What's the weather like there?'

'Very cold! Alex,' her voice was hesitant: 'I flunked out, I'm sorry. I just felt I couldn't reach you.'

The brandy made his lips clumsy: 'Marcia, for God's sake. I'm the one to apologize. Everything you said was dead on target.'

'Alex, come over – I must see you. Can't you take a few days off?'

'Now!'

'Yes, come down south with me.'

'Marcia, I can't. It's all brewing up. I can't leave now, you know I can't.' He paused.

'Alex – are you still there, Alex?'

'Yes, I'm here.' He yearned to hold her. 'Put it down to this brandy if you like but I want you back. Can't you come back. I want you very badly.'

'Likewise. But you can't come over – that's final?'

'You know I can't. Not right now.'

'Alex, my father's got a whole posse of doctors waiting to check me out. I don't know yet – my chest is bad. I guess I need some sun. Have you decided yet?' Her voice changed slightly, became more distant, he had to strain to hear.

'No, I haven't.'

'What did Jimmy say?'

'Oh, he's in favour, but he doesn't really want to know. Nobody seems to be able to come right out and say, yes, go ahead, it's right.'

'Alex, honey. Believe me, I wanted to help but I didn't know how. You shut me out.'

'Hell! I'm not very easy about these things.'

'I've got to go. Take care, Alex.' Her voice faded again. 'I'll ring again when I get to Florida, I promise.'

'Yes, please ring. Look after yourself. Get well soon.'

'You bet. Goodbye, Alex.' He wondered, dully, whether he would ever see her again, poured out another measure of brandy and then, with sudden revulsion, flung it away from him.

During the night he suffered a succession of dreams. They all had to do with running, but being unable to move.

He awoke to the sound of someone shouting. Stumbling round the bedroom, his pyjamas soaked in a cold sweat, he finally convinced himself it must have been his own voice. He looked at the clock – 8.30 – three hours to go! Three hours to decide.

The fluctuating whine of a vacuum cleaner filtered through from the living-room. He remembered the cleaner, Mrs Best. Over the sound he could just make out the chirruping of her five-year-old-son Robert.

He slipped on a dressing-gown, had a quick disgusted look in the mirror at his pouched haggard face and went in.

She was shuffling around the living-room, thrusting the cleaner at the furniture as if it was a weapon of attack. She beamed at him over the noise.

Robert was sitting curled upon the settee trying to fit the pieces of a simple jigsaw together. Mawn sat down beside him and watched. It was an abstract concentric pattern of colours, resembling a mandala. The boy was holding one piece in his hand searching for its place in the half-completed puzzle. Mawn picked up the box and studied the picture of the completed pattern on the lid. The separate pieces were cut in simple geometric shapes and some were inter-changeable in their position. Robert had made several mistakes, particularly with colours.

He glanced up and saw Mrs Best looking at him apprehensively. She switched off the cleaner: 'Don't seem to be no good at that – can't get the hang of it, he can't. Enjoys it though, keeps him occupied.'

'Is he all right at school?'

'You mean is he like all those people you been writing about in the papers? This brainrack thing!'

'Are you going to take him along to the clinic for testing?'

'Like they said on the telly? Yes, I suppose so – don't know what good it'd do!'

'Mrs Best, where do you live?'

She looked at him blankly.

'Do you live near a main road?'

'Wouldn't call it living. Used to be nice and quiet one time. Then they built that great flyover thing. Don't never stop now. All hours it is. Bleeding great lorries come banging by. Hardly worth living but what can you do – the council don't want to know.'

'How long has the flyover been up?'

'Five years it's been now.' She turned back to the cleaner.

'Please, Mrs Best, could I ask you something? Have you – are you going to do anything about Robert?'

'What can you do? You don't think he's going to grow up backward do you?' Her face held an expression of dumb sadness.

'Suppose there was a chance of putting things right, Mrs Best. Suppose we banned all the cars, lorries and buses. Took them off that flyover?'

'No buses? How'd I get to work? It's a mile or more to the tube!'

'Suppose we tried it over Easter. So you could have some peace and quiet for once. No fumes, no noise.'

'I work over Easter. How would I get in?'

'It wouldn't be easy. But if it helped to make Robert better? Could you get used to it?'

She pushed a straggling lock of grey hair back off her forehead: 'Get used to it in the end I suppose.'

'Would you resent it?'

'Dunno.' She jerked her thumb at Robert. 'If it would help him, wouldn't have no option, would we?'

'So you think it might be necessary?'

She looked puzzled. 'I thought you said it'd make him better, stopping the traffic and all.'

'Yes.'

'Then what are you on about? You'll have to do it, won't you? Not that you'd get them politicians to agree.'

'How do you mean?'

'Well they're never in a bleeding hurry are they? I mean they never more than half do a job. Mind you, my old man's just got us an old Morris, just about goes. He'll have a few words to say to you if you stop 'im using it. But if it's for Robert he'll just have to lump it won't he? Like we all will.'

Mawn reached into his wallet and took out two notes and gave them to her: 'Look, this is for an Easter present if you like.'

'Oh, yes!' She looked startled. 'What for? Miss Scott pays me wages. You don't owe me nothing.'

Mawn got to his feet. 'Oh, yes I do. Now, will you take Robert through into the kitchen for a bit. I've got an important phone call to make.'

He gave Lodge his decision.

'What finally made up your mind, Alex?' Lodge asked.

'A lady called Mrs Best. I don't think you've met her!'

As soon as the test was publicly announced an avalanche of reaction began. Professional media experts managed to prove that it was an event for which they had been campaigning for years. Car manufacturers made perfunctory objections and one, in a fit of pique, said that the car was being pilloried for no proven cause. Business chiefs showed how it would affect transport and how many thousands of pounds they would certainly lose, even though the test was to be carried out over a public holiday.

Students held open air parties to celebrate the occasion and a 'Roast an Ox in Oxford Street' party was organized. Even the Archbishop of Canterbury blessed the occasion.

For Mawn, the ten days leading up to the test were crammed with activity. There were conferences with transport chiefs, hospital officials and the police. No one representative seemed able or willing to integrate his own activities with those of his colleagues. He was continually hounded by the media and had in the end to set up a small press office.

There were union representatives and other scientists. There were even threats. Letters accused him of being alternatively a communist saboteur and an enemy of the working man. One even described him as the alien vanguard of a Venusian invasion. A dubious ray of comfort was provided by the Lord's Day Observance Society who opined that for the first time,

Easter Sunday would be properly celebrated as a day of rest.

Bicycle manufacturers organized a miniature 'Tour de France' race through the deserted city streets.

For the purposes of the test itself, the Greater London area was divided into one hundred arbitrary zones. In each, a small testing unit was assembled, where air samples were to be pumped into containers and taken by electric cars or on foot to the nearest laboratory capable of performing the analysis. From each laboratory, results were phoned to the waiting computer in Mawn's converted ward at St Olaf's Hospital.

Police had already begun to erect check points on all the major exit and entry routes to the capital and warnings appeared regularly in all media. The public were asked for their full collaboration and told that the Emergency Powers Act provided severe penalties for those who disobeyed the ban on driving. Car owners were told not to start their engines for any purpose. All garage repair shops and factories using petrol engines received a similar warning.

The public gradually accepted the idea that they were involved in a great and probably historic event which they would never forget. It was as if they were seeing, for the first time, a real possibility of relief from the stresses imposed on them by city traffic. As the first day of the test approached, people began to plan their Easter holiday without the family cars. For two days beforehand, trains out of London were packed with crowds leaving the city for relatives in the country. One telecast speculated that the city population had temporarily fallen by over a quarter.

Housewives who remained behind began to stock up with food almost as if they were back in the days of wartime siege.

The managers of the London Underground sweated over route maps to provide extra trains. It was already clear that they would not be able to absorb the extra passenger load and a special appeal was made for travellers to stay away from the subway unless their journey was essential.

On the evening of the Thursday before Easter the great exodus began. Every route out of the city gradually blocked solid with mile long lines of traffic as tired commuters jostled with each other to get out of the centre before their vehicles became immobilized.

The rush hours normally stretching between five and seven o'clock stretched on into the night. By ten o'clock jams were still present, particularly on the north-eastern exit routes leading into Essex and it was long after midnight before the streets began to fall silent. By two o'clock in the morning, a fine rain had started to fall as if nature was trying to wash the great metropolis free of the contamination.

The deadline set for the start of the test was eight a.m. on Good Friday.

By six a.m. Mawn's technicians had taken up their positions, having arrived in specially-equipped vans the day before. Now their equipment was being laid out in readiness for the collection of the first air samples.

As eight a.m. came and went, residents, long conditioned to the background roar of the early morning rush hour traffic, began to venture out into the streets, peering around fearfully, as if something essential to their feelings of security had been removed.

By eight-thirty, Mawn had completed all necessary checks on his equipment. The floor of the converted ward where he sat was covered by an interwoven network of hastily installed cables inter-connecting banks of computing equipment. Along one side of the room, a temporary telephone switchboard had been installed and three operators sat ready to receive the first measurements as they were phoned in by the laboratories.

Television cameras from the three major networks had been set up in one small corner of the ward from which to scan the scene, and were already relaying minute by minute coverage to the studios.

Mawn sat with his staff in front of a read-out screen impatiently waiting for the first results to appear. He thought that the room looked more like a studio rigged to show the results of a general election than a scientific test. The last encounter with the media had been a nationwide flop – this one could end up in a worldwide debacle.

There were satellite relays for viewers in countries ranging from the USA to Japan. He wondered if Marcia would be tuned in. There had been no further word from her since she had phoned from New York.

It had been arranged that samples were to be taken from each one of the selected measuring points on the hour, every hour, to enable Mawn and his colleagues to plot the atmospheric levels of the suspected acetylide on a series of graphs. The slope of the lines on the graphs would show a steady downward trend if the acetylide came from the car.

By 20.00 on Good Friday the results were almost totally confused. In some areas, there had been a drop in the atmospheric levels of the acetylide, but in others the level had remained the same and in six zones measurements showed that there had been a slight but definite rise.

The effect on Mawn was catastrophic. He had in his mind allowed for the possibility that the test might prove inconclusive, but that some levels were rising was almost impossible for him to bear.

For hours on end he sat furiously discussing possible causes for the increase. Nobody seemed able to suggest feasible cause. No cars were running, there was practically no wind to bring in contaminated air from other towns near to London and yet the levels were steadily rising.

By the early hours of Saturday morning, he sat haggard and red-eyed in front of the read-out screens as the measurements continued to build up, damning his thesis.

By six a.m. there was an apparent halt in the rise, but by ten a.m. twenty-three areas showed a continuous and definite rise. The test was failing.

At eleven a.m. Campbell Baxter and Richard Lodge walked over the river from Whitehall to the St Olaf's headquarters. Mawn scarcely seemed to notice their arrival as they went slowly over to the read-out terminals and watched gravely as the digits flashed over the screens. It was Lodge who broke the embarrassed silence.

'There must be another source, Alex!'

Baxter exchanged a glance with Lodge at the sight of a three-quarters empty brandy bottle standing on a pile of papers. Mawn shook his head irritably: 'Not a chance. It's directly related to the combustion of petrol. There is no other source.'

'I don't understand it,' Baxter began. 'I don't understand it at all. I really cannot begin to describe the consequences if this goes wrong. We would become an absolute laughing stock if it fails.'

Mawn stood up. 'We've got a change – all right, I haven't got any idea what it's due to. Just give me time.'

'You've only two more days,' Lodge said calmly.

Mawn turned to Baxter: 'I may have to extend the test period.'

'It's quite out of the question,' Baxter replied. 'It would be impossible to arrange. We're under quite enough pressure already. You'll have to complete it in the allotted time.'

Mawn's hand shook as he steadied himself. 'But it may take longer to find out why it's gone up. You can't force a conclusion if we haven't got the information.'

'I'm sorry,' Baxter replied curtly, 'but you have just three days to get it. I can keep public comment at bay for that long but after that I'm afraid you'll have to answer for the consequences.'

'Couldn't there be some other factor involved?' Lodge asked. 'After all, there's been some rain.'

Baxter gestured impatiently: 'Richard, even a layman could see that rain tends to clear the air, not increase levels.'

'Well, it's considerably warmer today,' Lodge continued, lamely.

'Warmer!' Mawn gripped the edge of the desk. He appeared to be talking to himself. 'Warmer – yes it is – it's warmer.' He brushed past the two men and strode over to a man seated in front of a weather chart: 'What was the mid-day temperature yesterday?'

The man looked up, startled at the interruption, then picked a paper off the desk: 'It was – let's see – fifty-nine – yes fifty-nine degrees.'

'What is it now?'

The man sifted through the paper nervously: 'It's – gone up a lot – almost ten degrees. Last reading came in an hour ago – yes, sixty-eight at ten a.m.

'That's warm for Easter,' Lodge said.

'Of course!' Mawn exclaimed excitedly. 'It could just be that the acetylide has absorbed on to surfaces – roads and buildings and so on. Now the warm air is driving it off in vapour – it's quite volatile. If it came off in vapour, then the atmospheric levels *would* rise.'

'And then if you're right about the car being the origin,' Lodge intervened, 'it should eventually come off in vapour form and . . .'

'. . . and disperse!' Mawn exclaimed. 'Yes, if that's right, and the car is producing it, then the level should rise to a peak and then begin to fall.'

He walked quickly over to the telephone switchboard. Once he was out of earshot, Baxter turned to Lodge: 'The man's in a shocking state. Can't you talk to him? He'll collapse if he goes on like that. Get him to rest.'

'He wouldn't listen for a moment,' Lodge began and then hesitated, 'matter of fact there is something I could try. I'll make a phone call back at my office.'

Over the following twenty-four hours, the levels of acetylide fluctuated unevenly. Television stations kept open with special late programmes and bookmakers raked in small fortunes by offering extended odds on the result.

By the middle of the afternoon of Easter Sunday, all levels seemed to be stabilizing, but no downward trends could be seen.

By six in the evening, Mawn gave way. In his mind he saw the whole edifice of his attempt to identify the brainrack poison crumbling around him. He took one last look at the folded pile of computer paper, desperately searching for some clue, some small indication of a change. There was none. Finally, the combined effects of two nights without sleep, little food and brandy gripped hold of him and he fell forward on the desk and slept.

There was a confused jumble of voices. Someone in the background was laughing, there was a clink of glasses. Somebody else was violently shaking his shoulder. He opened his eyes. Lodge was leaning over him brandishing a sheaf of computer readings, his face flushed. 'Extraordinary time to fall asleep!'

Mawn shook his head slowly forcing his mind to concentrate. 'What, what's happened?'

Lodge threw the paper down on the desk: 'You've been flat out for over five hours. Look at them, Alex. Look at them!' Someone forced a glass into his hand. 'They're coming down Alex – don't you see – the levels are falling, every single one.' A technician pounded his back: 'You've won man, you've won!'

Mawn woke early on the Monday morning. For some time he lay back thinking over the long weeks of stress. His body felt entirely different. Even the stiffness from the hard bench he had been lying on now seemed unimportant. The computer room was in total disorder. The floor was covered in crumpled piles of read-out paper and there were empty bottles strewn all over the metal instrument cases. Three technicians were still at work taking in the results of the night's air samples, but one glance at the numerals still flicking up on the read-out screen told him that the levels had maintained their downward trend overnight.

Quietly he told one of the technicians that he was going to walk to the sampling post in Piccadilly Circus. Once out in the street, the whole ambience of the city had altered.

The air was magically clean and the sun was already warm on his face as he walked slowly over the bridge towards Whitehall. The waters of the Thames glinted and sparkled and there was almost complete silence. With a great surge of pleasure he realized that the loudest sound he could hear was that of his own feet on the pavement. He paused, leaning over the balustrade. Below in the water, two men were hoisting the sail of a small dinghy. He waved his hand at them and they waved back smiling.

In Parliament Square, people were already pouring up through the exit from the underground. He smiled as one old man set his dog down on the pavement and released the lead, letting the dog run free, yelping with excitement, into the middle of the road.

In Whitehall a solitary Horseguard sat on horseback, already surrounded by tourists with cameras, his brass cuirasse reflecting brightly in the sun. A flower seller was already setting up a stall at the entrance to Trafalgar Square and, as he paused, Mawn was immediately aware of the scent of the blooms in the clear morning air. Somewhere in the distance he could hear the discordant wail of a police car speeding to an emergency. He worried vaguely about the effect its exhaust would have on the measurements and then realized it was no longer important.

The sampling van in Piccadilly was parked alongside the statue of Eros. Two men were detaching glass sample cylinders from the air pump and sealing them with paraffin film. He made a few perfunctory comments about their data but, in fact, there was nothing for him to do. He sat down on the edge of the steps at the base of the statue and gazed around in astonishment.

Even the grimy buildings with their covering network of extinguished neon signs seemed to have become brighter in the clean sunlight. People were emerging from the tube exits. For a moment they seemed to look around fearfully as if expecting a sudden release of traffic. One by one they began to step down over the edge of the pavement, treading gingerly on the surface of the road as if trespassing. Two dogs ran past barking. One triumphantly cocking its leg against a lamp-post as though to seal his ownership of that particular territory.

A group of bearded students appeared from Shaftesbury Avenue. One was playing a guitar and as the rhythm of his tune got faster his followers broke into a dance.

For over an hour Mawn just sat and watched as people shyly filtered in. As the crowds grew, strangers began to talk to one another. Somewhere a girl burst out laughing and the sound echoed back off the surrounding buildings. The effect was instant. All conversation died away and there was a silence followed by a man's shout, trying the echo again. As the voice bounced back, there was a shout of laughter, then everyone was trying.

An old sad-faced man wobbled his bicycle unsteadily through the crowd. A hand-printed poster on his back proclaiming the second arrival of Christ. Mawn started to wander down Coventry Street to Leicester Square.

From overhead came the growing rumble of a jet. Faces turned up grimacing into anger at the sudden intrusion of the noise. The students began to chant: 'Planes out, jets out, planes out . . .'

By St Martin-in-the-Fields a street trader wheeled his fruit barrow down from Cambridge Circus and parked in the middle of the roadway. A policeman walked ponderously over to him taking a notebook out of his pocket and began to take down his particulars, then stopped, picked an apple off the barrow, bit a large chunk out of it, nodded amiably and walked off.

The students had taken up a new position in the middle of Trafalgar Square and had lit a camping stove and were already frying sausages as Mawn arrived.

Mawn felt suddenly oppressed by the swaying movements of the crowds packed around him. He walked over to the cordoned-off sampling station and sat down on the plinth of Nelson's Column. There was nothing more to do, he felt drained.

Someone touched him on the shoulder and pointed. A police car was nosing its way up Whitehall, weaving through crowds who moved aside resentfully at the sound of its engine. It drew up alongside and Lodge and Campbell Baxter got out and walked over towards him. Reluctantly, Mawn stood up, scarcely noticing a third figure who had emerged and stood waiting by the car.

Baxter was the first to reach him, running easily up the steps and extending his hand: 'Many congratulations.' He looked around at the jostling crowd. 'Remarkable, really extraordinary. You must feel very pleased. I've just come up from number ten as a matter of fact, the PM was most complimentary.' Behind him, Lodge winked slowly at Mawn. 'Incidentally, he'd like to meet you, quite shortly I hope, to discuss all the implications . . .'

Mawn's attention wandered. The figure by the car. Her expression was unmistakable. He started to raise his hand. She walked towards him. Baxter caught his gaze.

'Oh, yes, Richard insisted we do a bit of taxi work for you!'

Mawn watched Marcia approach, trying to collect his

thoughts. 'You talk as if it were all resolved, Minister.'

'We're well on the road, don't you think? My problems are just beginning. We shall have to decide how to deal with the industry . . .'

She ducked under the rope cordon and walked up to them. He searched her face. The same nervous smile.

'. . . they will have to completely retool, of course, if we decide to develop the Stirling engine . . .'

'I'm afraid you've completely missed the point, Minister.' He looked from one to the other. 'I think you all have. I don't want any of you,' he looked directly at Marcia, 'to have any illusions about my future activities.' He saw her face fall, her eyes searching his anxiously. 'That's why I don't want to meet the Prime Minister now!'

Baxter smiled: 'It would be purely explanatory . . .'

'But that's the whole point. We've finished all that.' He forced himself to avoid her gaze and concentrated on the youthful face of the Minister in front of him. 'We've had all the experiments and the talking.' He pointed at the waiting police car. 'You used that to cover half a mile. It wasn't an emergency, you didn't need to, you could have walked. But *you* chose to use it . . .'

'I think you're rather tired, Dr Mawn.' Baxter was looking at Lodge impatiently.

Mawn nodded: 'Yes I am, but my brain is still working. I'm not affected.' He pointed to the crowd. 'But you and I haven't the first idea how many of those people out there are . . . It could just be that the use of your police car tipped one of them over the brink.'

He felt her hand grip his arm and then slip down towards his.

'Surely there can be no more doubts? We shall never be able to use cars again until the engines completely change.'

Baxter's smile had disappeared. 'I don't think they'll exactly bless you if you proposed such a Draconian solution.'

'I'm well aware of that and I'd get even less thanks from the Prime Minister.' Her hand gripped his. He still forced himself to concentrate on the Minister.

Baxter spoke lightly, glancing at his watch: 'It would be his decision, of course.'

'No.' Mawn's voice rang out. Faces in the crowd turned. 'It is *not* his decision. It is yours, it is theirs and . . .' he looked round at Marcia, 'and ours. Every one of us is going to make a full and final decision. From now on every car owner who starts his engine is going to be fully aware of what he's doing. There's no way for him to get out of it.' He put his arm round Marcia's shoulder and started to move away.

'Over the next forty years or so, we're going to be forced to adjust the whole of our life style – the whole of our technology to cater for millions of adults who are mentally retarded and who are never going to recover. So present my apologies to the Prime Minister and tell him that the choice is really quite simple. It's cars or the minds of our children, and God knows which we shall choose.'

Dick Francis

'If he ever opens a detective agency or joins the British intelligence service, some of the supersleuths of literature will have to tend to their laurels' TIME MAGAZINE

Odds Against 35p

'Galloping adventure stuff, with a spot of kinkiness in the delectable shape of a sado-masochistic *femme fatale* to lift it out of the blood-and-thunder bracket' SUN

Blood Sport 45p

'Instantly readable . . . attempted murders on the Thames and on the ranch, death in the Blue Grass country of Kentucky, three stallions hi-jacked, blackmail, burglary and bugging devices from dashboard to powder room' SPORTING LIFE

Forfeit 50p

'A racing reporter with a polio-stricken wife suddenly uncovers an ingenious racket and finds himself faced with blackmail, torture and mayhem of all sorts . . . the sex is more explicit than usual . . . a thundering good read' IRISH TIMES

Bonecrack 50p

'This time it's a rich monomaniac who will stop at nothing, not blackmail, not murder, to ensure his son will be a crack Derby jockey. A classic entry with a fine turn of speed' EVENING STANDARD

Enquiry 50p

'All the elements that Dick Francis handles so superbly: horse-racing so vibrantly portrayed that it fairly gallops from the pages . . . filled with suspense, high drama and the bristling hatred of revenge' NEW YORK TIMES

Rat Race 50p

'Top-class novel about a taxi-plane pilot involved in a fraud scheme . . . exciting (there is an in-the-air rescue sequence that would make you really and truly angry if you had to put it down) and a splendid read' THE TIMES

For Kicks 45p

'An absolute beauty . . . the detection is ingenious and detailed; the gimmick is a fine one; and the background of life among horses and trainers and stable lads (and criminals) is so real you can smell and taste it. As a puzzle, as a thriller, it's a winner' NEW YORK TIMES

Slay-Ride 50p

'Racing in Norway is the setting for this superstar of thriller-writers' latest adventure . . . a spine-chilling affair' FINANCIAL TIMES

Smokescreen 40p

'Certainly his best thriller . . . sets the scene of devilry in South Africa. Truly exciting' EVENING STANDARD

You can buy these and other Pan books from booksellers and newsagents; or direct from the following address:
Pan Books, Cavaye Place, London SW10 9PG
Send purchase price plus 15p for the first book and 5p for each additional book, to allow for postage and packing

While every effort is made to keep prices low, it is sometimes necessary to increase prices at short notice. Pan Books reserve the right to show on covers new retail prices which may differ from those advertised in the text or elsewhere